Linda Sealy Knowles

Anna
The Lawman's Problem

ISBN: 978-1-0880-6121-3

Dedication

To
Rachel von Eberstein
Anna Marie (AK) Knowles
Lauren von Eberstein
My three beautiful grandaughters who
Are taking giant steps into their future
Go Girls!

Chapter 1

"Please, Uncle Claude. Don't leave me here. This is a scary place." Anna peeked through her hands at the eight-foot gray, stone walls with a large, double-wooden gate. "Please, I wanna go with you." She dropped to her knees and wrapped her hands around his pant legs.

"Listen, child," he said to his ten-year-old niece, whom he had cared for during the last two years. "I have to go. Turn me loose now. You'd be left alone a lot, and that wouldn't be right. My men are waiting for me, and if I don't show, they will come looking for me." He glanced up at the sister who stood beside him. "Help me here, woman. I promise as soon as I can, I will send for her wherever I am." He pulled Anna's small arms from around his legs and strode away.

Anna fell to the ground and cried. Sister Melody stood before her and patted her on the back. "Stand, child. Gather your carpetbag and follow me. I will take you to meet our Reverend Mother. She will help you get settled here."

Anna wiped her eyes on the tail of her dusty skirt and stood. "I'm sorry to be a cry baby, but I told my uncle that I am old enough to care for myself. I don't want to be locked up behind these large stone walls."

Sister Melody smiled at the little girl's spirit. "This is not a bad place to grow up. You'll have a nice bed, three hot meals a day, schooling, and no one will ever beat you. There are worse places to live."

Anna stood, brushed the dirt off her skirt, and tucked her blouse into her waistband. "All right, I will meet this woman, but I ain't never going to dress like you." Anna peered at Sister Melody's white hat that covered her hair with a tight band wrapped around her neck. The wimple, as Sister Melody called it, had starched, stiff wings that were held with wire, and stood straight out on each side. Her long black dress looked like a hot robe with long, wide sleeves. When standing still, both of her arms were hidden in the oversized sleeves.

After several knocks on Reverend Mother's office door, a soft voice said to enter. Sister Melody immediately curtsied to Reverend Mother and kissed her hand.

Reverend Mother peered at Anna and said, "You've been crying, child. Please, Sister Melody, introduce me to our new resident."

"Reverend Mother, this is Anna Knight. Her uncle, Claude Moore, dropped her off at the gate a few minutes ago. He had to meet some men to do something but didn't say what." She shrugged and tilted her head to the side, the wimple almost touching her fingers. "Anna said that she is ten years-old. That's all I know about her." Sister Melody tugged on Anna's sleeve to make her step closer to the older woman.

"Welcome to Little Sister's Convent of Whitmire, Texas, Anna. May I ask if your uncle is your only living relative?"

"Yes, ma'am. Both of my parents are dead, and my uncle took care of me until he had to go somewhere. Although I begged him to take me, he wouldn't. I can take care of myself." Anna stood straight and lifted her chin. "I can cook, mend and wash clothes, and care for animals." Her lip protruded. "I could do a lot to help him and the other men, but he wouldn't hear of it."

"I can understand the position your uncle was in, child." Reverend Mother walked around her desk and stood in front of Anna. "So, you can cook? Do you like to work in the kitchen?"

"I like to make pies. Everyone says they're good, but I don't care about washing dishes." Reverend Mother raised her eyebrows and glanced at Sister Melody, covering her mouth with her hand.

"Do you like small children, too?" Before Anna could answer, Reverend Mother told her that they had several small children living with them who needed love and comfort every day, besides their basic needs.

"I like baking pies. Never been around small children before, but I am sure I could take care of them if I have to." Anna smiled into the face of the older woman. The lady's complexion was soft with pink cheeks and she had sparkling blue eyes. Anna felt comfort and safe in this woman's presence.

"All right, Sister Melody. Get Anna settled and allow her to nap before dinner tonight. She has traveled a good ways from home and I am sure she is tired. Tomorrow morning, she can help in the kitchen, and perhaps she can bake a few of her special pies for lunch." Reverend Mother grinned. "We all could use a sweet treat."

~

Early the following day, chapel bells were ringing before daylight. The patter of feet passed by Anna's room. She jumped out of her twin bed and opened her door. A swarm of white hats and black robes rushed down the hall into a big open room. Anna tiptoed in the same direction. She peeked into the room and watched as the black robes fell to the floor and bowed their heads. A large stained-glass window was on the back wall with a tall golden cross on the table below it. Suddenly, a man appeared from the side door wearing a long black robe, and he began speaking. The ladies repeated his words.

Loud footsteps came down the hall, so she hid behind one of the double doors. A teenage girl wearing practically all white flew into the room to join the others. She slid to a stop and fell forward on her knees. Several of the older sisters gave her a hard stare.

Anna shook her head and padded back to her room. Just as she slipped on a blue cotton shift that lay at the foot of her bed, she heard a soft knock. She opened the door to find a short, round woman dressed all in white.

"Are you the new girl who is going to help me in the kitchen?" the woman asked.

"I guess so. My name is Anna. Reverend Mother said that I was to help in the kitchen and cook pies." Anna tilted her head at the funny expression on the little woman's face.

"You are to come with me. Comb your hair and put on your shoes. From now on, you will report to the kitchen when you hear the chapel bells. After morning prayers, the sisters will all sit down for breakfast. I'll give you instructions about how things are done."

Anna was surprised to find the kitchen so large. There was one other woman in the room, and she was busy making coffee. She smiled at Anna.

3

"Gertie, this is Anna. She is going to help us with breakfast and then make a few pies for lunch. Anna says she's a baker." The little woman chuckled.

Anna watched the older woman walk to the ample counter. "What's your name, Miss Cook? You didn't tell me."

Gertie laughed. "Miss Cook. Now, ain't that funny?"

"My name is Sadie," she answered, giving Gertie a hard stare, "but Miss Sadie to you, young lady."

"All right, Miss Sadie. I'm starving." Anna cocked her head and smiled.

"You can have milk and a piece of toast while we're cooking. We eat after we have fed everyone. The priest will come in here and sit in that corner. He will have coffee and study a few of his lessons. Says he likes the smell of this room. For now, I need for you to crack about four dozen eggs in that big white bowl and beat them until they're fluffy. We will fry several dozen, too. Then we will place all the food on the sideboard, and the ladies serve themselves."

"Where do all the eggs come from? Do you have a chicken yard?"

"Yes, we have chickens, and little Jeffrey gathers and washes all the eggs each morning." Miss Sadie laid several pounds of sliced bacon in the big spider skillet.

"Will I get to meet Jeffrey?" Anna asked while beating the eggs.

"Of course. Jeffrey will have his breakfast with us. He is almost old enough to leave this place. We'll sure miss him when that happens."

~

After breakfast when all the sisters were fed, the kitchen help sat down to enjoy their daily breakfast. The priest arrived, greeted everyone, and took his place at the corner table. Anna was pleased to meet him.

Little Jeffrey, who stood nearly six-foot-tall, sat at the table and gobbled his food down. Anna smiled. Did he think this was his last meal? She was happy to have a boy around. Maybe they could go fishing.

Once the kitchen was clean, Anna gathered the flour, lard, sugar, fresh fruit, and other items she needed to make pies. Gertie and Sadie watched as they peeled potatoes and scraped carrots.

Sadie commented on how Anna's tiny fingers worked the pie dough and swirled the flour around into a perfect pie crust. Over and over, Anna prepared the top and bottom pie crusts until she made six perfect fruit pies. While in the oven, the fruit bubbled but never broke the crusts.

Anna walked outside to get a breath of fresh air. Jeffrey was outside preparing a hole in the kitchen-yard fence. "Hello again, Jeffrey," Anna said. "Do you ever have free time?"

"Free time? You mean if I can do anything I want during the day?"

"Yes, like go fishing or hunting?" Anna asked.

"Don't tell me you like to fish?" Jeffrey laughed.

"Why do you find that funny? Sometimes, when my uncle was gone for several days, if I didn't fish, I didn't eat."

"You're too young to have been left alone, much less, have to fetch your own food."

"Well, I did, and again, would you take me to a pond or lake where we can fish?"

"Sure. I will ask Señor Carlos if I can have a few hours off, and you get permission from Sister Melody. If they agree, I'll dig some nice, juicy worms for us to use." Jeffrey stared at Anna as if to find out if she was squeamish.

The next day, with two fishing poles and a bucket of giant worms, the pair went to a pond about a half mile from the convent. Jeffrey baited his hook and tossed it into the dark blue water. Anna looked around on the ground until she found a large leaf and picked a worm from the container. She held the worm, bent it double, and stuck the hook into its side.

"Why didn't your hook the worm closer to its mouth?" Jeffrey asked.

"Oh, no. I didn't want it to see me as I placed it on the hook." She looked up to see a smile on Jeffrey's face.

A couple hours later, the youngsters went into a shed with two large strings of fish. Anna had caught most of them. Jeffrey said he hadn't seen her hook bob up and down before she was pulling the fish onto the creek bank. "You're quite a fisherman."

Chapter 2

A couple days later, Anna entered the classroom at the convent for the first time. Sister Louise tested her to see which reader she should begin with. Nodding at her proficiency, she questioned Anna as to where she went to school.

"Oh, I have never been to school. My mama loved to read, and while she was sick, she taught me to read and to cipher by helping her cook. After I cleaned or washed clothes, I lay in the bed with her, and we read all about different countries. Papa had many books, and he loved to hear Mama or me read while he sat in front of the fireplace."

"But you're far more advanced than all my other students," Sister Louise said. "I'll have to speak to Reverend Mother about what I should teach you. Would you like to learn to speak a different language like Spanish, French, or Latin?"

"Oh, I would like to visit Paris one day. I would like to be able to speak French if I ever had the chance to travel that far away."

"Mercy." Sister Louise left the classroom murmuring to herself as she hurried to Reverend Mother's office. This small child knew all about a city like Paris, which was unbelievable. To travel out of Texas would be a dream come true, but to go to a foreign country like France would be a miracle, thought Sister Louise.

During the first few weeks in the classroom, Sister Louise began giving Spanish lessons to Anna. Reverend Mother felt that since Anna was now in Texas and living around many Spanish-speaking people, she should learn to communicate with them first. The Frenchmen would have to wait a few years.

Anna was a quick study and could soon speak Spanish fluently. Señor Carlos was instructed to only speak Spanish to her. Some of the other workers spoke so fast she had a hard time understanding them, but most of them were patient. With many repeats and hand signals, it wasn't long before she caught on to their dialect.

Chapter 3

Ten Years later

Over the next ten years, Anna grew into a lovely young woman. She cried each time one of the young people left the convent to go out into the world. Mary Lou, a young girl who decided not to become a nun, and Jeffery, her fishing buddy, left several years after she had arrived. Anna had grown to love them like an older brother and sister. She loved and nursed many of the babies that had been dropped off for adoption, and her heart broke each time one left with a new family. Often she was happy and sad at the same time.

Reverend Mother spent time chatting with Anna as she grew into a lady who had become the best baker around. Anna never desired to become a nun, so the sisters never pressed her to become one.

One morning, after Anna had placed eight pies in the oven and punched down ten loaves of fresh bread to rise again, Gertie said that Reverend Mother wanted her to come to her office. "But Gertie, I put pies in the oven, and the bread is rising. Will you watch everything very closely? Don't let the pies overcook."

"I will stand right here at the oven door. Is this good enough for you?"

"I guess," Anna replied, grinning at her sweet second mama. "I'm sure I won't be long. She probably has orders for more pies." Many times, customers would drop by to order some of Anna's pies for a party. Anna rushed as fast as her short legs would take her to Reverend Mother's office. The sisters were walking in a straight line, but Anna dodged in and out. The sisters tried to hold a straight face, but they burst out laughing watching her weave between them.

Arriving at the office door, Sister Maria motioned for her to go right in. "She's waiting for you."

"Good morning, Reverend Mother," Anna said and rushed over to give her a hug. "How are you this beautiful day?"

"Good, child, good. Please take a chair. I have a letter and package for you from your Uncle Claude. He's well, so please wipe that concerned look off your face. Your uncle writes that he has a home in Livingston, Texas, about one hundred miles from here. He has sent money for your passage on a stagecoach. What do you think about going to live with him?"

"Mercy, after all these years, he's sending for me. You don't know how many nights I have prayed for him to come back and get me. I was just a child when he dropped me off here, and now that I'm grown, he is wanting to take care of me. Doesn't that seem strange to you?" Anna pressed down on the package but didn't open it.

"You do remember he said that he would send for you whenever he could. It has been nearly ten years, but he kept his promise."

"You sound like you want to get rid of me." Anna stood and walked over to the window. She bit down on her bottom lip, trying hard not to cry.

"Now, my child, you know that's not true. It has been years since I fell in love with one of the children who came here to live. But, you were different from the first time I met you. At ten, you were independent and kind to everyone. You never requested anything frivolous. You worked hard and loved all the children. The sisters, the convent staff, and the boys and girls all love you."

"I love them, and I love this place. It's home to me, and I don't want to leave."

Reverend Mother joined Anna as she stood looking out over the convent yard. "As far as me wanting you to leave, that is not true. My heart is breaking, but I can't think of myself. I have to think what is best for you." Reverend Mother took her handkerchief out of her sleeve and wiped her eyes and mouth. "Child, I love you like my very own daughter and I always will. I will be here waiting for your return if you aren't happy with your uncle. You can always come home."

Anna looked at Reverend Mother as her eyelids welled up with tears. This old woman had been her mentor, friend, and surrogate mother. Just the thought of having to leave her made her feel as if she was going to lose her breakfast. "Do I have to go and live with him? I'm grown now, nearly twenty. Can't I decide my own future?" Anna lumbered back to Reverend Mother's desk and slumped down into a chair.

"Yes, you can, but you don't know anything of the outside world. I feel that you must go and experience a great adventure. Anna, you are not ever going to become one of us here at the convent. You're young and beautiful. Just imagine, you can have a life of your own, maybe a home, a husband, and children. Think about it—you can have your own bakery. There are all kinds of possibilities waiting for you to discover."

Anna rushed around Reverend Mother's desk and placed her face down in her lap. "How soon do I need to decide what to do?"

"As soon as possible. There's a stage leaving tomorrow morning. You need to be on it." Reverend Mother patted Anna on her back and pulled her up. With tears streaming down her face, Anna spun around and raced out of the office.

~

Early the next morning, all the sisters and convent staff, as well as the area men, and the boys and young girls who had duties, were lined in front of the convent double doors. Everyone was present but Reverend Mother, who said her goodbyes while Anna dressed in nun's clothing, hat, and shoes. For Anna's safety, Reverend Mother insisted that Anna appear to the outside world as though she was one of the sisters.

When Anna stepped through the double doors, everyone gasped. Never were they expecting a lovely nun with red-rimmed eyes to stand before them.

To break the silence, Anna joked, "Well, will I pass?"

All the sisters rushed to her and took turns hugging and pleading with her to write to them. Teary-eyed, each turned and went back inside.

With stooped shoulders, Señor Carlos reached for Anna's hands. "I will miss you, my child." He spoke in Spanish and grinned. "Please don't trust any man—never be alone with any of them. Promise, you will remember my words."

"Yes, I will remember and be careful. Surely, my uncle will help guard me until I make new friends." Anna suddenly hugged the old man. "Thank you for allowing the young men to teach me so many skills over the years. I feel that I can take care of myself."

He squeezed her hands, and in a flat monotone voice said, "Come home if you aren't happy. Remember, we will be eager to hear how you're doing." Anna swallowed hard and nodded. "James is going to drive you to the stagecoach depot. Remember my words. Trust no one but God."

James helped Anna up on the high seat of the wagon and tossed her two carpetbags behind it. He tapped the horses, and off they went toward the little village. Anna didn't dare look back because she was trying hard to keep her emotions in check. She needed to appear like a grown woman who was a nun from Little Sisters of Whitmer, Texas.

~

Señor Carlos motioned to two young brothers, Juan and Pedro. "I want you to follow close to Miss Anna. Don't let her out of your sight until she is in the arms of her uncle. Take this money." He reached inside his pants pocket as he instructed the boys. "Hurry and pack a few pieces of clothing. The stagecoach driver will let you ride on top all the way to Livingston. Now hurry." Señor Carlos turned to go back inside but stopped to yell, "Don't let Miss Anna see you!"

Chapter 4

Anna stood on the platform, fiddling with her headpiece, and watched as passengers prepared to climb in the coach. A fortyish-looking woman with a daughter who appeared to be about ten-years-old was the first in, and an older man who smelled of hard liquor was next. He pushed in front of her, grumbling, then grabbed the seat next to the window. Anna stepped back to allow another old woman to enter, followed by her husband.

A young cowboy who had been standing alone offered his hand to Anna and assisted her inside. He hopped in and sat across from her. She never dreamed the inside of the coach was so small. Anna jammed up against the little girl who complained that she didn't have enough room.

Once settled on the hard leather seat, she wiped her eyes and placed her hanky inside her sleeve. Anna glanced at all the passengers and greeted them with a smile but kept her eyes downcast like she'd seen the sisters do while in a crowd of strangers.

The coach rocked as the driver and armed-shotgun guard climbed onto the high seat and took up the reins. The driver yelled 'all aboard,' and the well-sprung coach swayed back and forth as eight to ten local men and boys climbed on top. Dirty boots dangled down beside the open window. She frowned thinking of the young men she was leaving behind at the convent.

As the stagecoach traveled slowly, Anna gazed out at the scenery. Since arriving at the convent, she had never been past the village of Whitmire. Everything seemed so flat, and red dirt covered the land. A cluster of short, green Saguaro cacti huddled nearby.

Every other minute, the young girl whined that she wanted to sit next to the window, but everyone ignored her. Finally, the coach's rocking and swaying silenced the child into a slumber. The older man pushed and elbowed the passengers, then he pulled out his bottle and took a swig of the stinking liquid it contained.

Anna tried hard to keep quiet, like any of the sisters would have done, but it was hard not to scowl at the old man.

The young cowboy had enough of the man's drinking. "If you take out that bottle again, I will toss it out the window. No one wants to smell you or that liquor."

"You're not my boss, young man. I paid to ride this stagecoach, and I'll do as I please." The older man sat up on the seat and faced the cowboy.

The young man leaned forward, stared into his eyes without flinching, and repeated his command, and the old man shrank back into his seat.

After several hours, the stagecoach pulled into a relay station to change horses, and the passengers had a few moments to refresh themselves. Anna was thrilled to be able to stretch her legs and go to the outhouse. One of the boys above jumped off the top and placed a box under the door. Several others stood and offered their dirty hands to help assist the ladies. Anna smiled, took their hands, and stretched her back as she headed toward the back of the building.

~

A few of the young men were sitting around a tree, watching a few rough-looking men gather near the stage. When the shotgun guard returned from eating, he went to look over the fresh horses. The men who were close to the stage quickly climbed on their horses and rode in the same directions as the stage would be traveling.

"Sir?" One of the young man was rubbing his hands up and down his pants. "Those men who just rode out of here are up to no good," he stuttered.

"What makes you say that?" The guard asked, not smiling.

"We—" He pointed at the other men sitting under the tree, "overheard them talking about what you might be carrying besides passengers."

Cursing, the guard tossed his freshly rolled cigarette on the ground. "Thanks. I'll alert the driver that we'd better be careful. You guys on top had better prepare to hunker down because if we see trouble, we'll be moving fast." The guard cornered the driver as the passengers were climbing back into the stagecoach.

~

Anna and the others adjusted themselves and settled back on the seats. The cowboy slipped down and covered his eyes with his brown Stetson. The older woman took out her crotchet. The older man leaned his head back on the side of the stage wall and fell into a drunken sleep. The little girl finally wiggled into her mama's lap which gave Anna a little more arm room.

The stage seemed to be traveling a little faster, making the coach rock and sway a bit more than before. After traveling for about thirty minutes from the relay station, gunfire exploded all around them. The driver shouted at the horses to go faster, and gunfire came from behind the coach.

The young cowboy shouted for everyone to get down and cover their heads. The mother tossed her daughter onto the floor and fell over her. The older couple hugged each other tightly while the old man continued to sleep.

Anna screamed for the young cowboy to give her one of his guns. He told her to get down and be quiet. "I can shoot. Give me one of your guns." Her tense body was on the verge of springing toward him and grabbing his gun, when he handed her the Colt 38 that he was using. Tossing her some bullets, he demanded that she load it for him.

The coach felt like it might be pulling to a stop.

Anna quickly loaded the gun and took aim out the window. She shot one rider in the arm and another one in the shoulder. Both riders pulled to a stop. Anna placed her wimple firmly on her head, leaned out of the window, and fired two more times hitting her targets. Her wimple made her feel like she might take wings and fly out of the carriage.

Her targets only appeared to be wounded as they fell forward on their horses' necks and rode off into the distance. She had never shot at a person before, and she was pleased that she had not killed any of the men. Slowly the driver pulled the stage to a stop and asked if everyone was all right.

The young men jumped down off the top and opened the door to the stagecoach. Anna practically leaped into one of the young men's arms as he set her on the ground. Her white wimple wings were folded down, and one side had a bullet hole in it. Her face was covered with red dust. Juan and Pedro stood close by, their large sombreros pulled down to cover their faces.

"Mercy, lady, I ain't never seen anyone shoot like you. You shot four of those men!" One of the young man exploded with excitement and began speaking in Spanish to his friends standing all around.

The driver congratulated the cowboy for good shooting. "You saved us from being robbed."

Turning as red as the dust flying all around, he shook his head. "Not me. The little nun there did all that fine shooting with my pistol. I told her to reload it for me, but instead, she took aim and shot four of those bandits. I took a shot, but I didn't hit any of them."

"What the heck! I never knew a woman who could shoot like that, much less a young nun." The driver pulled on his gloves.

The young riders climbed back on top while the cowboy held the passengers' door. As Anna straightened her hat, he took her arm and asked, "Where did you learn to shoot?"

Anna looked toward the ground and grinned. "I had a friend who taught me while I lived at the convent. He taught me to clean guns, load, and shoot at targets. Today was, well, my first time to shoot at a person or even a moving target."

Surprised with her answer, the cowboy burst out laughing as he helped Anna into the coach.

After spending the night at the next relay station, Anna was dubbed a hero all through dinner. She was embarrassed and kept her face down toward her plate of food. Anna was so used to working in the kitchen that she felt uncomfortable sitting and being waited on. She jumped up, carried her plate to the sink, and asked if she could help with the clean-up.

The lady in charge wouldn't hear of Anna's offer. "Let me show you to your room. The driver of the stage said you were to have the best room. You saved them from being robbed and most likely killed."

"Please, I don't need anything but a clean bed. Let the older couple have the nicer room." Anna had never been treated with any kind of luxury or praise other than for making delicious pies. All the fuss over her made her cringe.

"Honey, this is not a fancy place, but I do have clean beds, clean towels, and plenty of hot water. So, tonight you will enjoy all three. Now, here's your bed. No one will bother you, so sleep well. I will wake you in plenty of time to dress and have breakfast before the stage is ready to leave in the morning. Good night."

Anna stood in the doorway of her ten-by-eight room with a single bed located under a window. She strolled over to the bed, kneeled down beside it, and prayed.

Early the next morning, the relay station owner knocked on Anna's door and smiled at her. "My, don't you look fresh. You cleaned up your head gear nicely. The bullet hole on the right side adds some character to it." She laughed as she led Anna into the kitchen. All the young men jumped up and offered her a place beside them.

"Please sit. I want to help serve breakfast." Anna smiled and headed to the counter, collected an armful of tin coffee cups, and placed them in front of each man. She hurried to fetch the big pot of coffee, then filled all the cups before the owner could fuss at her.

"Please, miss. You don't have to work. I can manage."

"I am used to working in the kitchen, and I like helping others. What else can I do?"

The older woman smiled and said she could pour butter over the top of the hot, fluffy biscuits. Anna carried the jams and jellies to the table. She passed out forks and spoons, and all the men began to eat. The owner gave Anna a big plate of food and told her to sit and enjoy herself.

Chapter 5

Livingston, Texas

The red stage came to a jarring stop in front of the stage depot in the center of Livingston, Texas. The crippled stage-keeper jerked opened the door while many of the riding boys formed a circle at the entrance. "Get back," roared the old man as he offered his hand to the ladies in the carriage.

The older woman and her husband stepped down first, followed by the young mother and her daughter. The men grumbled to each other, losing their patience to see the sharp-shooter nun.

Anna stepped down onto the gray boardwalk and lowered her face, not meeting any of the men's eyes. She stood and waited for the shotgun guard to toss her two carpetbags down from the top. The men wrested each other for the bags. A tall, lanky young man snatched the bags away from the guys. He gave the men a hard stare, daring them to touch them as he positioned the bags against the stage-depot wall. The men, young and old, each bowed to Anna and backed away, still peeking a shy look at her.

The tall young man removed his hat and asked, "Is someone meeting you, Miss?"

Anna surveyed the young man and noticed he had a deputy badge on his vest. "My uncle is expecting me, but he didn't know for sure which stage I would be on since I didn't have time to correspond with him."

"Does your uncle live in town or on a farm outside of the city limits?"

"He said that he had a house in town. I noticed a few homes on the edge of town as we drove by them. Maybe he lives in one of them."

"Well, sure. What's your uncle's name, and I'll send a boy to retrieve him for you?"

"His name is Claude Moore. Do you know him?" Anna immediately noticed that the busy sounds of the town became very silent. Everyone who was within hearing distance looked away or moved on to do their business. The people who remained didn't say a word. She eased closer to the deputy and asked if she'd said something wrong.

"Uh, miss, I'll hurry and go get the sheriff for you. I know he'll be able to help. Why don't you sit here in this chair, and I won't be but a few minutes."

"Thank you, sir. It's kind of you to help me," Anna said, relieved that somebody knew Uncle Claude. As she took the chair near the stage depot door, she couldn't help but notice that people were whispering behind their hands. Perhaps it was because many of them had never seen a nun, especially one dressed in a wilted nun's wimple and covered in a dusty, black witch's robe.

The stage manager went back inside the depot, and some of the men wandered away toward a building that had swinging doors on the front. Anna noticed a dry goods store, where couples stood window shopping, a café, a millinery shop, and a building that had a lending sign that said Bank. She had never been in a store, but she had read about a town that had them.

People strolled past her on the boardwalk. Many ladies were dressed in lovely gowns and day dresses. Some wore hats with fruit or flowers on top. Anna thought they were kinda funny-looking, but she didn't dare laugh because that would have been rude. Horses and wagons filled with families drove by, and all of the people stared at her.

Anna was watching children playing in the street when she heard someone say, "Good afternoon, Miss."

Anna jumped and stood almost at the same time. "Hello."

"My name is Matt Jenkins. I'm the sheriff of Livingston. I was told that you are waiting on your uncle, Claude Moore."

"That's right. I'm his niece, Anna Knight. He sent for me to come live with him."

His Adam's apple bobbed up and down. "Would you mind walking down to my office? I have some information I need to show you."

Anna had learned that you always listen to a person before asking questions. Taking in a deep breath and releasing it, she nodded to the sheriff as he guided her to his office, out of sight of the nosy spectators.

Once inside his small office, he offered her a chair. After a quick glimpse of the quaint but business-like office, she took a seat while he sat in front of her.

Sheriff Matt decided to be straightforward with this young lady. There was no sense in trying to cover up who her uncle was and what he had done, since all the townspeople knew. "Miss, when was the last time you heard from your uncle?"

"Reverend Mother, at the convent near the border, received a letter from him last week. I don't know how old the letter was, but it had to be recent. In the letter, he sent me money for a stagecoach ticket and other expenses to come to Livingston and live with him. He said he has a small house at the edge of town."

Matt Jenkins didn't say a word. Anna sat as still as a mouse while waiting for him to make a comment. Finally, he broke the silence. "Do you mind if I ask why you were living at the convent, and why he sent for you?"

"First, do you know my uncle, and if so, do you know where he is? Have I made a four-day trip to Livingston only to find my uncle is not here?"

"I'm afraid that's right." The sheriff stood and rifled through a stack of papers on his desk. He flipped through the posters while Anna walked over to a small mirror on the wall.

"My goodness," he heard her say. When he glanced up, his breath caught in his throat, and his knees went weak. Anna had removed her headpiece and was shaking her long hair back out of her eyes. Hm. He had always heard that nuns shaved their heads and were practically bald. Matt had never seen such a lovely young girl, much less one with long raven hair that hung to her waist. The nun's outfit belied her petite form, her lovely, rosy lips, and her shy blue eyes. Clearing his throat, he approached and handed her a poster. "Is this your uncle?"

After studying the picture, Anna gave it back to him. "Well, he doesn't look exactly like I remember, but it has been ten years since I saw him. I'm pretty sure that's him."

Matt took the poster and placed it back on his desk with the others. He hated to have to tell this young woman about her no-good uncle, but he didn't have a choice. "The reason your uncle isn't here is because he's probably on the run from the law. You see, he's a wanted man. He and two other men robbed a bank in Brownsville, and they haven't been seen since. You said that he sent you some money. May I ask how much he sent you?"

Anna's posture slumped slightly as she stared at the old wooden floor. "Certainly more than I needed but not a lot." Anna looked at Matt. "I'm so sorry. Do you think that he might have sent me some of the stolen bank money?" Before the sheriff could answer, Anna huffed, "I had no idea I was traveling on stolen money."

Swallowing hard, his heart broke for this sweet nun. She looked so sad with a quivery smile. He wanted to console her, but he didn't dare touch her, with her being a nun. It was best to continue at a distance with more questions. "Now will you answer my question? Why were you living at the convent?" Why had this lovely girl spent her childhood at the isolated Little Sister's Convent in the small village of Whitmire, Texas? Leaning forward, he slid his chair closer.

"When my parents died, my Uncle Claude took over running the farm and cared for me. Well, you might say, I took care of him. I have always been independent, and my mama taught me to cook. After two years, fighting at the border broke out, and he felt that he needed to go and join. Later someone asked me what side of the border he was fighting on, but I had no idea. Anyway, he packed our things on our old mule and dropped me off at the convent. He said when things got better, he would send for me wherever he was. Now, nearly ten years later, he kept his promise." She peeked at Matt. "Since I never showed any desire to become a nun, Reverend Mother thought I needed to live in the big world outside of the convent walls. I can go back anytime I choose."

Relief flooded his body when he realized that this beautiful young girl wasn't a nun after all. He could barely speak. "Why are you dressed like a sister if you aren't one?"

"Reverend Mother thought I would be safer dressed like someone from the order. Men have respect for the sisters."

"I see, your Reverend Mother must be a wise woman who knows plenty about the outside world. You are a lovely girl and probably would have run into trouble with some wild cowboys traveling your way." He grinned as Anna's face flamed red from his compliment. "Do you have any idea why, after all these years, Claude wanted you to come here?" Matt Jenkins had his own idea why this man had sent for his niece, but he wouldn't voice his opinion, yet.

Anna's thoughts went to the package that he had mailed her at the convent. In all the time she had been there, he had never sent her anything. "No, I'm sorry to say. I just thought because Uncle Claude was ageing, he might need me to care for him."

"Old? He's not old, "Matt nearly shouted. "He's probably in his early forties, and believe me, that's not an old man." Matt Jenkins was twenty-five, and he didn't feel old at all.

"Well, as a child of ten, he was a lot older than me. I never thought about how old he would be now."

The sheriff paced around the small office.

"May I ask you another question about my uncle?" Anna said. "Does my uncle own a house in town? Do I have a place to live while deciding what I should do—stay or go back to the convent? I will need a place to rest and time to make my future plans."

"Yes, he does have a small house at the edge of town. He tried to sell it a year or so ago, but he asked too much for it. So, you do have a home. I'll walk you to your house and see if we can locate a key. If not, I will find a way to get you inside." Matt grinned as he helped her to stand. "Don't you think you should fix your headpiece?" Matt attempted to say with a hard, pronounced swallow. He didn't want to embarrass her.

Anna reached for the dusty, wilted wimple headpiece and tucked her hair under it. "Once I'm settled, I will dress plain like the girl that I am. I can't continue to pretend to be something I'm not. That wouldn't be honest."

Matt Jenkins took Anna's elbow and led her a few blocks to the edge of Main Street. A white picket fence surrounded the front yard of a small house with a cozy-looking porch. "Here's your new home for as long as you want to live here in Livingston," said Matt. "I guess it's yours, since your uncle can't come back and claim it."

As the two stepped on the porch, Anna noticed a swing lying on the porch floor. "Oh, look, Sheriff, a porch swing. Maybe I can get someone to help hang it up."

"I'm sure I can help you with that later," he said. "Let's get you inside first."

She covered her mouth with a hand. "Oh, I left my bags at the stage depot. I will have to retrieve them before the stationmaster locks up today," Anna said, as she glanced back down the way they had come.

"I'll have them delivered here for you." Matt thought he might bring them himself later. It would give him a chance to see how she was doing. He found the key located above the door lintel and shoved on the stuck door, then stood back and let Anna enter.

"Oh my, how nice. Look at the stone fireplace. It's spread across the whole wall." Anna removed some wood chips on the hearth and tossed them over the wood that was laid for a fire already.

"Would you like for me to light the fire to take the chill out of the room?"

"That'd be nice. I want to look at the kitchen. Hope it has a nice big stove with an oven." She hurried into the back room with windows across the wall and a door that led outside onto a small porch. "Oh, Sheriff, do you really think I can call this my house?"

Matt smiled at her excitement and said, "I don't see why not. You are your uncle's only kin?" After lighting the fire, Matt followed her around the house.

"I love this kitchen. The stove is wonderful, and now I know I can support myself."

"How is having a big stove going to help you support yourself?"

"Because I love to bake. I am called the baker at the convent. My specialty are pies and special bread." Her eyes glowed as she spoke about cooking.

"You will need supplies from the dry goods store. Mr. Pickle will have everything you need. I can come for you tomorrow morning with my wagon and help you carry your items." He grinned and said, "All I ask is a slice of your first pie."

~

Anna laughed for the first time since she'd left the convent. It felt good to feel happy again, and this man was indeed a joy to be around. "I think I may be able to pay you a little for all your help."

"I won't refuse anything you offer. For now, I'll go out to the pump and bring you a couple buckets of fresh water. There's a tub on the back porch." After hauling in the water, Matt said that he would have her bags delivered to her. "Good day, Miss Moore."

"Please, Sheriff Jenkins, call me Anna."

A grin spread across the handsome man's face. "Matt to you, Miss Anna, not Sheriff." He placed his Stetson on his dark brown hair and left. Anna stood in the doorway and listened to him whistle as he hurried up Main Street to the stage depot.

Anna stepped onto the porch and called, "Pedro, Juan, come out of hiding. I know you are somewhere near."

A shy Pedro poked his head around the corner of the little house. "How did you know I was here?" he said, as he held his giant sombrero.

Before answering she looked at the other side of the porch. "Hey, Juan. You might as well come out because I know you are here, too."

"Shoot fire, Miss Anna. Señor Carlos said we weren't supposed to let you see us. How did you know we were here?"

Anna waved a dismissive hand. "Now, boys, we have grown up together. I can almost smell your presence."

"Hey, we don't stink."

Laughing, Anna said for them to come inside her little house. "Now, were you two on top of the stagecoach?"

"You bet. It was scary, but once I saw you hanging out of the window, I knew those men were in trouble. I am so proud that I taught you to shoot so well."

"So, now you are taking credit for her being able to shoot those bad men?" Juan said with a snicker to his brother.

"I am the one who spent hours loading her pistol to shoot at the targets." Pedro snorted and looked around the little house.

"Hey boys, it doesn't matter who taught me to shoot. You, Juan, taught me to defend myself and to use a hammer. I learned from both of you and I'm able to take care of myself because of your lessons. Now, I want to know when you're heading home."

"We can't leave until you are with your uncle. Señor Carlos said for us to watch over you until you are in your uncle's arms. Why didn't he meet you? We watched the sheriff take you to his office and then here. Is this your uncle's house?"

Anna hung her head down and sighed. "I'm afraid my uncle won't be here. The sheriff told me some sad news about him."

"Oh, Miss Anna, I'm so sorry. You traveled so far only to find him dead." Pedro placed his arm around her shoulders.

"Oh no. My uncle is not dead. He's wanted for robbing a bank."

"Mercy, that terrible," Juan said. "When he's caught, he's going to prison for years. We need to make arrangements to take you back before he returns and tries to take you away from here. You know the convent is your home."

"I know I can always return, but since you boys are here, I feel safe. But I need to stay, and just maybe Uncle Claude will come here and give himself up, while trying to see me."

"But, that could be dangerous. Your uncle may only want money. He might try to kidnap you and use you as ransom for protection from the law," Juan said, as he looked into the bedroom.

"Stop being such a scaredy-cat, Juan. If her uncle does come, we will be here. He'll have to go through us to abduct her," Pedro said as he stood in front of the fireplace.

"Listen, fellows, I'm not afraid. The sheriff will be watching me, and with you two staying here, I will be fine. This small house has two bedrooms. You both can share a room. If you don't want to sleep together, I can buy a cot to place in the room."

"Shoot-fire, we ain't never slept apart. I wouldn't know how to sleep without hearing Pedro's loud snoring." Juan walked into the bedroom and flopped onto the bedcovering. "Nice," he said.

Chapter 6

After warming the two buckets of cold water and washing her hair, face, arms, and feet, she sat down in front of the fireplace in the oversized rocker. Anna rubbed and brushed her hair to help it dry while waiting for her carpetbags to be delivered. She instructed the boys not to let anyone know that they were going to be living with her. "People might not understand even though we're practically kin." Then she sent them to bed because they were worn out from riding for days on top of the stagecoach.

Anna rocked and watched the flames dance in the fireplace until her drooping eyes closed. Suddenly, she heard a loud banging on the front door. She peeked out the window and saw a gray-haired lady, dressed in black, with a black veil tossed over her hair. A tall, younger man stood next to her. Wrapping the towel around her head to cover her wet hair, she opened the front door.

"Oh, miss, my name is Henrietta Winters, and this is my son, John. I have come to you because you're the only godly person this town has. Would you help because I can't just let my husband, Big John, go without a few Christian words said over him."

Anna didn't know what to say or do. These people thought she was a Catholic nun and could perform a funeral by praying and saying words from the Bible. Before she could give them an answer, Sheriff Jenkins stepped upon the porch with her carpetbags.

"What's going on, Henrietta? I thought you would be at the graveyard by now."

"Now, Matt, you know what a God-fearing man Big John was, and I can't let him go to his Maker without proper words. When I heard that this woman…uh, girl…was a nun, my problem was solved. She can send him off."

"Didn't you make arrangements with the preacher?" Matt asked, his eyebrows knitting together.

"He left to go to Madison to marry a couple. We didn't think that big John would pass so soon."

Sheriff Jenkins smiled at Anna, who appeared sleepy. She was still dressed in her long black robe, barefooted with a wet towel wrapped around her beautiful hair. "You can see that she must get dressed. John, take your mama to the graveyard, and we'll be along in a few minutes." Sheriff Jenkins motioned for them to continue on their way. Then he stepped inside the house and immediately saw two men peeking out from behind the front bedroom door. "What are they doing here?"

"Listen, please don't concern yourself about them now. What do you mean I will perform a funeral? I've been to many services, but I have never had to do anything. Certainly, I can't do what that woman wants me to do."

"Look at me. These people don't know you aren't a nun. You want to get off on a good foot with the townsfolk since you may be staying here for a while. I'm sure you can come up with a few choice Christian words to say over Big John. You don't have to preach a sermon." Matt reached for Anna's shoes and placed them in front of her. "Now fix your hair, and let's get a move on. It will soon be dark."

~

With a death grip on her elbow, Matt walked side by side with Anna to the crowd of people that had come to pay their condolences. She was glad that she hadn't eaten anything because she was sure she would have thrown it up right there on the spot.

Everyone parted for Sister Anna as she slowly walked to the pile of dirt surrounding the six-foot hole where the casket was already placed. Two men lifted Anna on top of the dirt to use as a platform overlooking the crowd. With a glazed stare over the crowd, she could visualize the old priest at the convent saying words over a graveside. Clearing her throat, she stole a glimpse down into the hole and saw the casket. She prayed silently that she wouldn't tumble forward and fall headfirst on top of the deceased.

A heavyset woman stepped forward and waved her arms in the air. On the count of three, voices rang out in the song, "Shall We Gather at the River." Anna's thoughts jumbled, and she wanted to run and hide, but she knew that she had to do her Christian duty. In her mind's eye, she could see and hear the old priest. This gave her reassurance.

The song leader stepped back in the circle of people as everyone settled down to listen to Sister Anna.

Scanning the faces of the townspeople, Anna began. "My name is Sister Anna from Whitmire, Texas. I'm sorry to say that I didn't personally know John."

"His friends called him Big John," A burly-looking fellow bellowed loud enough to wake the dead. "We want you to get the right John buried."

Several of the men laughed, and the women giggled. "Sorry, Big John." Anna paused as she witnessed Matt ease over to the man. Clearing her throat, she continued. "I know that his wife, Henrietta, and his son, John, thank all of you for attending Big John's departure from this earth to his heavenly home. Today, we come to cherish Big John's memory. Your memories of his life will help you through the difficult times ahead. Words can't take away the hurt you're feeling, but your family and friends will give you the strength to go forth. I know that your love will continue for him, even though you are parted. Death ends a life, not a relationship."

With blurred vision, Anna looked up for the first time at the crowd. With her silence, several people tossed pretty wildflowers on top of the casket. Once everyone was settled back in their places, Anna ended the service with lasting remarks.

"Ashes to ashes, dust to dust, we commend to Almighty God, our brother, Big John, and commit his body to the ground. The Lord bless him and keep him." Anna made the sign of the cross with her hand. "Amen."

The response from the crowd was surprising as all said Amen after her.

The two men helped her down to the flat ground as Matt stood next to her. "Thank you, Gentlemen," Anna said, as the men nodded and walked away.

Henrietta rushed to Anna and gave her a bear hug that lifted her feet off the ground. "Those were the prettiest words I have ever heard over someone. I shall always be grateful to you." She turned to her son as he nodded his agreement and led his mother to their family carriage.

In a softer voice, Matt said, "My goodness, you did a fine job. I have had to attend many funerals performed by preachers who proclaim to have preached for years, and I have never heard one as nice as the one you just did. Oh, Big John would have been proud."

Shaking from her head to her toes, she pleaded with the sheriff. "Please take me home before I'm asked to perform a wedding ceremony."

~

Matt and Anna arrived back at the house. Several times he thought he might have to carry this beautiful girl. She was almost ill from having to pretend to be an instrument of God.

One of the young men was sitting in the repaired porch swing. He jumped up, leaped off the porch, and ran to them. "How was the service?" he asked, twisting his hat. "You look sick. Are you?"

"No, I'm fine now, and the service went as well as expected with no time to prepare," Anna remarked.

"She is modest. It was great, and the family was very pleased," Sheriff Jenkins replied to the young man.

"Good, I will go on to bed now that she's back," he said, as he shifted from one foot to another.

Matt watched as the young man entered the house, then he took Anna's hand in his, led her over to the porch swing, and helped her sit. "Can I bring you some water? Why don't you remove that wimple? I always feel that you're about to take flight." He grinned and sat down.

Anna smiled and removed the hairpins that held the wimple in place. She rubbed her hair, and it fell down across her shoulders.

Matt wanted to run his fingers through the long curls that looked as soft as silk. He was going to have a hard time keeping his hands to himself. Swallowing hard, he looked out over the small yard. "Now, will you tell me why those two young men are in your house?"

"Pedro and Juan are like my brothers. We were raised at the convent together. Señor Carlos sent them to make sure I arrived safely in the arms of my uncle. They will live with me, but I did tell them not to let anyone know of our living arrangements. I have to admit that I feel safe with them."

"I feel better knowing that you won't be alone. There are some unsavory characters in our town, and you're not just a nun; you're a lovely young girl." Matt spoke softly so Pedro wouldn't hear him.

"I'm not too tired to know when I have been complimented. Thank you, and thank you for bringing my bags. Is the offer still good about taking me to the dry goods store?"

"For sure. I will be here around nine. Good night and thank you again for helping with the funeral this afternoon."

~

Before the sun had risen, a loudmouthed rooster sat on someone's fence and announced a new morning. Anna stepped out onto the porch, stretched her back, and smiled. What an exciting day she had ahead of her. Being an early riser at the convent, Anna walked to the pump and filled a bucket with cold water. She glanced again at the old bird who was crowing his head off, then saw Pedro standing on the porch.

"Leave that bucket, Miss Anna, and I will bring it in. Would you like another one filled?"

"Yes, I need plenty of water to clean this house. The bed linens and towels need washing and every inch of the house needs to be wiped down. After Juan gets dressed, ask him if he can find a store open and bring us something to eat. Later, Sheriff Jenkins is going to take me to the dry goods store to purchase supplies."

"Let me put my boots on, and I'll wake Juan. We have a full day's work ahead of us. Might as well get busy."

Anna smiled at the handsome, young man as she walked over to the woodpile and chose small pieces of wood. Later, she would have one of the boys make a wood box next to the stove. Baking pies and bread would require a lot of dry wood, and she didn't want to have to run outside to keep the stove hot.

After Juan returned with pastries and a jar of milk, Anna realized that the town needed a good baker. She enjoyed making donuts and cinnamon buns, and they would sell like her hot cakes first thing in the morning.

Anna found soap and other cleaning supplies in the pantry, so she washed sheets, towels, and the boys' dirty clothes. Pedro had repaired the clothesline, and all the clean items were blowing in the cool breeze to dry. With several buckets of hot water, every inch of the kitchen was scrubbed clean. She had Pedro wash the outside windows while she wiped them down on the inside. Last, she found a mop and bucket, then poured scalding hot water over the floor.

When the floor was clean, Anna and the boys sat on the front porch to let it dry.

A glance in the mirror reflected her dirty face and errant tendrils of hair sticking to her cheeks. The white towel wrapped around her waist was stained with dirty handprints. She was a sight, but she didn't care. The house was spotless, and the kitchen was ready to use to cook her delicious pies, once she had her supplies.

"Oh, my goodness. I need to clean up for the sheriff. He's coming for me later this morning to buy supplies."

~

Juan and Pedro were sitting on the front porch when Sheriff Jenkins, driving a single horse and wagon, stopped in front of the house. He jumped down and tied the horse to the fence post. "Howdy, boys," he called out. "I'm Sheriff Jenkins. Do you know if Miss Anna is ready to go?"

~

Juan stepped inside the house just as Anna was coming out. "Miss Anna," he said with wide eyes. "You don't have on your nun things. What are people going to think?"

"I have to stop pretending to be something I'm not. You know that I'm not one of the sisters. I am going to live here for some time, and I need to let the townspeople know the real Anna Knight."

"What will Reverend Mother think when she learns you are dressing like a commoner?" Juan said.

"Reverend Mother only wanted me to dress like the sisters while I was traveling, for safety reasons. She gave me instructions before I left. Now stop fretting and let me pass. The sheriff is waiting."

Hurrying through the gate, Anna gave Sheriff Jenkins a big smile. He was a solid, well-built man with a handsome face, broad shoulders, big hands, and narrow hips. His good looks nearly took her breath away.

He tipped his head to the side. "You're as pretty as a pup this morning, Miss Anna."

"Well, I have never been compared to a dog before, but most puppies are cute." She gave him a lighthearted smile.

"Believe me, I meant it as a compliment. Maybe I should have said you look as fresh as a daisy?" He gave her a cockeyed grin.

Both of them laughed.

As Matt helped Anna down from the wagon, she felt as if someone was watching her. She peered around, but there was no one that she could see. Taking a step forward, she stumbled over a small child sitting in the doorway. The little girl was the dirtiest urchin she had ever seen. Anna bent over to tell the child she was sorry for bumping into her, but before she could say anything, the child raced away.

Anna watched the child disappear into an alleyway. Why would a small child like that be running loose without one of her parents? Some people were just plain irresponsible when it came to taking care of their precious children. As Anna and the sheriff entered the store, a bell jangled over the door. Anna glanced at the silver object. What an excellent idea. This was the first store that she had ever been in, and she was fascinated with all the pretty things.

On the back wall behind the counter were high shelves filled with a lot of small items. A glass case under the counter displayed pretty objects that were too expensive to buy. The tables upfront were piled with all types of fresh food items, and further back were household goods. Closer to the rear of the store, tables held piles of men's pants and stacked shirts. Dress goods were on several tables and a rack of ladies' homemade dresses hung on the back wall, close to ladies' personal items. Giddiness flowed over Anna's body. She wanted to whirl around in the room to make sure she didn't miss anything.

Henrietta came out of the storeroom. Seeing Anna dressed in plain clothes, she stumbled and nearly fell on her face. Sheriff Matt was close enough that he caught her arm. "Lord have mercy, child," she said, as she smiled at Matt. "How come you're dressed like that?" She inspected Anna from her head to her toes.

Anna gave Henrietta a shy smile. "When I left the convent, Reverend Mother dressed me like one of the sisters for my protection. When you came after me to say words over your husband, the sheriff said I had to help and do the service. I never meant to fool you or anyone," said Anna, as she looked down at her shoes.

"Oh, honey, it's all right. You did a fine job sending Big John off to his Maker. Nun, sister, or just a plain young lady, I'm pleased." Henrietta hugged Anna.

"I'm so glad you understand," Anna said, beaming red from embarrassment. "You have a wonderful store. This is the first one I have ever been in, and it's like the ones I have read about in books. I do have a list of things I need for my new kitchen."

"Are you telling me that you've never been in a real store before? Mercy, child, did they keep you behind those stone walls like a prisoner?"

"More for my protection than a prisoner. You see, I looked different than the other children in the orphanage, so Reverend Mother was afraid that some bad men would take me away. I really never questioned her decision because I was happy there."

"Well, I guess that explains things," Henrietta murmured. She wiped her hands on her apron and said, "So, you have a list made up for me?"

"Yes, ma'am. Here it is. I want to make pies and special breads to sell. I saw several ladies selling their wares on the street. That is what I will do to sell my pies and bakery goods early in the mornings."

"You bring me one and let me taste it. I might want to sell them in my store," Henrietta said, peering at Anna over her wire-rimmed glasses.

"I can do that, but I also make hot doughnuts, cinnamon and sweet bread, and of course plain loaves." Anna smiled at Henriette and chose fresh strawberries and blueberries. She pointed at the canned peaches and asked for six cans. Her customers loved fresh peach pie, but she was sure she could use the ones in the cans.

Once the sheriff carried out the items in boxes, Anna still had the feeling that she was being watched. She peered all around the street but didn't see anyone. Matt helped her onto the wagon bench, and they headed back to the house.

After the boys carried the boxes into the kitchen, Matt said he had plenty of work waiting for him at his office. If she needed anything, she was to only send one of the boys after him.

Standing on the porch, she felt the wind as it stirred the leaves on the large oak tree next to the house. It was a beautiful morning, but she still had a creepy feeling that someone watched her every move. She would speak to Juan and Pedro about her feeling if she continued to have it.

Anna hurried back into the house, and after preparing six pies to go in the oven and setting bread to rise, she quickly penned a letter to Reverend Mother.

Dear Reverend Mother,

The trip to Livingston held a lot of excitement. Several bad men attempted to hold up the stage, but we managed to hold them off. After arriving in Livingston, Sheriff Jenkins informed me that Uncle Claude is a wanted man for robbery. The sheriff has taken me under his wing and took me to Uncle Claude's house in town. I guess you know that Señor Carlos sent Juan and Pedro to protect me until I was in the arms of my uncle. Tell Señor Carlos thank you, and the boys are safe and are living with me in my house. The three of us plan to stay in Livingston. The sheriff has questioned me about the money that Uncle Claude stole from a bank. Will you open the package that I received the day before I left? It might contain stolen money. I am praying daily before making any decisions, and I feel God's presence is with me. Please write and tell the sisters I miss them.

Your faithful servant,
Anna

Later, Anna asked Pedro if he would walk with her down Main Street and help her choose a small alleyway where she might be able to put up a stand to sell her baked goods every morning. She wanted both boys to go with her, but Juan had left the house very early to search for a job. He wanted to help support himself and Pedro while living in Livingston.

As they strolled down the old, wooden boardwalk, she was aware that many of the townspeople craned their necks and whispered about the young girl who pretended to be a nun and the handsome young man tagging along beside her.

Anna smiled at everyone as she strolled by and occasionally stopped to view an open space between buildings. Finally, they stopped at an alley between the boardinghouse and the dry goods store. They stepped inside the empty space, and giant rats peeked out from several crates that had fallen over. The big rats ignored Anna's approach and scuttled and scurried about the crates.

Pedro picked up a big stone and threw it at the critters, and they hurried away.

"They gave me the creeps," Anna said.

"If you like this space, I will put out some rat poison and get rid of them." He reassured her by patting her on the shoulder.

"I wonder who I need to get permission from to use this area—the boardinghouse or Mrs. Henrietta in the store." She stepped onto the boardwalk and decided to stop at the boardinghouse first since Mrs. Henriette didn't say anything about space when she spoke of selling her baked goods on the street.

"Good morning," Anna said to a tall, hawk-faced man who was dressed in a three-piece gray wool suit. He had to be burning up in that heavy woolen suit. It was nice and cool outside, but the weather wasn't ready for winter clothes yet.

Wiping his forehead with a clean white hanky, he asked Anna how he could help her. She smiled and looked around the room for Pedro, who remained standing in the doorway.

"My name is Anna Knight, and I would like to sell my baked goods in the mornings in the alleyway next to your building. Does the alleyway belong to the boardinghouse?"

"My goodness, no one has ever made such a request." He smiled and turned his head as if he was giving her request some thought. "Well, young lady, the space between the buildings was left like that for safety reasons, such as a fire. I personally see no reason why you can't use the space in the mornings. You might want to ask the owner of the dry goods store since they are next door. I would like to tell my clients that there are baked goods right out the door. Will you be selling coffee, too?"

"Thank you so much, Mister?"

"Beans, Beans' Rooming House."

"Mr. Beans, I thank you again, and I will have to think about making coffee to sell with my baked items. You gave me something to ponder." Anna hurried outside and stood beside Pedro. "He's so nice, but he suggested I ask Miss Henrietta if she cared if I set up beside her store. Mr. Beans asked if I would be selling coffee with my baked items. We will have to figure out how to do this."

After a lengthy discussion with Henrietta about using the alleyway to sell baked goods, Henrietta volunteered her kitchen stove for Anna to make pots of coffee. "You can come and go out the back door of my kitchen. Just pay me two cents a cup, and you can keep the other three cents. We both make money that way."

Chapter 7

Near the border of Texas

Claude Moore rode his mount along the creek bed until he came upon his two companions with whom he had parted ways after the bank robbery in Danville, Texas. He dismounted near a few trees and walked over to the fire by the water's edge.

"Looks like you made it without any trouble, Claude," Slim Smith said without looking up from the bacon he was frying over the fire.

"Not too sure about that. I might have a posse on my trail since I robbed the payroll car hooked on the train headed to Abilene. Had to shoot the conductor. He looked dead when I stepped over him." Claude laughed. "Speaking of being dead. You two should have been goners. I rode up and could have gotten the drop on you buzzards before you ever noticed I was anywhere near."

Slim scrambled to his feet. "Dad gum, how did you find us so quick?"

The other man swung around, cocked his rifle, and aimed it directly at Slim and Claude. "You two go to Mexico. I won't go to jail for killing a man I never seen. It's time I go home, away from here."

"I reckon that is your decision, Red Eagle," Slim said, shaking his head. Before the man could walk away from the fire, Claude's pistol exploded, and Red Eagle's spirit went to the afterlife in the sky.

"Damnit, man, why did you have to kill him?" Slim raced over to the small man, lifting his head into his lap. "Red Eagle, can you hear me?" He was fighting back the tears as he witnessed the old man's last gasps of breath. They'd been partners for as long as he could remember. Despite his age, Red Eagle was still a great tracker and cooked any critter that was killed for their supper.

"Come on, man. Bury the old fool." Claude started to walk toward his horse.

"Why did you have to kill him?" Slim fought back the tears welling up behind his eyelids.

"He'd talk when he was away from us. I never trusted him. Besides, the split of the money will be more for us."

"Well, thanks to you," he said, disgusted, "he won't be talking to nobody now. I'm gonna miss this old man," Slim said, and he darted a look at Claude. "Let me get my shovel so I can bury him. We need to move on from here if you think a posse is hot on your trail."

"You still want to travel with me?"

"Shoot fire, man, I ain't stupid. I want part of the payroll you got off the train," Slim said, as he tossed the shovel on his shoulder.

"I planned that we could hide somewhere in these hills until that posse has passed by. They're going to have to get fresh horses, too."

After Slim wrapped Red Eagle in a blanket and lowered him into a deep hole, he walked to the creek to wash the dirt and sweat off his body. His mind was filled with hatred for Claude, and the first chance he had, he would make him pay for killing his old friend. After pouring himself a fresh cup of coffee, he asked Claude if he was ready to break camp.

"Yep, but I still need to go into town and see my niece. I sent her the bank money, and I am sure she brought it to Livingston." Claude grinned at Slim.

~

As the two rode around in the hills looking for a hideout, Claude couldn't stop remembering his sister, Lilly, who adored her baby girl, Anna. He still grieved for her even though he had planned the killing and raid on their farm. Lilly had covered her eight-year-old daughter's body with her own when the men rode in, shooting and looting everything in sight.

For nearly two years, Claude had stayed on their farm, trying to put it back together. Once the judge told him that he couldn't sell the farm, rage filled him. Anna was the heir, but she was too young to make any legal decision. Since he was her guardian, he had access to the money in the bank account that belonged to his brother-in-law and sister. He spend it on whiskey and women.

Remembering the murder of his sister, he was too bitter and angry with himself to remain on the farm any longer. He had tried for over two years to forget what he had done, but Anna was always a remembrance. A war had broken out between two groups of men near the border, and he hoped this would remove the thoughts of what he had done. With the bad decision he had made festering in his gut, he packed up his ten-year-old niece, Anna, and dropped her off at the Catholic convent and orphanage close to Whitmire, Texas. Claude promised to come back for her as soon as he could. Smirking, he thought, that was ten years ago.

~

Anna stood on the front porch and listened to a rooster break the silence of the quiet dawn. The early sunrise of pink and reddish-orange filled the light blue sky. Tears filled her eyes as she remembered the morning she had said goodbye to Reverend Mother. She loved the older woman like a second mother, and she missed her very much. Sighing, Anna turned to the kitchen and helped herself to a fresh cup of coffee that Juan had prepared while she stood outside.

Anna and the boys dressed for their first Sunday service. Livingston had only one church at the edge of town—a small white Baptist church that had stained glass windows. As the trio entered the wide double doors of the building, a short, round man wearing a long black coat and a wide-brimmed black hat welcomed them.

"My name is Reverend Melvin Stubbs, and I am happy to have you attend our worship service today. Please take a seat anywhere."

"Thank you, kind sir. My name is Anna Knight, and this is Pedro and Juan. We are pleased to be here," Anna said as the boys removed their large sombreros. Anna pulled her black lace shawl over her head and walked down the center of the church aisle. The three of them kneeled at the altar, making the sign of the cross before backing away and then turning to sit in a pew near the front.

Anna could sense a hush coming over the congregation as they watched their every move. Finally, the organist began playing the opening hymn. She reveled in the beautiful music coming from the front of the church. The stained-glass windows reminded her of home, which was a surprise and a joy. All the people stood and sang along with the music. Some of them held songbooks while others sang from memory.

After settling in their seats, it appeared that everyone was preparing to listen to the preacher. Suddenly, a loud woman's voice rang out from the middle of the church. "I'm not staying in the Lord's house with that girl who pretends to be a Christian. She's a fraud, parading around in a nun's outfit. I insist that you remove her immediately from this house of our Lord, or my family is leaving."

"Who is she talking about?' Juan whispered, looking around.

"Me. She's talking about me. We'd better go now," Anna said softly to Juan and Pedro. Before they could move out of the pew, another voice rang out from the opposite side of the church.

Henrietta stood as straight as an arrow pointing her finger toward her. "This is God's house, Mrs. Tarver. Our newcomer is a good Christian girl who was raised in a convent near the border. She never pretended to be a nun. It was me who mistakenly took her to be a sister from the convent. Me and me alone. In my grief, I didn't give the child a chance to explain anything to me. Because I didn't allow her to identify herself, Sheriff Jenkins said that she would say words over Big John's grave, and Lord, have mercy on his soul, she did."

Henriette scanned the congregation and continued. "Anna said beautiful words over him, and many of you were there and heard them." She pointed at a few of the people sitting near her. "Now, Mrs. Tarver, sit down or leave. Most of us here today don't care what you do." The two women stood glaring across the heads of the congregation until the preacher spoke to them.

"Ladies, please take your seats. You both have had your say. Let's remember we are in God's house, and we are all God's children. It is no surprise that God has given us instructions on loving others." Preacher Stubbs held up his worn black Bible. "The scripture tells us that God is love, that He first loved us, and that he sent His Son to die for us. God created all people valuable and worthy of love. Jesus even tells us that the greatest commandment is to love one another." He laid his Bible down on the podium and said, "Let us pray."

When the service was over, Anna, Juan, and Pedro stood and peered around at the strangers staring at them. Henrietta moved through the crowd, took Anna's elbow, and led her and the boys out the front door. When they reached the bottom step, she told Anna how surprised she was that the old woman said those ugly things about her in church.

"Please don't judge our town by one crabby old woman. She wasn't even at Big John's funeral, so she didn't know what she's talking about."

~

Sheriff Jenkins walked up behind Juan and Pedro. "How are you young men doing?" he asked as he watched Anna. He'd been sitting in the back of the church and saw how Anna and the boys conducted themselves.

"Fine, I guess," Pedro said. Looking down at the ground, he kicked the dirt with his boot. "I found myself a job at the livery starting tomorrow morning. Juan will stay home to help and watch over Anna."

"Good for you, but don't fret too much over Anna. I'll be around."

Henrietta said her goodbyes and hurried off with her son.

"Pedro, you didn't tell me that you have a job. You know you don't have to work. We'll talk about this later." Anna smiled at him and then turned her attention to Matt.

"It's nice to see you this morning, Sheriff. Would you join us for lunch? We have a lot to talk about," Anna said.

"I'd be mighty pleased to. Wish I had brought my carriage today, but since I didn't, we can walk the short distance to your house."

~

Anna hurried into the kitchen and warmed the roasted chicken, carrots, and small potatoes. She placed her yeast rolls in the oven to cook while she set the table. With a mallet, she chipped pieces of ice off the block in the bottom of the small icebox to serve with the tea.

Later, all three men rubbed their full stomachs until Anna brought a strawberry pie from the kitchen.

"I wouldn't have believed I had room for anything else, but I'm going to enjoy a piece of this," Sheriff Matt said as he took a small plate that was running over with juicy strawberries. Once lunch was over, Matt waved for the boys to run along, saying he would help Anna clean the kitchen. Anna quickly pinned a large dishtowel around Matt's middle, then took the hot water from the stove and poured it over the dirty dishes.

Later as Anna and Matt sat in the swing on the front porch, he asked softly, "Have you heard from your uncle?"

She gave the swing a shove with the toe of her shoe and replied, "No, nothing."

~

As the sun began to rise over the tall trees, Anna and the boys carried armloads of long boards to the alleyway and made a long table using turned-over barrels. Anna tossed a clean white tablecloth over the table, and all three hurried back to the house to collect the baked goods. After setting out pies, hot doughnuts, and several pans of brownies, they stood ready for customers.

Once the sun came out, men came from all directions.

Anna rushed into the dry goods store and met Miss Henrietta coming out the back door with a large pot.

"Go fetch the milk and sugar off the counter and you'll be set to serve this steaming coffee."

Juan set out cups, saucers, small plates, and cloth napkins while the men waited patiently for Anna to slice the pies and brownies. In less than thirty minutes, there wasn't a crumb left to purchase.

"Mercy, child, you gonna have to bake a lot more goodies if you want to make money. When word spreads about your delicious baked goods, there'll be more customers than you can handle, and if you can't serve them, some won't come back." Henrietta picked up her coffeepot and went inside.

Anna suddenly felt the sensation that someone was watching her. She glanced around but didn't see anyone but a small child's face which was pressed against the upstairs window pane. The child jumped out of sight, but not before Anna knew she had seen the girl before. The girl was hungry. She had seen that same expression on many young faces when they entered the orphanage.

"Boys, we can leave the table set up, but we'll need more boards to make a few tables and benches for the customers on which to sit and eat. I'll walk to Matt's office and ask if we can use his horse and flatbed wagon. Maybe we can find a small pull wagon or two to help carry the baked goods from the house. What do you think?"

"I think you two had better get busy. After work, I can help— about six," Pedro said. "Now I need to leave for the livery."

"But Pedro, we were going to talk about you working. You don't have to, and besides, Juan and I need your help."

Pedro shook his head. "We're going to need my money to live on shortly. Your money will run out. Remember you have to spend your profits on supplies to make all your baked goods. When business is good, I will be able to quit and help you more." He turned and headed toward the livery stable, leaving Juan and Anna dumbfounded.

"Well, I'd better be going," she said. Anna smiled and nodded at the townspeople as she made her way to the sheriff's office. A light was on inside, so Anna knocked and opened the door at the same time.

"What a pleasant surprise so early in the morning," Matt said as he looked at Anna from her head to her toes.

She glanced down and cringed. Her white apron was smeared with strawberries and chocolate icing.

"You look good enough to eat," he said, fingering a taste of strawberry off her apron while pulling out a chair for her to sit.

"Thank you, kind sir, I think." She giggled and felt her face flame bright red.

"What can I do for you this morning, Miss Anna? I know you have a reason for coming to see me." He leaned against his desk crossing his boots at the ankles.

"I need your flatbed wagon and horse to haul some lumber to my house. Juan is going to build a few benches and a couple of long tables where my customers can sit while sampling my baked items. You forgot that I opened my alleyway café this morning."

"Shoot, I sure did. You didn't happen to save me anything, did you?" Matt raised his eyebrows in question.

"Sorry, I didn't. The men came at us so fast I didn't have time to do anything but cut pies and pour coffee. All the food was gone in just a few minutes. I need to hurry home and start baking for tomorrow. While the pies are in the oven, I'll help Juan."

"I'd be happy to loan you my wagon and horse. You can use it anytime. Come on, I'll walk you to the livery and have Pedro hitch my old mare up. She's very gentle, so you will not have a problem with her."

After the wagon and horse were ready, Anna turned to Matt. "Do you know anything about the little girl who is running wild all

41

over town? I saw her watching me from the boardinghouse window, and she looked so pitiful and hungry."

"Yep, that little hellion belongs to Mary, a saloon gal, who works all night and sleeps all day. She ain't got any time for that child. That's why she does whatever she wants."

"But, she can't be more than three or four."

"I know, but what can I do? I can't catch her, and believe me, I've tried. Her mother tans her hide and makes her stay in her room all day if I go to the saloon and complain."

"That's awful, but maybe I can coax her down for breakfast. I would feel better if I knew she wasn't hungry."

Chapter 8

The grand opening of Anna's Alleyway Bakery was a wash-out. Thunder and lightning and a heavy downpour spoiled a few pies and some fresh baked goods before they could be carried into the back door of the dry goods store. With much laughter and confusion, Miss Henrietta helped Anna and Juan carry the delicious pies and not-so-hot doughnuts to the front of her store where men were lined up to be served despite the lousy weather.

After most of the baked goods were sold, Anna confessed that they had better watch the weather more closely. "I saw the clouds, but I never dreamed we were going to have a flood." She pinned her wet black hair to the top of her head.

"One good thing, your baked goods brought in many more customers than I would have had normally on a rainy day," Henrietta said.

A voice sounded behind her. "You know, Miss, I own the café up the street. How would you like to sell your baked goods and hire on as my cook?"

Anna spun around, surprised that the small man with grayish, curly hair stood before her offering a solution to her problem. "Sir, we haven't been properly introduced. My name is Anna Knight. And besides, I have never been in your café." She smiled at the man who still wore his white apron.

"This is Herman Godwin. He's had the café in town for a hundred years," laughed Henrietta. "You know, Anna, this might be the perfect answer to selling your pies and baked goods and make good money to boot. You need to go with Juan and look his place over. At least, you'll have a roof over your head and be out of the cold weather."

"Mr. Godwin, let me clean up my things, and Juan and I will walk down and talk with you some more. I don't make quick decisions."

"You just take your time, Missy, and you and your fellow come and have some lunch. I want you to look the place over. Maybe you could give it a nice touch."

"Juan is a very close friend of mine. We're more like family than what you're suggesting."

In less than an hour, Anna was thrilled with the idea of working in the big kitchen. She could prepare pies, doughnuts, special breads, and other simple desserts before she started the food that would be served for lunch and an early dinner. Mr. Godwin served a simple fare, and she would have his help in preparing vegetables and meat. Country men worked hard and they enjoyed large helpings of meat and bread.

Mr. Godwin had a nice glass case beside the big double doors. It was the first thing that customers saw when entering the café. He sold blocks of cheese and small brown bags of crackers, apples, and other seasonal fruits. Anna asked him if she could decorate the glass shelves with nice paper and display her pies and specialty breads on them. They could sell slices of pies or the whole pies and loaves of bread.

After looking around, she asked him if he had tablecloths and large napkins for the tables. He said no, he'd never thought about dressing up the area like that. "Mr. Goodman, I can sew, and I will be happy to make tablecloths and matching napkins if you purchase the material. I can make enough for several days, but you'll have to have a washwoman to keep them clean and ironed. Cleanliness is next to godliness, and people like a clean place to eat."

"Goodness, woman, you are costing me a lot of money and you haven't even turned on the stove. I'll need to sit and reflect on all of the expense you're requesting me to spend." Making a humming noise in his throat, he grinned at Anna. "All right, Miss. I'll make these changes for you, but you'd better not up and quit on me." Mr. Goodman instructed Anna to purchase the material she needed for the tables and any other items she thought would help to make his place nice.

While selecting the material, she chose some oil lanterns with decorated shades. They would be perfect to set around the café when darkness came. She purchased more flour, lard, and fresh berries to help make her pies. Of course, she couldn't ask Mr. Godwin to purchase her supplies *and* collect the money for herself. He'd pay her a fair wage to cook, and she would have the money for the homemade baked goods. Anna was pleased that she would soon have a nice nest egg and could pay back the money that her uncle had sent her to travel and live off of. The last thing she wanted was to live off of stolen money.

~

The next morning while Anna worked at the café, Matt and Juan broke down the tables and benches in the alleyway. Using the flatbed wagon, Matt carried the wood to the back of Anna's little house. Later, Juan might want to make something out of the lumber. As Matt was loading the lumber, he glanced at the boardinghouse and saw the little girl looking down. She jumped back when she saw that he had seen her.

Juan thanked Matt for helping him and requested that he come to the café and have lunch. "I know Anna will be happy to see you."

As he drove the wagon back to the livery, he looked forward to seeing Anna and eating her cooking. Mr. Godwin's café offered good home-cooked food, but with Anna's touch, his place would be full every day.

~

The kitchen was warm, compared to the first cool day of fall. As Anna lifted the two windows, she saw the little girl sitting on the back steps. "Mr. Godwin, do you know the little girl who's perched on your steps?"

"Yep, that's Susie. She comes every morning when she can sneak out of her mother's room, and I feed her. Some days she doesn't show up, but when she does, she can't get enough to eat. I try to make her a small lunch to take with her."

"I can see that she needs a bath and clean clothes, but she looks like she's crying. Will she let you approach her?"

"I'll take her some cheese and bread, and maybe she will tell me what's wrong." He picked up a knife and cut a slice of cheese off the golden block and broke off a hunk of bread.

"Good morning, Susie," Anna heard Mr. Godwin say. "Why are you crying? Did your mama hit you again?"

Anna watched as the little girl shook her head no. "She's gone.

She got on the stage with a man. He had on a tall, ugly hat."

"So, you are telling me that your mama left you here all alone?"

"No," she said, shaking her head side to side. "She gave Miss Goldie money to watch me." Susie wiped her runny nose on the back of her hand.

"So Goldie is going to be your new mother?" Mr. Godwin quizzed her.

"Goldie is mad at Mama. She's going to sell me to one of the drunks. Said he'll take me out of her hair." Susie frowned up at Mr. Godwin. "How can I get in her hair? That's silly, but I ain't going with no dirty man."

"So, what are you going to do?" Mr. Goodman asked.

"I'm going to live with the sheriff. You know, he don't have a girl to help him. When I get bigger, I will cook for him."

"Susie! You'd better come to me, girly!" Goldie's voice came from the balcony across the street.

"Hurry, child. Let's go inside the kitchen and hide from the old witch." Mr. Godwin took her hand, pushed her inside, and locked the door.

"The woman has gone for now, Mr. Godwin," Anna said, looking down at the small, beautiful child. She stooped down on her knees and wiped tears from Susie's eyes. "Don't cry anymore, little one. We aren't going to let anyone give you away to a stranger. You can come and stay with me. Now, sit at the table and eat your food. I will pour you some milk."

"Coffee with a shot of whiskey in it—that would be better." Anna and Mr. Godwin stared at the little beauty. "That's what I have in my mama's room."

"This morning you can have milk or a little coffee with milk in it." Anna waited for her to make a choice.

"Just milk, I guess."

As the child ate, Anna rolled out pie dough and whirled the pie crust into a perfect circle. She dropped the crust into a pie pan and, using her fingers, pressed the dough around the edges. Chopping small berries with other ingredients, she filled the pan with the filling. Covering the pie with another pie crust, Anna cut a cross in the center of the pie and placed it on the cabinet. Anna repeated the process several times and then poured canned peaches into the center of the crust. She glanced up to see Susie standing so close to the worktable that Anna could only see her eyes.

Anna opened the door and placed six pies into the oven. She glanced at the clock sitting on a shelf across the room. She had time to make six more pies and bake eight loaves of bread.

"Can I play with that dough?" Susie asked.

"When a person cooks or plays with the dough, they have to be clean. I will fix you a big tub of warm water and help you wash up. Then I'll show you how to bake a pie that you can give to the sheriff. How would you like that?" The little one seemed to like Matt.

"I wanna make him something, but I don't want a bath. Mama and Goldie always hurt me when they put me in a tub."

"I promise—" Anna held her hand up and placed it over her heart. "I won't hurt you at all. Your hair needs washing, but I will be gentle."

While the child was bathing, Anna took her clothes to the sink and hand washed her pantaloons and dress. She hung them on the porch to dry in the cool wind. Mr. Godwin offered to bring down one of his undershirts for her to wear while her clothes were drying.

While Anna dried the child's small body, she saw dark bruises covering her thin frame. "Do you fall down a lot, Susie? You have bruises on your legs and back."

"I got hit by my mama's friends."

"Are you telling me strange men hit you?"

"Yep. But I didn't cry. They pushed me out of my mama's room or sometimes locked me in the closet. If I begged to get out, my mama would tell them to shut me up."

"Well, I can tell you now, if and when your mother comes back for you, I will not let her take you from this place. Mr. Godwin, the sheriff, and myself will not let her abuse you again."

Little arms wrapped around Anna's legs, and Susie asked, "What's abuse? I don't want any of that stuff anymore."

Mercy, thought Anna. I must pray for this child and her mother. Anna allowed Juan into the kitchen and whispered to him to go to their house and bring back a pillow and quilt. She wanted to make a pallet for Susie to rest upon while she was cooking lunch.

After Juan returned, Anna coaxed Susie to lie down and rest. Juan helped Mr. Godwin prepare vegetables and cut up a dozen chickens.

With a pan of hot grease ready, Anna made a batter, and Juan rolled the chicken into it and dropped the pieces into the pan. For an alternate dish, she made a large meatloaf. With fresh green butter beans, mashed potatoes, dark gravy, hot rolls and biscuits buttered, lunch was ready to serve.

Mr. Godwin insisted that Anna greet and seat the customers and take their orders. Many chose the fried chicken while others selected the meatloaf. After the customers had finished their meal, Anna, speaking in a low tone of voice, asked if they would like to select a dessert from the glass case. "We have four different pies. Blueberry, strawberry, apple, and peach cobbler."

Nearly everyone selected a piece of pie, and after sampling the dessert, many requested a whole pie to take with them. Anna was thrilled, but she had to get busy and refill the glass case with more pies before the supper hour.

Chapter 9

"She said what?" Sheriff Matt nearly yelled loud enough to wake Susie from her nap.

"Lower your voice. The child is exhausted from being hungry and tired." Anna led Matt outside on the back porch. The afternoon breeze felt good to her face. She had stood over the hot stove most of the afternoon preparing baked pork chops and chicken. Then she had made eight pies and a big batch of blueberry cobbler for the supper crowd, although Mr. Godwin had said that he didn't usually have many customers for the evening meal.

Matt shook his head. "Anna, I have no idea why that little girl would want to live with me. I bet I haven't said ten words to her. Can't believe that mother of hers would just leave her here."

"Well, she did, and that old woman told Susie she was going to sell her to a man, and he would take her away." Anna was almost in tears as she repeated what Susie had told them.

"The only thing I can do is carry her to the orphanage in Selma, nearly forty miles from here," Matt said, looking down at his boots.

"That is not going to happen. I lived in an orphanage for ten years, and I was old enough to take care of myself. The sisters and Reverend Mother were kind to me, but over the years I have heard about other terrible places where children are forced to live. Susie can stay with me and the boys. She can stay here during the day and when she grows up, she will be in school."

"So, you have her future planned out. What about the law? I have a responsibility to this child now," Matt said.

"You just said that you will have to take her to an orphanage. That is your solution to *your* responsibility?" Anna scrambled to reverse what Matt had just said.

"Now wait a minute, Anna. I have to make out a report."

"Why? This child has been running wild since before I came to Livingston, and you haven't done anything about it. If maybe you had, you would have seen all the dark bruises on her legs. Some man has taken a strap to the little one and, remember, I told you before that she was hungry."

"Calm down, please. I'm not the enemy. But I have to do what's right for the little girl," Matt confessed, running his hand through his dark hair.

"While you are figuring out what to do, Susie can stay with me. I will not let that old woman sell her to anyone. At least I'll purchase some clothes and make sure she is fed and safe." Anna was disappointed in Matt. The little girl wasn't going to live with him, even though she had said she wanted to. The child wanted to feel safe, and now Anna would make sure she was.

"All right," Matt said, rubbing his hands down his pants. "Susie can stay with you for a week or so. By then, if her mother hasn't returned for her, then we'll have to make plans for her future. Word will soon leak that the saloon gal has left town. The old chuckling hens will be glad that another fallen woman has left. Soon, they will flap their feathers and make it their business as to what to do about Susie. But no group of busybodies are going to tell me how to do my job." Spinning on his heels, he muttered he would see her at supper.

"Thank you, Matt," Anna said, "I will pray for you."

He stopped and gave her a lopsided grin. "You do that."

~

Mr. Godwin was in shock when he raised the shades on the double doors and unlocked them for the supper hour. He glanced over at the clock. It was only a few minutes before five and a long line of cowboys, miners, and a few riffraff were lined up outside waiting for him to step out of their way. Anna quickly moved in front of the line and asked the men to wait while she seated them.

As the customers took their appointed places, she said, "Gentlemen, please remove your hats."

A few grumbled but did as she asked and hung them on the back of their chair. After all the tables were filled, Anna took their orders while Mr. Godwin and Juan dished up their food. When Anna reached the riffraff in line, she smiled at each one of them and said, "Boys, if you return tomorrow with clean faces and hands, I will give each of you a piece of pie on the house."

"What if we wash up now? Can we have a piece today?" One of the men questioned.

"Give me your order for supper, and then go out the back door to the pump. Hurry now," Anna said sweetly. Before she could collect everyone's order, the men rushed back to their table and looked like three young schoolboys waiting for a treat. "My, don't you gentlemen look nice. Now eat your dinner, and I will serve you an extra-large slice of pie."

During the hour, several men had poured themselves some alcohol into their coffee. The conversation became loud and rowdy. Anna whisked herself over to their table and posted her hands on her hips. "Gentlemen, please refrain from using your strong drink here, and remember, you are inside a building, not on the playground. May I offer you something sweet from the glass case—pie or cobbler?"

"Yep, and I want a taste of your sweet lips to go with it." A scruffy, but good-looking man pulled Anna into a tight grip.

She didn't struggle, but leaned down to his ear and latched on to it. "Should I bite it soft or hard?"

Suddenly he pushed her away, and the man immediately asked her to forgive him. "I didn't mean to get out of line."

Anna smiled at the young man and said he was forgiven. "Now, which pie would you like?"

~

Matt had just walked into the café when he saw the young man pull Anna into his arms. He started toward them when he witnessed him letting her go and heard him apologizing.

Anna waved at Matt as she went to get the men their desserts. "Come with me, Sheriff Matt. I have a special table for you." In a few minutes, Juan and Susie walked over to his table. Juan pulled out a chair for the child to sit while Matt stood until she was in position.

"Well, this is a pleasant surprise, Miss Susie. You sure look mighty pretty today."

"Miss Anna washed me and my clothes. She fixed my hair, too. Tomorrow she is going to buy me a new dress. I don't need it now that my old dress is clean."

"Anna is a nice woman who believes in being clean all the time.

You will have to get used to that if you stay with her."

"Can't I come and live with you? You ain't got a gal," Susie said matter-of-factly. "I am small for my age of four years old. That old woman said she would tell the old man that I was three. 'People like little girls,' she said."

Matt was getting madder by the minute. He was going to have a long talk with that old woman who worked upstairs in the saloon. If she came near Susie again, he would put her on a stage to Mexico. "Why don't you stay with Miss Anna? She has a nice little house, and she will teach you to cook. Anna's a great teacher and she'll never hurt you."

"Well—" Susie stuck out her lower lip, and her eyes filled with tears. "I will stay for a while if you don't want me."

Matt pulled the child into his lap. "It's not that I don't want you. It's better for a girl to stay with another girl."

"Is that one of those *manner things* that Mr. Godwin said I had to learn?"

"I guess that would fall under manners," Matt said, thinking how smart this little child was.

"Okay," Susie said, rubbing her runny nose on the front of Matt's clean shirt.

He glanced up at Anna's friend. "Juan, how are you doing? Is Anna keeping you busy?"

"Mr. Godwin hired me to work here in the café. I am Anna's helper and the repairman for this place. He wants me to build some more shelves behind the glass case and organize his storeroom. This room needs more cabinets. He has food sitting everywhere, and it needs to be off the floor."

"Goodness, Mr. Godwin hit the jackpot when he hired Anna." Matt smiled and used his napkin to wipe gravy off Susie's mouth. And how nice and quiet the customers in the café were behaving. Several times a week he'd had to toss men out into the street who were causing a disturbance. He studied Anna as she moved from one table to another, speaking softly to the customers. She was definitely a charmer.

Chapter 10

The longest day of her life had ended, but she had a smile on her face. Mr. Godwin had decided to pay Anna on a daily basis for the number of pies and other baked goods she sold. And he trusted her.

After showing Susie around the little house and tucking her into bed, she sat in front of the fireplace with the letter that Pedro had brought home. Both boys sat cross-legged on the floor and listened as she read news from the convent.

"Oh, listen to this," chirped Anna. "Reverend Mother and Sister Melody are coming to Livingston in a few days. Gosh, they are probably on their way by now. It had to take this letter a few days to reach here."

"That's right. We need to start meeting the stagecoach each time it rolls in," Pedro said.

"That won't be much trouble for us, Anna, because the stage depot is practically next door to the café. When we hear the stage coming, one of us can stand near the door and watch the passengers get off," Juan suggested. "Come on, go on with the letter. Maybe she will tell you why she is making this long trip." Juan straightened out on the floor and propped his hands under his chin. He was tired from the long day of serving customers and chopping wood for the stove.

"She said that the authorities have been snooping around the convent. They want to catch the man who robbed the bank and a military payroll from a train. The lone thief shot the conductor, but before he died, he described the man who had shot him. The authorities are sure it was my uncle." She read aloud.

"*My dear, I have prayed about making this trip, but I feel I need to be close to you. We will pray for your uncle together. I shall look forward to being with you soon. Tell Pedro and Juan that Señor Carlos prays for them every night."*

Faithfully yours,

Reverend Mother

"You know Reverend Mother left out important information in her letter. She wants us to read between the lines because she's afraid that the authorities might read her mail. Let me see that envelope." Pedro took the piece of paper and said, "Yep, this was opened and resealed by someone."

Anna held the letter to her chest. "It's so unbelievable that Uncle Claude could be such a bad man who would rob, steal, or even kill another person. Neither one of you have ever met him," Anna remarked as she peered down on the two young men. "I was only ten years old when he dropped me off at the convent. The letter Reverend Mother received from him requesting that I come and live with him was the first communication that she had received since he left me."

"If he's done all these bad things, why would he want you to come and be with him? That's doesn't make sense," Juan said.

"Right before I left the convent, I received a package from Uncle Claude. I was so sad about leaving that I forgot about it and left it on my bed in my room. Reverend Mother said that she would send it to me after she went through it. Now, I am thinking that he might have sent me stolen money to bring to him." Anna pondered for a moment. "He was going to use me!"

"I bet he thought you would pack up the money, bring it with you, and then he would take it from you and skedaddle, leaving you here all alone." Pedro sat up on his knees in front of Anna's rocker, building up a steam of anger.

"You know, we need to alert Matt as to what is going on concerning your uncle," Juan said.

"We don't have any proof. Since I have arrived, I haven't seen hide nor hair of him or even received a note. Let's wait until Reverend Mother arrives before involving Matt with my problem. He has a wanted poster on Uncle Claude, so he knows that he's a wanted man."

~

The next morning, Anna stood on her front porch watching the sun rise well above the eastern hills. The day had come to life with sounds of chirping birds. A screeching hawk circled high, hunting for food in the cloudless light blue sky. It was going to be a beautiful cool day, but Anna wasn't going to enjoy it.

As she sat in her swing, she said her morning prayers. She loved this time of day—the quiet, God's creatures singing, the morning coming alive. She missed hearing the ringing of the church chimes, and the sisters practically trotting in a straight line to the spacious church where together they hummed their prayers. She was enjoying Livingston, but she missed her home—the convent. Smiling, her heart jumped with joy realizing that the most special person in her life would be arriving soon.

She heard the boys moving around and preparing the fireplace and kitchen stove with small pieces of wood. Anna entered the house. Susie was still asleep on the bed that they shared.

"Good morning," Anna called to Juan and Pedro. "I'll have coffee and breakfast very soon."

Once breakfast was over, Pedro left for his job at the livery. Juan washed the breakfast dishes while Anna prepared eight pies and ten loaves of bread. While the pies were cooling, she rolled out six dozen doughnuts and a few other pastries. She dropped the doughnuts in the hot grease. As they drained on the board, Anna sprinkled white sugar over them.

Susie finally woke up. "Can I have one of those things with the hole in the center? Man, oh man, they smell good."

"Susie, you must say, 'may I have a doughnut, please.' That's the way a big person asks for something to eat."

"But, I ain't big—yet, so can I have one or not?"

Juan laughed and started to give her one, but not before Anna slapped his hand. "Juan, you must help me teach Susie manners."

"There's that word again. I don't think I like to hear *manners* again."

Anna placed Susie in a chair at the kitchen table. "Susie, people with nice manners receive things a lot faster than people who are impolite. Now, say 'May I have a doughnut, please?' and see how fast you'll get it."

"Well, poop. If I have to," Susie said and did so.

"Mercy sakes, don't ever say that ugly word again. Do you understand me? Little girls don't say nasty things like that."

"Maybe I'd better go live with the sheriff. I bet he'll let me talk the way I want."

"I am sorry, sweetheart," Anna said, tapping her finger on the tabletop. "I am trying to teach you to be a sweet girl, so please don't be upset with me when I correct you."

"Oh, okay. Can I…I mean…may I have another one of those round things?"

"Yes, you may," Anna replied, feeling like she'd just climbed a mountain.

~

Sitting tall in their saddles, Claude and Slim looked down on the town of Livingston. Claude knew that his niece, Anna, should have arrived already if she left the convent soon after she received his letter. "Slim, if I go into town, I'll be recognized by someone. I lived there for a couple years before I made plans to join up with your group of friends. I was tired of doing odd jobs and gambling to make ends meet. Tried to sell my house, but I had no takers. You'll have to nose around in town for news of my niece. She won't be hard to spot since she is a sister from a convent." Claude gave Slim a hard stare. "You do know what a nun looks like, I hope."

"Sure, I do. I ain't ignorant. My folks were hard-shell Baptists although they didn't believe in the Catholic ways. Ain't sure why they felt that way, but I never could talk to either one of my folks. The only attention I got from my old man was when he got drunk and beat the hell out of me, which was pretty regular. Ma never tried to stop him."

"Sorry, you had bad folks. I can't say I did, but they sure would be disappointed in me right about now. Good thing they've passed on." Claude shifted in his saddle and saw a large pile of rocks about fifty yards ahead. "Follow me, Slim, and let's make camp over there near those rocks."

After scouting around, Claude spotted an opening in the rocks, behind which a narrow path that led into an old mine. "Hey, look at this place. This cave will make a good hideout." Slim joined him and picked up a large limb and lit the dry branches with a match.

"Give that to me. You go tie up the horses." Claude pushed through the narrow rocks and waved the torch all around. A few bats flew in all directions, but other than that, it was empty.

After Slim tied their horses behind some rocks, he joined Claude in the cave.

Claude smiled. "Yes, this will do nicely. I will remain here while you go into town and scout around for my niece. Don't draw any attention to yourself and find out if she is staying in my house and if she came alone to Livingston."

"Maybe I'd better get a room at the boardinghouse, if they have one, and stay for a day or so. What do you think?" Slim said.

"No, as soon as you find out where she's living, come on back here. I'll go into town and get her and the money. She'll come with me without a fuss."

~

Juan pulled the wagon around to the front of the house, while Anna held Susie's hand down the steps. "We have to hurry to the café with these fresh baked goods. You can help me set the tables." Later, between breakfast and lunch, she would go to the dry goods store and buy some much needed clothes for Susie. She was so happy not to have to worry about the child running wild all over town.

Henrietta seemed thrilled to see Anna and Susie enter the store. "Well, look at who we have here? Two of the prettiest girls in Livingston," she commented, as she bent down to touch Susie's long blond curls.

Susie smiled and walked over to the case that held several jars of peppermint sticks. She pressed her nose into the glass.

"Let's head to the back of the store and look at some girl's clothes, Susie. Maybe, you will get a treat before we leave." Anna took Susie's hand, but the little one continued to look back at the jars of candy.

Anna selected four little dresses, four white shifts, six pair of pantaloons, and a pair of sturdy brown shoes. After trying the shoes on for size, Henrietta chose six pairs of white socks for Susie. "These will fit nicely."

Back at the front counter, Anna chose long, colorful ribbons to go into Susie lovely blond hair.

"I don't won't those things in my hair," Susie said.

"Well, I want you to look pretty in church, so I am buying some anyway." Anna smiled down at her.

"I ain't going in that old white building where that old man screams." Susie shook her head and folded her arms across her chest.

"I didn't know you were a scaredy-cat. Afraid of an old man? I don't believe that," Anna teased.

"I ain't scared of nothing!" Susie spun around to run out the door but ran right into Matt's tall legs.

"Hey, what's your hurry, little one?" Matt said, as he picked her up. Susie immediately laid her head on his shoulder and said that Anna wouldn't give her a peppermint stick.

"Susie, don't you dare start telling lies. If you do, you will not get any candy." Anna shook her head as she looked into Matt's handsome face. He became better looking to her every day.

"Henrietta, please give me a dozen sticks of peppermint and put them in a small bag for me. I am not ready to share them with anyone until they can apologize for telling tales." Anna retrieved her packages and the bag of candy.

Matt nodded good day to Henrietta and walked with Anna to the café. He held the door of the café open for Anna and Susie.

"Thanks, Matt, for helping me, but I'd best go to the kitchen and start lunch. Will you come back and eat with Susie? She may give you a treat for being a good boy." Anna smiled sweetly and reached for Susie.

"If duty doesn't call me, I'll be here. Good day, ladies." He bowed to Anna and Susie.

Chapter 11

Mr. Dunner, the old man from the stagecoach, stood at the bar in the Silver Slipper Saloon. "Man, I ain't never seen anything like it. The little gal begged the cowboy sitting across from me for a gun. She screamed at the cowboy that she could shoot. He gave her his pistol and said for her to reload it for him, but instead, she looked down the barrel of the pistol, leaned out the window, and started shooting. Bang! Bang!" He pointed his finger like a gun. "She shot one bandit after another. I bet there were a dozen riders that fell by the wayside." Dunner had the men's attention now. "Give me another beer, Sam, and bring my friends one, too," demanded Mr. Dunner, feeling like a big shot now that he had an audience.

"Hey, old man. I heard that she only shot four men," one of the men shouted.

"Excuse me, sir," the old man snorted and cursed under his breath. "I was there, and I witnessed it all. Thought we were all going to be killed." He wiped his mouth with his sleeve. "The young cowboy continued shooting, but I never saw him hit any of the bandits. Suddenly a rider was so close to my window I could smell his nasty breath. The old woman in the seat next to me screamed like she was being scalped. The little nun pulled herself inside, stretched across my lap, and shot the man. The cowboy in the stagecoach never even saw the man." Dunner turned up his glass and drank half of his beer, then belched. "I tell you, fellows," he said, "I was scared out of my wits, but that little gal saved us all."

"You called her a nun, but we've heard that she ain't one. She was only dressed like a sister of the order for her protection," A bearded man standing close to the bar spoke out.

"Maybe she ain't a nun, but she's shore a sharpshooter. Since you know that she ain't a nun, who is she?"

One of the men spoke up. "Some of us were standing on the stage depot when she arrived and heard her say that her uncle was expecting her, but he didn't know what day she would be arriving. The deputy asked the name of her uncle, and she said he was that bad-ass outlaw, Moore." The man paused for a minute. "He may have been expecting her to arrive, but he didn't dare come into town." The men chuckled, and one declared that there would be a hanging for sure if that murderer and thief showed his face in Livingston.

"What did the gal do?" The old man was interested in the nun's welfare.

"The deputy notified Sheriff Jenkins that Claude Moore's niece was at the stage depot. He came and took her to his office."

~

All morning, Slim had been lazing around in the far corner of the saloon sipping on glasses of bug juice. He had tasted better whiskey, but he couldn't afford the good stuff. In his drunken state, he heard Claude's name. Slim turned to watch and listen to the men gathered at the bar. He understood from their conversation that Claude's niece wasn't a nun. How in the world would he find her now? A nun stood out like a totem pole in a western town, he thought.

"Shut your face. You're as dumb as a dead stump," A drunken cowboy said to another man standing at the bar. "I done told you that she's the little cook at the café. She ain't no upstairs floozy."

"Hey, you," screamed a painted-face woman with bleached blond hair. "You been cozying up to me all morning, and now you have the nerve to call me a floozy. Who do you think you are?" Grabbing a glass of beer, the bar fly tossed it in the man's face.

Suddenly, a fist hit the loud-mouthed cowboy, and blood squirted all over his face and down his shirtfront. The cowboy landed on his backside in the middle of the saloon floor. He quickly sat up, shaking his head and rubbing the blood onto his hands and neck. "Who do you think you are, butting into our quarrel? I'm going to clean your plow." The bleeding cowboy stood and started swinging his fists, and the whole room exploded into a brawl. Tables slammed on the floor and chairs became weapons, hitting each participant across the head or backs. Two men were tossed out the front door, and another was thrown through the picture window before Sheriff Jenkins arrived.

Surveying the room, Sheriff Jenkins shot his pistol in the air to stop the ruckus. All the men pushed and shoved their fighting partners away and eased back from each other. "All right. Who started this mess?" The sheriff demanded.

When no man spoke up, he looked around, then spoke to the bartender. "Jim, stand at the door, and each man here will drop money into your apron as they make their way out. It looks to me like everyone had some part in ripping this room apart. Now I'm going to stand and watch each of you gather your hats and go home or back to work."

In less than ten minutes, all the men had left the bar, and Jim was satisfied with the money collected to pay for damages.

"What started this fight?" the sheriff asked Jim.

"It started about the little nun, whom I'm guessing isn't a nun. One thing led to another, and the barmaid got upset for being called a floozy." Jim gestured toward the upstairs with a smirk.

Slim was angry because he only had one silver dollar left, and he had to toss it into the bartender's apron. He wanted to tell the sheriff that he wasn't in the brawl, but he suspected he'd better not draw attention to himself. Now he'd have to go back to the hideout and get more cash from Claude if he was going to continue searching for his niece. Slim rode toward the hideout, a half mile from town. He shaded his eyes and looked to the hills to see if he could spot Claude watching the trail, but his partner was well hidden from people passing by.

As Slim approached their hideout, he whistled so Claude would know that it was him. He sat in his saddle and waited for a response. When Claude didn't appear, Slim rode to the cave and was surprised not to see Claude's horse. He slid down and slowly made his way to the entrance of the cave and peered inside. No fire or any sounds came from the open dugout.

Slim was afraid to enter the cave, so he stepped back and studied the ground. He should have noticed all the hoof prints on the ground when he first rode up. Claude and his horse had disappeared, and the ground was all torn up by many horses—a posse.

Claude must have escaped because the posse didn't bring him into town and report their action to the sheriff. His first thought was to head to the border town in Mexico and hopefully locate Claude.

Anger wouldn't describe how Claude would be when Slim told him that he had not discovered his niece's whereabouts. If he didn't need a share of the stolen money, he would disappear from the meanest man he had ever met.

Chapter 12

Anna was sitting at the small worktable in the corner of the café. It was all she could do to keep her eyes open, Mr. Godwin thought. But she rallied on, finishing the meals before the lunch crowd came. He knew she was up before the sun rose and was the last person in bed each night. She cooked pastries and pies every free moment she had for the café. "Anna, today is Sunday, and I am going to start closing at two o'clock. I want you to take Mondays off. You are not to come back to this café before early Tuesday morning with your fresh pies. Is that understood?"

"Are you closing the café on Mondays?" Anna asked.

"No, but Juan and I can cook and serve. The crowd is always small the first of the week. I won't hear any argument." He turned and hurried over to the stove to dish up the boiled potatoes.

~

Matt stood on the back porch of the café talking to Susie. The young girl was saying that she was being good, so Anna would give her a treat. He laughed and entered the café.

"Guess what, Matt, tomorrow I'll be free to go fishing, if you would like to take me. I'll fix a nice picnic if you dig some worms and find us a couple of strong poles."

"That's the best offer I have had in weeks. I can leave my deputy in charge and this trip will be our secret. I don't want to be discovered while catching the biggest fish in the creek."

"No, I will catch the largest fish, my dear sir. I am the best fisherman in the south," Anna said, grinning.

"We may have to make a wager tomorrow." Matt stood and curled a dark strand of Anna's hair around his finger. "I'd better get busy stringing up our new fishing poles. May I come over this evening—maybe sit on your swing with you?"

"I would like that."

Early the following day, Matt apologized for showing up with his flatbed wagon. He had loaned his carriage to Jim Martin, a young farmer who was courting a gal a few miles from town. Jim would be returning it today, but Matt and Anna needed to reach the creek early.

"Your choice of wagons doesn't impress me, Mr. Matt Jenkins. I'm just happy to be out in the fresh air doing something I haven't done since leaving the convent." Matt lifted Anna onto the bench and placed the picnic basket in the bed behind the seat.

"How far is this fishing hole away from town?"

Oh, I guess less than five miles. It is shady on one side of the bank which is really nice in the summer and pretty sunny this time of the year. I have fished at the same spot for many years. You will enjoy building a fire and sitting in the sun while we eat the wonderful lunch you have brought along." He smiled down at Anna as they traveled toward the creek.

"I only brought bread and water." Anna attempted humor but couldn't pull it off. She burst into laughter.

"I may not know much about your personal life before you came to Livingston, but I feel I know a little about the prettiest little lady that showed up a month or so ago. I hope to get to know you a little better today." Matt pulled the single horse over to the creek bank, unhitched him from the wagon, and hobbled his legs so he could eat the tall grass but not wander away. He helped Anna down from the wagon, grabbed a pail, and filled it with water for the horse.

Matt watched Anna as she retrieved the blanket and basket from the wagon and placed it near a flatbed of grass close to the creek. He carried the two fishing poles and the bucket of worms to the edge of the water. "This is as good as any place to begin with. Sometimes I move around the bend when the water is moving slowly."

Anna unwound the fishing line from her pole and baited her own hook with a fat, juicy worm. She tossed it out and watched her cork move around until it settled in the water.

Matt grinned as he readied his pole and swung it near Anna's.

"Hey, you creek hog, you have a lot of space out there without having to hug my line."

"Don't be calling me names, Missy. The wind carried my line. I'll toss it further away from you." Matt started pulling his line in when Anna quickly began backing up and pulling her own line into herself. "Hey, you, look at my big catch."

Matt laid his pole on the ground and grabbed the fishing net. Laughing and splashing in the creek, he nabbed Anna's big fish. She stood on the bank, yelling for him not to lose it.

In a few minutes, Matt held the fish up for Anna to see. Sure enough, it was at least six pounds. "All right, Missy, you caught the first one, but the game is on. I'll now show you how a real fisherman catches the big ones."

For several hours, Matt and Anna laughed and praised each other for catching a string of catfish that would feed a dozen people. Both of them stood at the edge of the bank, washing their arms and hands.

"I am starved, Missy. I believe I would love to have some of your 'bread and water' from your lovely picnic basket." Matt grabbed Anna's hand and led her to the spot where she had left the blanket and basket.

~

When Anna tossed the blanket in the air to spread out on the grass, a sensation came over her. Again, she felt that they were being watched. She stood still, then she slowly turned and looked all around.

"Anna, what's wrong? You're white as a bedsheet." Matt reached for Anna's hand and touched her cheek.

"Nothing really. I just feel like we're being watched," she said. "It's a funny feeling I get when I sense something's wrong."

"You don't have to be afraid. I am here, and I am your big, brave protector." Laughing, he said, "Now feed me, woman."

Anna's eyes were as large as saucers as she looked over Matt's shoulder. A tall, sunburned-faced man stood with a pistol pointed directly at them.

~

"It looks like your hero is not so *big and brave* now," the stranger said, mimicking Matt. Slim, Claude's partner, had followed Matt and Anna. He had been to the border and received instructions from Claude to bring Anna to him, no matter who he had to hurt.

"You, girlie, are going to be reunited with your uncle. He's anxious to see you after all this time. He sends his apology. Claude wanted to come in person, but too many men, like this one, are after him. Now, you move away from your soon-to-be ex-lover—" Slim snickered at his own comment, "while I tie him. You do as I say, and I won't hurt him."

~

Anna stepped slowly away from Matt, never taking her eyes away from the stranger. She tried to remember if she had ever seen him in the café or somewhere else in town, but nothing came to mind. He fumbled with a rope tied on his saddle and motioned for Matt to turn around. Suddenly, Matt twisted around, and with a swift kick, knocked the man's feet out from under him. A blast of gunfire found Matt doubled over on the ground. The bullet had lodged into Matt's left thigh.

Anna screamed and fell to Matt's side as he lay bleeding. The stranger grabbed Anna's blouse, causing buttons to fly. He squeezed her shoulder and pulled her to a standing position. Anna's fingers reached for the blanket and, pulling it off the ground, tossed it over the stranger's pistol. With both hands covered, he clutched at the heavy blanket while Anna knocked him in the head with the picnic basket, causing him to drop the gun.

They both scrambled near Matt for it. Anna clawed at the man's face with her sharp fingernails, causing him to loosen his hold on her. She reached the pistol first and pulled the trigger. The stranger's eyes bulged, and he rolled over on his side and vomited. He died almost instantly.

Anna's body was shaking, but she pulled herself together and swooped down over Matt's body. He was unconscious and his pant leg was soaked. Blood ran down his neck and back. Anna turned him over and saw a large gash in his hair. A bloody stone lay under Matt's head. His leg was bleeding badly from the gunshot wound. Over the years, Anna had learned a few medical techniques from Reverend Mother. She knew that she was going to have to control the bleeding or Matt would die.

Anna lifted her skirt and, grabbing her shift, she tore off a long strip and tied a tourniquet onto Matt's leg to stop the flow of blood. She searched in the basket for clean napkins and carried them to the water's edge wetting them. Wiping his face softly with a wet napkin, Anna repeated his name over and over but failed to rouse him.

Anna knew she couldn't carry Matt to the wagon, but she had

to get him to the doctor. She placed the blanket back under his tall frame and tugged him over to the flatbed wagon. Hurrying to the horse, Anna tried to untie the rope that had his hoofs hobbled. Finally, using a table knife, she loosened the knots and slipped the rope off the animal's hooves. The horse tossed his head and reared his front legs. Anna moved backward and reached for his reins. Being a stranger to the horse, he shied away from her and took off across the field that led to the main road.

"Oh, Lord," she prayed as she watched Matt's horse racing across the open field, "Please let him go back to the stable in town. Pedro and Juan both know that Matt and I have gone fishing. Please send help." Anna turned and hurried back to Matt. He was still out cold. Placing the blanket firmly under his body, she leaned Matt up against the wagon wheel. Maybe it was a blessing Matt wasn't able to use his two-seater carriage.

Anna shook Matt's shoulder several times. Finally, Matt blinked his eyes, dazed and unsure if he was still alive. She called his name and begged him to look at her. "I'm here, Matt. You've been shot, but I'm sure help is on the way. I need to get you in the wagon. Please try to help me by standing on your good leg."

After ten minutes of struggling to stand, Anna pushed Matt over into the bed of the wagon. He had lost consciousness again. "It's probably for the best, Lord. Maybe he can't feel pain." Anna shook her head. She had been talking aloud to God ever since the stranger appeared.

Attempting to make Matt comfortable, she pulled tall grass up until she had enough to make a soft pillow. She took two clean napkins and covered the grass before positioning his head. All the while, Anna continue to pray silently.

Suddenly, Matt's body started shaking. He probably had chills from losing so much blood. With nothing to cover his body, Anna climbed into the wagon and lay down beside him. His body was shaking so hard she could hear his teeth hitting together. Anna removed her skirt and covered his shoulders with it. She rolled over on his chest to cover him, and finally his body calmed.

"Please Lord, please send help." This was Anna's last thought as she closed her eyes and fell into an exhausted sleep.

Chapter 13

The three o'clock stagecoach arrived precisely on time in Livingston. Like always, a crowd of people stood near the stage depot, waiting for their loved ones or just curious to see the strangers coming to town. Today was no different except the sheriff wasn't in town today. The deputy was on duty to help meet and greet the strangers.

"Look out, look out. A runaway horse is coming down the middle of the street. Get those children out of its way," someone was yelling at the top of their lungs.

"Whose horse is that?" the deputy asked, as people were unloading from the stage.

"I'll go to the stable and see," a young man called to the deputy.

"Welcome, ladies, to Livingston," the deputy said to an elderly sister." He took the nun's hand and helped her down the shaky steps. He reached for the younger nun's hand and assisted her onto the platform.

"Hurry, Deputy," a young man called. "The black horse belongs to the sheriff. Pedro said that he and Miss Anna went fishing early this morning and they took the horse and wagon. Something must be wrong."

"Excuse me, ladies, but I have to go and see what has happened." He hurried with the young man to the stable. Pedro and a few other men were already saddling their horses. The preacher was on the stage platform, and he raced after the deputy, quickly unhitched his horse, and said that he was riding along.

~

After what seemed an eternity to Pedro, he saw Matt's wagon. The men rode to the area where the couple had been fishing. One man yelled he had found their bucket of fish. Another rider had discovered the picnic basket and poles. The loudest cry came from a man who had found the dead body.

Pedro and Preacher Stubbs found two bodies lying tangled into each other's arms, seemly fast asleep, in the back of the Matt's wagon.

Slowly, the other riders walked their horses over to the back of the wagon and sat, looking at the two cozy lovebirds and then glancing from one to another.

Finally, Pedro climbed onto the wagon and called Anna's name. "Wake up," Pedro said.

Anna slowly lifted her head and immediately she was fully awake. "Thank the Lord, you have finally arrived. Matt has been shot in the leg and we have to get him to the doctor. He has lost a lot of blood."

"He looks dead," one man said.

"If he ain't, he'll soon wish he was, because he'll soon be a married man." Laughter and hooting came from the older men.

"Preacher Stubbs, should you perform a funeral or a wedding?" Another man said, as the wagon was being hitched up to a fresh horse.

"All right, fellows, you've had your fun," yelled the deputy. "I need a couple of you to wrap that dead body in my bedroll and tie him over Pedro's horse. We'll discover who he is once we return to town."

"Shall I tell all the men at the Silver Slipper to prepare for a big shindig?" one of the younger men shouted and waved his hat over his head.

"Listen to me, fellows. Most of you know what a nice gal Miss Anna is, and she would never do anything improper," the deputy said, as he climbed on his horse. "I'm asking you to keep quiet about this until we discover why there's a dead man, and the reason Matt's been shot."

There was no reply from the men as they followed the deputy into town.

~

Reverend Mother and Sister Melody were soon greeted by Juan, and after claiming their carpetbags, he carried them to the café for some refreshments.

"What do you suppose happened to Anna and the man she went

69

fishing with?" Reverend Mother asked Juan.

"Anna's friend is Sheriff Jenkins. He has been so helpful to us since we arrived. The sheriff helped Pedro, Anna, and me with many things. Anna would never go off with a bad man." Juan headed to the café doors and saw Pedro driving Matt's wagon to the doctor's office.

"Reverend Mother, Anna and Matt are back. They're heading to the doctor's office," Juan said, as he grabbed his sombrero from the hat rack.

"I'm following you," Reverend Mother said to Juan. "Sister, let's go see what has happened."

~

Matt had been moved to Anna's little house and placed in the middle of her double bed.

He did remember someone holding up his head and shoulders and telling him over and over to say, "I will." He tried to focus, but the room spun around and around. "Say, 'I will,'" he was told again, so he mumbled, "I will."

Matt could hear people talking, but they stood too far away from the bed for him to make out what they were saying. He was sure he heard a woman crying and saying, "No" over and over. Was he going to die? "Hell, no," he murmured to himself. "I've got too much living to do before I ride off into the sunset."

"What did you say, Matt." Preacher Stubbs leaned closer to Matt's mouth. When Matt didn't respond, he called to the doctor. "Hey, Doc, I'm sure I heard him speak."

"That's a good sign that his head injury might not be as bad as I thought." The doctor felt Matt's forehead and said that he didn't have a fever. He also said Anna would have to watch his leg wound for infection which could give him a high fever later.

Matt inched open his eyes to see an old woman in nun's clothes peering down at him.

"Don't fret about this young man, Doctor. Between the three of us, he will have all the attention he needs," the woman commented.

~

Juan and Pedro had given up their bedroom to Reverend Mother and Sister Melody. They would sleep on bedrolls in front of the fireplace. Susie slept on the small sofa next to the dining room table, while Anna rested on a pallet next to Matt's bed. The little house was bursting at the seams with people, but no one complained.

~

Matt had been unconscious for three days. He had awakened for only a few minutes at a time. Anna realized that she needed to check on Matt's leg wound because blood had seeped through the bandage, and it should be cleaned. She lowered the bedcovering and realized that he lay stark naked from his waist down. Flaming heat traveled from her head to her toes, and she looked away and quickly covered his private parts and his good leg. As gently as she could, she pulled on the tape that held the gauze over the stitches. She removed the dead skin, trying hard not to breathe while cleaning the wound. The smell nearly gagged her.

Anna knew that Matt had awakened during the time she started changing the bandage on his hurt leg. Long and raspy groans erupted from him as she rewrapped the wound. He clasped the sheet with one hand while patting the mattress in rhythm with the other. His eyes remained closed.

~

On the fourth morning, Matt woke up, sniffing and smiling. "I smell buttered cinnamon toast." His stomach growled, he glanced around the round and attempted to sit up.

"Oh, Matt, you're finally awake. Are you dizzy?' Anna asked with excitement in her voice.

"No, but I am going to pee everywhere if you don't get yourself out of my way." He tried again to sit up.

"Juan, come and help Matt with his personal needs." Anna left the room after giving Juan a bucket and a wet cloth. She could hear Matt fussing and asking what the hell had happened to him. Juan was patiently helping him with his long johns and explained that a man shot him in the leg.

Anna hurried into the kitchen, heated chicken broth, and softened toast in some warm milk. She placed it on a tray and waited for Juan to come out of the bedroom.

"Anna," Juan leaned over and whispered, "He's in a bad mood. I've never seen him act this way. Maybe the gash on his head has caused him to be...difficult."

Anna shook her head and carried in the tray of food. "I have some broth and toast. You haven't eaten in four days, so the doctor said to only serve you something light."

"I'll eat in a minute, but first I need to know how I got shot. Since you and I were the only ones fishing, how and why did it happen?" Matt grimaced every time he moved. When Juan had turned him onto his side to relieve himself, he screamed at Juan to get out of the room.

"The doctor left some medicine to help relieve your pain." Anna picked up the brown bottle of liquid and showed it to him.

"Later, maybe when I need to sleep. For now, I want answers." Anna had never witnessed the scowl on Matt's face before. He had always been pleasant and gentle in his actions.

"Who shot me?" he demanded.

"My uncle sent a man to get me. A stranger who I'd never seen before. He followed us to the creek and watched until he had the chance to sneak up on us. The man was going to tie you up, but you knocked his feet out from under him. His gun went off, hitting you in the leg. I tossed the blanket over the man's handgun, and we wrestled on the ground. I got his gun and pulled the trigger. The bullet hit him in the stomach, and he died instantly," Anna said as tears streamed down her cheeks. "I never intended to shoot him, and I have asked God to forgive me for taking another's life."

"Damn it, girl," Matt yelled, causing her to jump back from the bed. "Don't you have any idea what that man would have done to you before taking you to your uncle? Don't stand there crying over killing an outlaw, one that wouldn't think twice about killing you." Before Anna could answer, he continued. "Don't you realize now what danger you're still in? That fool uncle of yours will be sending someone else after you when he learns his partner is dead—killed by your hands."

"I can't believe that Uncle Claude would ever harm me. I know he wants the bank money, but once he gets it, he will go on his merry way."

"Don't you have any brains in that head of yours? No, he won't go waltzing off into the sunset as you think. I'll have him behind bars the minute he shows his face. There's a posse right now on his trail."

~

Matt sighed and stared at the ceiling, grinding his teeth to keep from crying out with pain from his leg and the back of his head. "I can't believe I was foolish enough to take you away from town without some of my men hiding in the woods."

Anna looked stunned at Matt's statement. "Are you telling me that the only reason you have become my friend is so you can catch my uncle when he tries to see me? You have been 'using me' to catch the most notorious outlaw in Texas." Anna waited for a response which never came. They both scowled at each other until his stomach growled.

Realizing he had let his anger get the best of him and told her his plan to catch her uncle, he felt like a big dope. He had hurt Anna's feelings, and that was never his intent. "Are you going to feed me? I'm starved."

Anna eased over to the side table rearranging the food on the tray. She looked like she wanted to smash it over his head, and she had already killed one man. Whipping around, she reached for the doorknob and slammed the bedroom door.

"Get your tail back in here and bring me some decent food. This is slop, and I want real food," he said.

Anna quickly opened the bedroom door and tossed his pants and shirt to him, hitting him in the mouth. "Put them on. I'm sick of looking at your hairy legs."

"What in the world is going on in here? It sounds like the Civil War all over again," Reverend Mother said.

Matt didn't say a word but gave the older nun a sweet smile. "I'm starving and Anna won't feed me," he mumbled like a four-year-old.

"Do what you want, Reverend Mother. I'm going to the café and relieve Sister Melody for a while. Need to get away from this baboon before I put another bullet in him."

"Now, Anna, that's no way to speak about your husband," Reverend Mother said, as she stepped out of Anna's way.

"Husband?" Matt screamed, as Anna looked to the ceiling, saying something that he couldn't make out.

"Yes, husband." Reverend Mother hummed as she removed the soft milk toast and prepared to go to the kitchen.

"I'm not anyone's husband and never will be." Somebody here had lost their mind, he thought.

"Sorry, son, but you and Anna are married. Preacher Stubbs married you two, now, three days ago." Reverend Mother came back into Matt's bedroom.

"That's impossible. Anna would never marry me. I'm the man who is going to put her uncle in jail and most likely watch him hang."

"Maybe that's so, but it's too late to fuss over that matter. You and Anna were caught in—let's just say, Anna was practically lying on top of you, asleep in the back of your flatbed wagon. She was partially undressed, and you were unconscious."

"Why would you, a godly woman, tell me this bunch of lies? I'm sorry, but I don't believe a word you just told me."

Reverend Mother walked out of the room and went straight to the kitchen. She placed a small piece of pot roast on a slice of bread and motioned for Juan to come into the bedroom with her. "If you keep this down after you have eaten it, I will give you more. Now, Juan, tell Mr. Jenkins what Pedro told you about them being discovered in the wagon."

Juan looked sheepish and peered at his boots.

"Go on, and don't leave anything out." Reverend Mother stood straight with both hands folded in front of her.

Juan took a second and swallowed hard while repeating the same story that Reverend Mother had told. He left out the part where all the men said that they would string up the sheriff if he didn't agree to the marriage.

"If I was unconscious, how did a wedding take place? Did I have a proxy?" Matt asked, feeling as if he would scream from the pain in his leg.

"A proxy? What's that?" Juan asked, glancing at Reverend Mother.

Ignoring Juan's question, Reverend Mother explained more of what the preacher had told her about the situation. "You came to for a few minutes, and two of the men held your head and shoulders up so you could speak a few words. It was a very short ceremony but legal just the same."

"When Anna was in here earlier, why didn't she say something?" Matt asked as he took a forkful of food. He chewed and swallowed. Food never tasted so good. He stuffed the remaining roast and bread in his mouth. "Get that pail," he demanded, but it was too late. The few mouthfuls of food came spewing out all over the floor. Matt was embarrassed, but his head and leg hurt too much to talk.

"Juan, please bring a mop and bucket and a glass of water. I need to give the sheriff some medicine, then we can clean the floor and open that window. This room needs some fresh air."

Chapter 14

Anna returned home to find a wonderful aroma of food cooking. Reverend Mother had taken two safety pins and placed an apron on front of her black flock. She smiled at Anna and walked over to her.

"You haven't given me a proper welcome yet, young lady. Ever since Sister Melody and I exited that stagecoach, I've witnessed more excitement than I have in my lifetime."

"Oh, Reverend Mother, I'm so pleased to have you here with me—even if it is only for a while." She took the older woman's hand and led her over to the table, peeking into the bedroom to check on Matt.

"You don't have to worry about him for a while. I gave him a big dose of medicine, and he'll most likely sleep all afternoon. He had to have *real food* as he called it, but it wasn't long before he regretted it. Matt won't want anything to eat anytime soon."

"I'm so sorry I stormed off the way I did. I was surprised and hurt to learn he had only befriended me so he could catch Uncle Claude if he showed himself. I feel so foolish because I have feelings for him." Anna couldn't meet the good woman's eyes.

"Child, Juan told me how nice the sheriff has been to all of you—you especially. It's only natural that you could lose your heart to a young, handsome man. You have only been surrounded with men whom you grew up with, because I never allowed outsiders to come inside the convent to be near my girls."

Reverend Mother paused and took a sip of hot tea. "The sheriff knows you two are married. He's not too happy with the situation. Juan and I explained what had taken place between the two of you, and how the men of the town forced you to marry."

"I'm sure if Matt had been fully conscious, no man would have forced him to do anything he didn't want to do." Anna fought back the tears. "I kept telling them that nothing happened between Matt and me. That he had been shot and he was unconscious, but they wouldn't listen." Anna wiped tears off her face with the back of her hand.

"Now, I'm going to have to suffer his anger. He'll hate me." Anna glanced at the bedroom door and prayed that Matt wasn't in any pain. "Reverend Mother, did you find money in that package that Uncle Claude mailed me? I was so upset about leaving the convent that I forgot all about it. After Matt told me that my uncle was a wanted man for robbing a bank, I remembered the package, but I didn't mention it and he didn't ask."

"After I received your first letter, I opened the package, and yes, it contained a lot of money. Claude had instructed you to bring it to Livingston with you but not to tell anyone. I decided that I'd better bring it, but I didn't dare breathe a word." She motioned for Anna to look down at the hem of her long black skirt. "I sewed stacks of money all around the hem, then padded the money so it wouldn't make a rustling noise. If the stage got robbed on the way here, no bandit would touch an old nun. Thankfully, we had a very nice trip."

"As soon as we can give the money back to the bank, then I can go home with you. Uncle Claude won't have any reason to see me. Matt can stay here." Anna glanced at Matt's bedroom door. "Let's wait to tell Matt that you brought the money. He may want to travel to the town and return the money to the bank in person." Her sigh held sorrow. "I read something about a princess marrying a pirate, and the king declared their marriage wasn't real. Matt might be able to persuade a judge to do the same for us. Then he would be free from me."

~

"And, you free from him," responded Reverend Mother. Trying not to smile, Reverend Mother thought that once Matt warmed to the idea that Anna was legally his wife, he would never let her go. Anna was too young to know that a married woman had no legal rights. Her money and property belonged to her husband, and he had complete control over her actions.

After a long day, Sister Melody, Susie, and Juan came home from the café. After a pleasant supper, Reverend Mother read scriptures from the Bible and heard prayers from everyone.

Susie surprised all of them by asking for food for her little friend who was sitting on their front porch. "He ain't got no pa and ma and nothing to eat or a place to sleep," she said.

~

Matt was wide awake and lay listening to the family as they assembled in front of the fireplace. Suddenly, he wanted to sit up, but he knew he had better stay still. He needed to relieve himself, but he didn't want to disturb Reverend Mother. "God, what is this place turning into?" he said low to himself. "Another orphan? Anna doesn't need someone else to care for."

"Susie, where is your friend?" Matt heard Anna ask with a shocked tone. "Please bring him inside. We have plenty of food, and we can't allow the child to sleep outside in the cold."

"Come with me. He's on the porch, but it's dark," Susie said to Anna.

~

When Anna and Susie stepped onto the front porch, Pedro was down on his knees holding onto a young boy. The child was struggling to escape.

"Jamie, stop. Pedro won't hurt you. Look, I have Miss Anna. She is going to feed you some supper. Come with me," Susie said, taking his hand and leading the small boy into the house.

"Pedro, you come to the kitchen, too. We saved you some supper," Reverend Mother spoke softly and put her hand on Pedro's back.

"How's Matt doing?" Pedro asked.

Anna and Sister Melody washed the boy's face and hands, sat him at the table, and gave him left-over roast and potatoes. The child shoveled the food into his mouth like someone might try to take it away from him.

"Slow down, little one," Anna said. "You will not go hungry again."

Matt's raspy voice came from the other room. "Close the door and help me with the bedpan, please."

Juan came out of Matt's bedroom and left the door open. Anna noticed. "Sister Melody, I need to go check Matt's wounds. We can bathe Jamie in the morning, and I will ask the deputy to try to find his family. He can sleep on a pallet next to Susie tonight." Anna took a deep breath and walked into Matt's bedroom.

"So, you finally decided to come home and check on your patient?" Matt said sarcastically.

"I need to check your leg and the gash on your head." Anna flipped back the blanket on the bed and saw he still didn't have any clothes on from his waist down. Turning her head, she whipped the sheet over his private parts and left only the wounded leg uncovered.

"Tomorrow you can dress in some clothes," Anna said, feeling her face flame red.

"I think I could eat something. Not that slimy milk toast either."

"Reverend Mother told me that you need to eat something light on your stomach tonight. I'll make oatmeal with a little honey. That will stick to your ribs and stay in your stomach." After Anna changed the bandage on his leg, her hands were covered in gooey black. She had smoothed a yeast paste and ground charcoal over the stitches to help fight infection. "Bend down and turn your head toward me so I can see the stitches." After examining and nursing Matt's wombs, she turned toward the bedroom door. "I'll be back with a pan of hot water so you can shave and wash your body."

"I thought that's what a wife is supposed to do for her poor, hurt husband," Matt yelled at her as she exited the room. She stopped at first, then bolted to the kitchen where she noticed that she had an audience listening to their every word.

Suddenly everyone busied themselves, Anna was too embarrassed to offer an explanation as to what they overheard coming from the bedroom.

Entering the kitchen, she placed a pail of water on the stove to heat. She got a bar of soap and a clean washcloth, then she placed his razor and cleaning items on a tray and walked back to the bedroom. Pedro jumped up from the floor and opened and closed the door for her. She prayed that Matt would behave himself while bathing.

"I was thinking that you might be too weak to stand and shave. Would you like for me to hold the mirror?" Anna asked.

"Yes, that would be nice. Man, I can't wait to get this itchy beard off my face," he said, rubbing a hand over his jaw.

Anna sat on the side of the bed and held the mirror with trembling hands. He began making circles on his face with the wet bar of soap, but his hand looked weak. Anna noticed how easily he had grown tired. "Maybe I could help by shaving you myself." She took the brush and wiped it from his eyes to the bottom of his jaw.

"Make circles like this." He took her hand and show her how to go around and around with the brush. Afterward, he allowed her to lather the soapy lotion until the fragrance was like a cloud surrounding them. Stroke after stroke, she slid the sharp blade over his face, down his jaw, chin, and over his Adam's apple. She took a wet cloth and wiped the remaining lotion off his face and watched him smile at her. A warmth crept up her neck.

"Well, my little bride, I wondered how long it was going to take before you told me that we're married? I had to hear it from your guard dog."

"I'm sorry this happened to you…us, I mean…but don't you dare speak about Reverend Mother like that. She's not a dog. Reverend Mother is the most wonderful person in the world. I pleaded with Reverend Stubbs not to listen to the men, but your deputy couldn't control the situation."

Quickly changing the subject, Matt said, "Finish here before the water gets cold. I'm ready to feel clean again."

Matt made a real sideshow out of his bathing. With her back to him, she could tell everything he was doing. He seemed to be in a good mood for a change. She hoped that meant his wounds weren't giving him too much pain.

Anna gave him a half glass of soda water and he rinsed out his mouth.

"Come close and smell me. I'm as fresh as a daisy." Matt reached his hand out to pull Anna closer. Her back was straight as a ramrod.

Placing her hands behind her back, she said, "Believe me, I'll take your word for it."

Matt fluffed up his pillow and watched Anna, who looked like she had swallowed a bug. "Now, don't you think it's about time you gave your bridegroom a kiss? We've been married for what—five days now?"

Horrified and shaking, she gave him a hard stare. "You know our marriage isn't real. You were unconscious for goodness sakes!" Anna stepped away from the bed.

"Come here, closer to the bed," Matt demanded softly as he patted the mattress.

"I need to take care of these things," she said, reaching for the shaving mug, razor, and mirror.

Matt took advantage of her being busy and grabbed a tight hold on her wrist. "Tsk, tsk, my dear bride, it's too late to run. A little kiss to bind our marriage is all I'm asking."

"Please turn me loose," she pleaded. With her free hand she placed the items on the side table.

"Come now, a little kiss and I'll let you free." Matt had a cockeyed grin on his face.

Taking a deep breath and saying a silent prayer, Anna leaned over his soapy-smelling chest, and with eyes wide open, touched his lips with hers.

Matt jerked his head back. "You mean to call that a kiss? That was like kissing a dried, dead frog."

"Oh you. You know I haven't ever kissed a man." She twisted and pulled on her wrist.

"Come on now, and try again. Close your eyes and pretend you're kissing a knight in shining armor, like all ladies dream about." She had told him that she loved to read.

"Please, I beg you—" Anna was fighting back tears. "Leave me alone. I told you I couldn't stop the preacher from conducting the ceremony. I did try." Why was he punishing her?

"Kiss me again, my little pretend nun." He gave her hands a shake.

She lowered her face to his, and with her eyes closed, kissed him softly on the lips.

"Better," he grunted. "Next time you'll give me some tongue."

"Dear God," she murmured.

"He's not going to help you now, my sweet bride."

Anna jerked her wrist free, rushed into the kitchen, and leaned against the kitchen counter. She could feel her face blushing.

"Are you all right?' Reverend Mother asked.

"Yes, I guess. Matt's feeling better, thank goodness. He didn't have much to say about our marriage. Don't know what he will do once he's well enough to walk around on crutches and can return to work."

After preparing oatmeal and a couple pieces of soft, buttered toast, Anna stood over Matt as he gobbled every morsel. He drank a small cup of water and lay back on the bed. "Now, maybe I can sleep. Good night, wife," Matt said. "Will you be nearby if I need you in the night?'

"Yes, I have a pallet beside your bed," she commented, but Matt was already asleep.

Chapter 15

Anna looked over at Jamie as he lay snuggled close to Susie. "I need to go and talk with Jamie and see if he can tell us anything about his folks. I heard him whispering to Susie, so I know he's still awake," Anna said softly to Reverend Mother. "You need to go to bed, too. This household rises early in the morning."

Anna watched as Reverend Mother walked into the bedroom that she shared with Sister Melody. She turned to Anna and blew her a kiss goodnight. Smiling, Anna tiptoed into the living room and sat down between Susie's and Jamie's pallets.

"Hi, Jamie. I heard you talking to Susie, so I know you're still awake. We are all happy to have you staying with us, but we must help you find your folks. When was the last time you saw them?"

Jamie turned his face into his pallet's pillow. "I don't wanna talk about them. Go away."

"I'm sorry, but I'm not going away. You must try to answer me. I don't want to have to turn you over to the sheriff and get you into trouble."

"I ain't done nothing wrong. Just begged my pa not to leave me. He hit me a bunch of times and told me to shut my sniveling up. I didn't want to be left all alone, but he drove away anyway. My two sisters waved goodbye to me."

"Did he say why he was leaving you?" Anna couldn't believe that a family could just drop off their child in a strange town all alone.

"He told Mama that he couldn't feed us anymore. He was going to give us away to strangers and let them take care of us. Folks like you."

"Do you think he was going to drop off your sisters in a

different town?" Anna asked, thinking that was his pa's plan.

"I ain't sure. Told him I wouldn't eat much, and I would work harder. He said to shut up, or he would beat me again."

"Is that how you got the bruises on your face?" Anna asked softly.

"Yes, ma'am. Mama didn't let him hit me much. She cried and begged him to leave me be."

"Well, it's late, and you need to go to sleep. Please don't worry about having to go back to your folks. I won't ever allow anyone to hit you again."

Jamie leaped upon his knees and hugged Anna tight. "I love you," he whispered.

Anna stood over the children's pallet and looked down at Juan and Pedro, who lay listening to Jamie's every word.

"Poor little fellow," Juan said, and Pedro just shook his head. Anna walked into the water closet and changed into her long white flannel nightgown. She spread her pallet on the floor beside Matt's bed and whispered prayers for her family, then fell into a deep sleep immediately.

Anna was awakened by the bedsprings of Matt's bed. He twitched restlessly and called out in his sleep. "No, no, I'll kill you!" he said.

Jumping up off the pallet, she peered under his bedcovers and saw the bandage on his leg was still intact, and it wasn't bloody. He just was having a bad dream.

"Anna, is that you?" Matt asked as he flopped over on his good leg. He felt like he was in a fog and he was being pulled back down into darkness.

"Yes, it's me. Now go back to sleep. You had a bad dream." Matt's hands were on her arms. He pulled her closer to the bed as he tried to open his eyes. His body ached all over. "Come close. Let me hold you."

She pulled away and refused, but he tugged her closer and begged, "Please." One hand relaxed in her hair, and the other was around her middle, under her breasts.

~

Anna woke earlier than Matt, remembering that she had crawled in the bed with him. Thank goodness he didn't have her wrapped in his arms like last night before she fell asleep. Slipping her legs off the bed, she eased up and slid her feet onto the floor. Reaching for her robe that lay on the chair, she put it on and ran her hand through her long raven hair.

"Where you going, dearest?" Matt said, leaning up on one elbow, watching her every movement.

"Oh, my. I hope I didn't wake you," she said softly. "I have to light the stove and assemble everything to make pies," She reached for a small basket. Placing her hairbrush, comb, and her other toiletries in it, she turned around and gave Matt a sweet smile.

"Why are you taking all your personal items with you?"

"Well, you're doing well enough that you don't need my help. I will be moving into the room with Reverend Mother and Sister Melody."

"The hell you will! You're my wife and you'll be staying right here with me." Matt dangled his hairy legs over the edge of the bed and sat straight up. "Whoa, the room is spinning around."

The sheet didn't cover his lower body, giving her a good view of his private parts. Anna was sure her face turned as red as a beet. "I can't believe you slept without any clothes on. You are a barbarian." She took a step to the door, but he hopped off the bed on his good leg and slammed his large hand on the door.

"You aren't moving out of this room, so put your items back where they belong."

"You listen to me, Sheriff, I will not only be moving out of this room, but as soon as this issue with Uncle Claude is settled, I will be leaving Livingston without your permission. I have no idea where I'll go, only far away from you."

~

With one hand, Matt held onto the sheet wrapped covering his lower body and the other held onto the door to keep his balance. His leg felt like he had been stabbed with a hot poker.

Quickly, Matt grabbed the back of her robe and jerked her back toward him. "Now, you hear this. Just try to leave me and see what you get for your trouble. There's no place you can go that I won't find you. And when I do, I will tan your behind. Do I make myself clear?" Something grabbed his leg. "Ouch!" Matt yelled as he dropped his covering and nearly fell over on his face. He grabbed up a little boy and shook him loose from his leg. "What the—?"

Juan jumped off his pallet and pulled Jamie away from Matt

who screeched at Juan. "That brat bit me."

Pedro jerked the sheet off the floor and helped Matt back to the bed. "Sit. Let me look at your leg. It's bleeding again."

Reverend Mother raced into the bedroom to help Pedro with Matt. "Get me a bowl of water and a clean cloth," she said to Pedro and then asked Matt if he needed pain medicine.

"No, I need attention from my wife and some peace," Matt said only for Reverend Mother's ears. As Reverend Mother attended to him, he watched Anna talking to that new child, Jamie, who they had taken in yesterday.

"Why did you attack the sheriff?" Anna held him in her arms, rocking him back and forth as he cried.

"Will he put me in jail?" he wiped his nose on the back of his hand as Sister Melody gave Anna a clean, wet cloth to wipe his face.

"Tell me why you bit him?" Matt could see the smirk on Anna's face.

"He said that he was going to beat you. I would never let him hurt you," Jamie said, laying his face on Anna's chest.

"Oh, sweetheart, the sheriff would never lay a hand on me. Juan and Pedro are my protectors. They would never allow anyone to hurt me."

"Anna can feed that child all that bull, but if she even attempts to leave here, she will be sorry. I will put *her* in jail if I have to," Matt ranted, then lay back on the bed and bellowed for pain medicine.

Reverend Mother sent Juan to take him some meds. "Finally. Maybe we can get this day started. Anyone hungry?" Reverend Mother covered her giggles with a hand.

Chapter 16

Livingston's Main Street was quiet except for a sweet tune being played by a lone piano player in the Silver Slipper Saloon. The streetlights were dim, casting shadows on the storefronts as the posse from Langston, Texas, ambled toward the corral and stable at the end of town. The deputy, Martin Lowe, walked out of the sheriff's office and watched the men. The Langston leader, Sheriff James Watkins, turned his horse around and stopped in front of the deputy.

"It kinda late, isn't it, Sheriff," Martin Lowe questioned.

"We were close to town, so the men wanted to come on in and hopefully sleep in a good bed. Hate to wake anyone up, but it can't be helped." He glanced over Martin's shoulder and asked, "Where's Matt?"

"Well, he's been shot, but he's recovering."

"Who shot him, and how bad?"

"Claude Moore's partner shot him while trying to kidnap Moore's niece." The deputy grinned. "He shot Matt in the leg, but he should be moving around on crutches soon." Martin grinned and said, "I'll tell you this. He messed with the wrong gal. Moore's niece grabbed his gun away from him and shot him dead after he shot Matt."

"That sounds like a story I need to hear from Matt." He kicked his horse in the sides and rode on down the street behind his men.

~

Early the following morning, Deputy Martin knocked on Anna's door. Sister Melody let him in, and the deputy smiled at the wonderful smell coming from the kitchen. "Good morning. I'm sorry to be here so early, but I need to talk to the sheriff."

"Certainly, come in. I will tell Anna that you are here. May I bring you a cup of coffee and a pastry?" Sister Melody asked as she led him into the kitchen. "Anna, this young man needs to visit with the sheriff." She poured Deputy Martin's coffee and placed a hot doughnut on a small plate. "Please sit while Anna prepares the sheriff for your visit."

Martin raised his eyebrows and took a seat at the kitchen table. Across the table, a cute little girl and a small boy sat staring at him, like he was a monster.

"Is that a sheriff's badge on your vest?" Jamie asked.

"Yep. I work for the sheriff." Martin has seen the little girl before, but the boy was a stranger to him.

"Martin, get your butt in here now," Matt yelled from his bed.

Grabbing his doughnut and cup of coffee, he hurried to Matt's bedside.

"Shut the door," Matt said.

Anna tapped and called from the door.

"Go away," Matt yelled.

Anna opened the door and entered as if she hadn't heard Matt's demand. She slammed a tray of coffee and pastries onto the side table, spun around, and stormed out.

"I get no respect from that one," Matt said to Martin, "but I'll train her soon enough."

Martin laughed and pulled up a straight chair. "I wanted to tell you that Sheriff Watkins came into town late last night. The posse looks tired, and their horses are worn out. He'll be here to see you this morning, but they're sleeping late and will have breakfast before he comes here."

~

An unfamiliar feeling came over Anna. She shifted, realizing that she was standing in the same place since she came out of Matt's room. Anna had too much to do to daydream and just stand and listen to the deputy talk to Matt. *I have pies to make and money to earn to help feed this large family. I am not an invalid.* Even when she lived behind the convent walls, she cared for herself. Pushing away from the bedroom wall, she headed back into the kitchen mumbling, *I can take care of myself.* She slammed the pie dough on the counter.

~

Matt listened to the pounding coming from the kitchen. He

looked at the deputy. "Thanks for coming to tell me. I can't wait to hear how far the sheriff and his men have traveled." Someone was knocking on the front door. "Maybe that's the sheriff now."

"Matt, you have more company." Sister Melody led the older man into Matt's bedroom. "I'll bring in some more coffee for your guest."

"If you aren't a sight, all laid up in that nice bed and with pretty nuns waiting on you hand and foot. Maybe I need to get shot." Sheriff Watkins laughed as he stood at the foot of Matt's bed.

"Personally, I can't wait to get back on my feet and back to work. Martin, my deputy here has been taking care of the town, but I want to help catch that Claude Moore. You know Moore sent his partner to kidnap Anna, his niece. He knows she has the bank money. His partner shot me, but thankfully Anna managed to grab his gun and shoot him."

"That must be some brave little lady." The sheriff took a cup of coffee from Sister Melody and waited until she exited the room. "You say that this Anna has the money that was stolen from the bank in Langston? How did she get it?"

"About a month ago, he sent for Anna, who lived in a convent in Whitmire. He took her there when she was about ten, and it seemed he was ready for her to come and live with him. Before she left the convent, he sent her a package, which she forgot to bring. Later, Reverend Mother of the convent opened Anna's package, and it contained the money, so she brought it here to Anna. By this time, Anna had learned the money was stolen."

"How did she find out the money was stolen?" Sheriff Watkins rubbed his whisker-laden face.

"I had to tell Anna that her uncle was wanted by the law for robbery and murder. Of course, she was devastated, but I showed her a wanted poster which convinced her of the truth. I have stayed close to her and have two friends protecting her when I'm not close by."

"How did that man nearly kidnap the girl and shoot you?"

"I let my guard down and took Anna fishing. While we were preparing to eat our picnic lunch, he jumped us." Matt shook his head. "I will not be that stupid again. Several men are watching her every move around town."

"Moore will send someone else after her. Do you think the same thing?" Sheriff Watkins said, taking a big bite out of one of the pastries from the tray. "This is wonderful. Who's the cook?"

"I would lay my life down on a bet that someone will try again to take Anna. Her uncle wants that money, and he'll do any and every thing to get it. As far as the good pastries you are stuffing down your throat, Anna made them. She's a wonderful pie maker and cook," Matt said, trying not to show how proud he was of her skills.

Dusting his hands together, Sheriff Watkins questioned Matt about his health. "When do you think you'll be able to ride with us?"

"I won't be leaving Livingston. Anna will be with me at all times when I am up and around again. Guess you haven't had time to hear the gossip. Anna is my wife, and I am going to guard her day and night. Her uncle's men will have to kill me before they put their hands on her again."

"You—married? Is this some kind of joke?" Sheriff Watkins laughed. "A womanizer like you—married? What do all the other women think about it?"

"Hey, most of what you heard about women and me were just made up by women I rejected." Matt tried to get out of bed, but the pain in his leg was still too great to move around without assistance.

"How did that little lady out in the kitchen rope you into matrimony?" Sheriff Watkins snorted while retrieving his hat.

"It's a long story, but I was unconscious most of the time. If I had been fully awake, things might have been different. I must say, between us, being married to Anna ain't half bad."

"Well, I will say you lucked out. At least your bride ain't ugly as the backend of a mule." Sheriff Watkins laughed before he walked back toward the kitchen.

~

After the sheriff left, Matt yelled for her to come. She wiped her hands on a dishcloth and hurried to Matt's bedside. "Did you have a good report about my uncle from the other sheriff?"

"No, but I'm sure they have him on the run. Listen, I need a pair of crutches. I have to get out of this room. The sooner the better. Will you ask Pedro to check around and see if he can find me some?"

"Of course. You will still need to be careful. Your wound could still break open again."

"Just find me a pair. What are you cooking that smells so

good?" Matt held his head high to smell the air.

"Reverend Mother is cooking another pot roast with vegetables, and I have peach cobbler in the oven for lunch. I can't ask Mr. Godwin to feed this large family so we're cooking here. Juan and I will be taking most of my pies to the café to sell. I need the money."

"Hey, you're my wife now, and I can support you and the others. You don't have to continue to slave over a hot stove at the café any longer."

"Thank you for your offer, but I'll continue as always until my uncle is captured. Then, I'll make plans for the future. Now, I'll ask Pedro to find you a pair of crutches. Juan and I will be late if we don't leave now." She hurried back into the kitchen.

~

Later in the day, Sheriff Watkins' posse entered the café for lunch. Juan and Mr. Godwin whipped up pounds of potatoes, fried pork chops, and cooked green snap beans with bacon. Anna had prepared dozens of yeast rolls and fresh buttery cornbread. The men ate heartily without much conversation. Anna finally got the nerve to ask one of the men if they had found Claude Moore's trail.

"Well, ma'am, we followed him for miles but lost him once he went across the river into Mexico. You know we aren't allowed to arrest anyone once they cross the border," the young man said, giving Anna a sweet smile. He took his napkin and wiped his mouth. "Miss, this is the best grub I have eaten in a long time. Reminds me of my ma's cooking back home. I'm sure thinking about leaving this town and heading home. I miss her home-cooked meals."

Anna returned the young man's smile. "You should do just that. I know you're mama misses her boy, I mean…son." Pouring more coffee for the other men, Anna headed back to the kitchen.

"Did you find out anything about your uncle, Anna?" Juan asked as he served up another plate of food and placed it on a tray.

"They followed him to the border. That's all one young man said."

After the men finished off big helpings of dessert, they left for entertainment at the Silver Slipper. Mr. Godwin, Juan, and Anna relaxed for a few minutes. "Man, those men put away some food." Mr. Godwin sighed. "All your pies and peach cobbler are gone. You had a good payday, Anna."

"I need to go to the stable and talk with Pedro, then I need to make more pies for the evening meal." Anna removed her apron and started for the door. Juan was directly behind her. "Where are you going?" she asked.

"With you. Matt said that I wasn't to let you out of my sight. So, if you're going to see Pedro, I'm going, too."

Anna rolled her eyes. As they hurried down the boardwalk, Anna sensed every eye in town on them. She was relieved to find Pedro pitching hay to some new horses.

"This is a surprise, Anna, Juan. What brings you both here?" Pedro propped his arm on the pitchfork.

"Matt needs a pair of crutches, and he asked me to see if you could find a pair for him, since you are around so many people. Maybe you could ask if someone has some he can borrow. He is dying to get out of bed, and he feels that he can hop on his good leg."

"Sure, I'll start asking today and when I leave here for lunch."

"Great. I will stop on our way back to the café and ask Miss Henrietta. If there's a pair to be found in this town, she'll know. See you at home."

As Anna and Juan entered the dry goods store, Anna looked up at the jingling bell and ploughed into a big burly man. He stood nearly six and a half feet tall and had a full red beard.

"Well, hello, pretty little gal," the stranger said, as he held Anna tightly.

"Pardon me." Anna pulled on her arms and looked to Juan. "You can turn me loose now."

"Maybe, I don't want to let you fly away. I like where you landed."

"You heard the lady, Mister. Let her go!" Juan brooked no argument.

The big giant freed his hold on Anna and turned to Juan. "Now, young fellow, you wanna take this outside? No little piss ant like you is gonna' tell me what to do."

"Leave my friends alone, you big brute, before I take my broom to you. Go on about your business." Henrietta stood like a warrior ready to pounce on the stranger's head.

"I'm leaving, but I'll be back next month," the man said, leering at Anna.

"You do that. Try to make it in before it snows. We can use

more of your soft fur pieces." Everyone watched as the big man slowly moved out the door.

"Mercy, Miss Henrietta, that man gave me a fright. Is he a trapper?"

"Yep, and a good one, too. I buy all of his fur pieces and they sell like your hot doughnuts. The ladies will make gloves, moccasins, lined vests, and the inside of hats. When winter hits, mostly January and February, the men and little children will be wearing some of his fur pieces."

"If I'm still here, I will have to purchase some." Anna smiled as she stood at the window and watched the big man ride off with his pack mules. She turned to the proprietor. "Miss Henrietta, Matt needs a pair of crutches. He is ready to get out of bed, but he still can't walk on his hurt leg. Do you have any or know of someone who might have a pair he could use?"

"John," Henrietta called to her son in the storeroom. "Look in the back closet and bring out those crutches we've had for years. Sheriff Jenkins is in need of them."

"Here's the crutches. They need dusting, but they are still good." John carried them out from behind the counter and gave them to Juan.

"Sheriff Jenkins will return them after he has no more use for them. Thank you so much." Anna smiled and hugged Henrietta. "Reverend Mother would love to have you both come to Sunday dinner. Please say you'll come."

"We'll be happy to come," Henrietta replied and smiled at John.

Chapter 17

Darkness had settled on Matamoros, the border town in Mexico, as Claude Moore sat at the corner table in the smoke-filled room, drinking the last of his whiskey. But he was stone sober. Young senoritas danced from man to man while men strummed their guitars and sang.

Claude wore his Stetson down low over his three days' growth of dark beard. He needed a bath, clean clothes, and a shave—all in that order. But he had heard rumors that a couple of his men were in town, and he waited for them to show their faces. He didn't have long to wait.

The swinging bat-winged doors burst open, and bigger than life, one of his desperados stood. Craning his neck, he surveyed the crowded room until he spotted his prey. Backing out of the tavern, allowing the swinging doors to hit him in the back, he returned quickly with another man.

Claude Moore watched the two men saunter over to his table. Tucker Mills, the big bushy-faced man, placed one booted foot on a chair and leaned over the table.

"Well, boss man, it took you long enough to get here," the foul-smelling man spewed his words over Claude.

"Don't you ever stop and take a dunk in the Rio Grande? You smell worse than the pigpen on my farm."

The man straightened and stood over his boss. "Now, that ain't no way to talk to the man who saved your hide several times. I plan on getting one of these senoritas to scrub my back after I've said howdy to you."

"Where's that young Willie you took on?" Claude asked, looking around the room.

"Oh, we left him outside holding that piece of crow bait he calls a horse," Tucker said. "He wants to eat before doing anything else. Neither one of us can cook like you."

"Get out of here and come to my room around ten tonight. Upstairs in room number 10. We'll make plans after I can breathe around you."

~

Matt sat on the side of his bed where he could see Anna standing at the dry sink washing dishes. Her long raven hair hung down over her narrow shoulders, and the big white apron bow swished back and forth on her backside. He was sure his two hands could span her tiny waist.

With his crutches, he paced back and forth in the bedroom. He had to get his mind off Anna. Even though she claimed not to be his wife, Matt wanted to officially make her his, but it was impossible with a houseful of people. His thoughts went to the future, and he could imagine her being with child, her belly stretched out to the size of a watermelon. He remembered his pa telling him that his mama was never as beautiful as she was when carrying a child in her belly. Well, Anna was beautiful now, but having a child would only make her more so. His body reacted from his thoughts, and he was almost ashamed. She was a virgin, just like all the other nuns, and would remain so until he caught her uncle and threw him in jail.

Anna and Juan had gone to work and Reverend Mother prepared his lunch. He chewed on a piece of steak slowly. His sore leg ached like the very devil, and it was his fault. Matt had spent most of the morning standing on it in the bedroom and then went outside on the porch. He walked up and down the steps trying to bring strength to his leg. Now, he was paying for all the activity.

He pushed a few more potatoes around on his plate and listened to Reverend Mother and Sister Melody talk about their plans to help build another much-needed room onto Anna's house. Lord, help me, he thought. When will I have time to start a building project?

Matt had lain in bed thinking about the best way to get a bead on what was happening down in the border town across the Rio Grande, where Claude was hiding out. He finally laid out a plan, but he couldn't tell anyone but the sheriff. Anna and Reverend Mother would never agree to his plan.

Sister Melody showed Sheriff Watkins to Matt's room and offered refreshments, but he refused. The sheriff pulled up a chair and straddled it. "Well, my boy, it's time my posse and I return to work. A few of Moore's men have been spotted crossing over the border. So, I guess his gang is back together. We'll just camp out in the woods and wait until they try to re-cross the Rio Grande when it's low enough."

"I have an idea, but it is of the utmost importance that not a word of this leaks out to anyone." Matt stared at the sheriff.

"Let's hear it, man. We need to catch this gang before they do more killing."

"Anna has two young men who came with her from the convent. They can take care of themselves. Juan is with Anna all the time, working with her at the café, but Pedro is working at the livery at the end of town."

"I met the young man you are speaking about. He helped us with our horses," Sheriff Watkins said.

"I'm sure he did. Well, I thought he could slip across the border and hang out in the town—watch and listen out for Moore and his men. The men in the saloons gossip worse than women, so Pedro will hear about what they plan on doing next." Matt listened to make sure no one was near his bedroom door. "Pedro would do this, I'm sure, but Anna and Reverend Mother would skin me alive if they knew I put him in danger."

"I need to get him off by himself and ask if he will do this, right," Sheriff Watkins suggested. "Does he have a good horse and bedroll?"

"He can use my black horse and saddle. Everything is at the livery. Pedro knows what's mine, but he must not tell anyone what he plans on doing."

"This sounds like a good plan. The young man will fit right in with the other locals, and he's a handsome lad. The girls will fall all over him."

"That's another thing," Matt said, as he leaned over the bed and opened a drawer on the table next to the bed. "Give him this money. Then he can say that he worked on a cattle drive in Texas and just came home to rest before he takes another job."

"Good idea. I will take care of all this. If I don't come back, you'll know your plan has been put into action." Sheriff Watkins placed his chair against the wall and walked out into the living area. Matt could hear him saying goodbye to the ladies as he departed the house.

~

Pedro was excited beyond words to help catch Claude Moore. He had heard many tales about the killings and robberies that this man and his gang had done in the past. Anna was hurt and disappointed in the man who'd raised her for ten years, but she would never have come to live with him if she had known how he had changed over the years. She realized that the only reason he had sent for her was for her to bring the stolen money that he had mailed her. Moore had only used her.

Pedro's memories came back. She had told him and Juan one night in front of the fireplace how her uncle had worked alongside her papa and mama, and his sister. He was a fun-loving man whom she tagged after for years on the farm. After her parents were murdered, Moore had worked hard, but he wasn't the fun-loving uncle anymore. Anna had learned to cook and clean, so she had taken on more chores than a small child should have to do.

Then one day, her uncle told her he had to go off to fight in a war, and she needed to stay at the convent until he sent for her. Moore waited ten years, and he lied about why he wanted her to come to him. So sad, but Pedro would never forgive Claude Moore for hurting his sweet friend. Of course, God would make him forgive the man. Still, he wanted to help put him in jail.

After giving his employer a sad excuse for being gone for a few days, he saddled Matt's horse, tied on his bedroll, and secured his money down in his boots. He couldn't afford to be seen with the posse, so he'd leave now and would purchase clothes in Mexico.

~

Later that evening, when Pedro didn't return home for dinner, Anna sent Juan to look for him. He returned with a message that Pedro had taken a horse and bedroll and rode out of town. "His boss man said that he didn't say where he was going."

"But Juan, Pedro didn't say a word to any of us." Anna looked at Juan as he patted his hat on his knee. She felt that he wasn't telling her everything about Pedro's immediate departure. "Something has to be very wrong because this doesn't sound like him at all."

Juan kept his face turned toward the floor and finally said that he was going in to check on Matt. Anna watched him hurry into Matt's bedroom and close the door. She slowly eased over to the bedroom door to hear the conversation between the two men.

"Anna, do you think Pedro will be coming home tonight? What should I do with his dinner?" Sister Melody's voice. Anna jumped away from the door and tiptoed into the kitchen.

"Pedro rode out of town for a few days. Just dump his food into the slop bucket." Anna walked over to the rocker in front of the fireplace and sat down. She bowed her face and prayed softly, "Lord, please protect our loved one, Pedro. Keep him safe wherever he is now. Amen."

~

Juan stood at the foot of Matt's bed. "Sir, I know you think that I am just a dumb boy that followed Anna to Livingston. I may be young, but I'm not dumb. I know you know where Pedro went, and I want to know the reason he left his job and home."

"I don't think you are dumb. I respect you and Pedro, and I know you boys are smart and hard workers." Matt started to sit up on the bed.

Juan rushed to the head of the bed and pushed Matt back down on the mattress. "Tell me before I cut you."

Matt realized that Juan held a sharp blade near his throat. "All right, Juan, I'll tell you, but first put away that weapon before you hurt someone."

"Sorry, Mr. Matt, but I have to know, and I'm sure you know something about his disappearance." Juan pushed his knife back in the scabbard on his waistband.

"First, peek out the door and make sure Anna is not listening. She's a nosy little thing when I have company." Matt sat up on the bed and ran his palm through his dark hair.

"All clear. She's sitting in the rocker talking with Sister Melody. Now, tell me before she decides to come in and go to bed." Juan said, moving close to Matt so he could hear him.

After describing what Pedro would be doing in Matamoros, Juan was satisfied. "If he doesn't return in a few days, I will travel across the Rio Grande and look for him. He and I have always done everything together. I really should be with him." Juan hung his head down to his chest.

"It's better that he's working alone. Once he locates Moore and learns his plan, he will return to the posse across the border. Sheriff Watkins will take over, and Pedro will return home."

Chapter 18

Claude Moore sat upstairs in the Mexican Cantina near the open window enjoying the pleasant breeze. The streets of Matamoros never slept. There were always drunks shooting guns in the air, guitar players strolling up and down the boardwalks and young girls running and giggling away from the young and old wanted outlaws. The breeze felt good on his face as he watched his three men ride up and tie their horses to the hitching rail.

In minutes, a loud knock sounded at his door. "Come on in," Claude called as he lowered the window to block out all the noise coming from below. Three men came into his room wearing leather vests and chaps over the front of their pants. Each sported two pistols wrapped on their waist.

"How did you manage to score the best room in this wonderful establishment?" Tucker joked, as he bounced his rear on the double bed, covered with colorful quilts and four plush pillows.

"I have a standing reservation. When I come into town, the owner tosses out anyone staying in this room, and the servants make it ready for me. Money talks." Claude said, dangling a cigar from his lips. He stared at the other two men who came in the door with Tucker. He knew Tucker, but these men were strangers. Before getting down to business, he peered at the man he knew. "Is Tucker your real name?"

"It ain't polite to scoff at a man's name. If I wasn't a tolerant man, I might just get good and roused," he said.

"Tucker . . . that can't be your real name."

"You're right, but I've been called Tucker since I was a small lad. My real name is Homer."

The three men busted out with laughter. "Well, I can't blame you for allowing people to call you Tucker. Homer is a sissy name," Claude said, signaling for the men to sit down at the small table.

'First, why did you ask about my name?" Tucker quizzed.

"Well, I guess all famous men needs some kind of handle, beside the one they're born with," Claude replied.

"Hey, I ain't famous," Tucker said.

"You will be if you keep hanging with me," Claude remarked. "You haven't introduced me to your new friends."

The big fellow pulled out a chair and flopped down. "Name's Bull from Waco, Texas." He was over six feet, wore a black patch over his left eye, and his front tooth was missing.

Claude couldn't take his eyes off the big man.

"What the hell are you staring at?" Bull glared at Claude.

"I'm looking at one of the ugliest varmints I've ever laid eyes upon." Glancing at Tucker, he asked, "Why didn't you ask Bull to wear bells around his neck. People on the street will remember him just by his appearance."

"I don't have to take that kind of talk from nobody." Bull stood quickly.

"Tucker, you'd best tell your friend to behave himself if he wants to live to see daylight," Claude said without even looking at the young man who was ready to draw his Colt to defend Bull.

"What's wrong with you, boy? Do you want to work with us or not?" Tucker asked the young one.

"Guess he didn't like the way I talked to your friend here. I'll say he has grit for sure, but he'd better sit down before he provokes me into killing him."

"All right, Claude, let's get down to business. Willie and Bull are good men. I'm sure Slim is ready to get down to business and collect his share of the bank money, too." He realized that Slim wasn't in the room, so he turned to Claude and asked if Slim was going to join them.

"Slim is dead. He went into Livingston to grab my niece, but he got into a scuffle and shot the sheriff, but somehow my niece shot him. That's all I know. Once we find my niece, I'll discover the whole story. You see, it's hard for me to believe that my Anna killed Slim because she's a Catholic nun. The nuns that I know wouldn't hurt a fly."

"Why did you want your niece brought to you?" Tucker asked.

"Slim and I robbed a bank and we parted ways when the posse got on our trail. I stopped in a small town and mailed my niece the bank money. She lived in a convent near the border. I sent her a letter telling her I wanted her to come and live with me in Livingston. You see, I'd dropped her off at the convent when she was about ten and I promised to send for her when I got settled. Of course, I knew she would jump at the chance to come live with me, and she'd bring the money." Claude stood, ambled over to the window, and pulled back the shade to look over the street.

"While traveling to Livingston, I went by Abilene and had the opportunity to rob the train that carried the Army payroll. Unfortunately, things didn't go smoothly, and I had to shoot the conductor, but before he died he described me to the Army soldiers. Every little town that I passed through had wanted posters plastered all over. The Army is up in the air about their payroll. The captain of the fort is so angry because only one man robbed the train. Therefore, I couldn't go to Livingston and retrieve the bank money from my niece. Since I lived there for several years, the sheriff and most of the townspeople know me."

Silence reigned all around the table. The two new men didn't know what to say or what questions to ask. Finally, Tucker spoke up. "You're saying that your niece still has the bank money? Since you can't go into Livingston and get your niece, one of us will have to do it. You say she's a nun? She should be an easy prey to find and bring back here."

"Why do you say that?" Willie asked.

"Boy, don't you know anything?" Tucker said. "Nuns are shy, quiet ladies that will do most anything that is asked of them. And, there aren't many nuns that live in a town. They're like a flock of geese—they live together."

Claude eyed Willie and Bull and smiled. "Have you two ever been to Livingston, Texas?" He knew that he and Tucker couldn't go to Livingston. "Tucker will be easily recognized since he's been to Livingston. But, since you two haven't been there, I'll give you directions in town to find my niece. You just tell her that I want her to come with you. If she puts up a fuss about leaving, then you'll have to gag and tie her. But bring her here unharmed." Claude tossed a coin in the air over and over. "Now, time is playing against us. I was told that Sheriff Watkins is going to get a warrant to cross the border. We need to nab my niece so we can cross the border while the posse is searching for us over here."

Bull stood straight and looked Claude right in the eyes. "Willie and I want part of the bank and Army payroll money."

"I see," murmured Claude.

~

Pedro sat on Matt's black sorrel, chewing on his bottom lip and trying to decide where to cross the Rio Grande. The water was dark and swift, but he'd been told that it was only about waist deep. He bent over the horse's neck and whispered in his ear," Take me across, boy," then kicked the animal in his sides.

The horse took one cautious step, then another into the sandy, rock-filled bottom of the river. It was only a few seconds when the water was up to his boots and stirrups. The horse stumbled but soon found his footing and climbed the sandy slope onto the Mexican border. A worn trail cut a gap between two low mountains that led to an opening in a grove of cottonwood trees and a small creek bed running by its side.

Pedro yawned again, stiff from riding hard and fast to the border. His stomach rumbled. A decent meal would be mighty good. Anna and the other sisters would know by now that he wouldn't be joining them for supper tonight. Juan would have gone in search for him, and his boss would have told him that he had took a horse and left town. He prayed that Juan wouldn't come in search of him.

Pedro was ready to stop for the night and ride into town early the next morning. He was tired of riding and looking over his shoulder. Peering ahead as the sun was going down, his eyes caught the sun bouncing off something shiny. Was that a rifle?

Holding tightly to his saddle horn, Pedro squeezed his knees into the side of his horse just as a blast from a rifle missed his sombrero by an inch. Jerking his hat off, he leaned over and steered the horse into the cluster of trees, trying to settle him down, but he was spooked and bounced him around on the saddle. Leaning close to his sorrel's neck, he whispered, "Whoa, whoa." Slowly the black horse calmed, and they stayed hidden for several hours.

The late evening was overcast with dark clouds, causing Pedro to shiver. He pulled up his collar wishing he had worn his sheepskin coat. It was time to use the dark of the night to reach Matamoros without being seen.

Kicking his sorrel in his side, he rode slowly close to a mile before giving his animal his head, allowing him to trot into the noisy town.

Pulling his sombrero down over his face, he stopped in front of a cantina that rented rooms. After securing his horse at the livery and registering, he took the stairs two at a time to his room. He immediately locked the door and placed a straight chair under the door knob. A man couldn't trust no one, not even the proprietor, in this lawless town.

Using the cold water in the pitcher on the small table, he scrubbed his face, neck, and arms clean. He was starving, but this wasn't the first time he'd gone to bed hungry. Pedro wasn't about to go out and be seen tonight.

Chapter 19

After a long day at the café, Anna talked Juan into going with
her to pick the last of the wild strawberries. Since the weather had
turned cold, this would be her last chance to pick the berries.

Juan stretched out on the soft grass, covered his face with his
wide-brimmed hat, and pulled his jacket close around his neck. In a
matter of minutes, Anna smiled at his snoring.

Anna hadn't had the chance to pick berries or work in the
garden after work since Reverend Mother and Sister Melody
arrived. She worked from early in the morning making pies and
other pastries to late in the evening. Arriving home, she cooked
dinner and then got busy preparing more desserts to sell at the café.
With Susie living with them, she had to bathe her and spend time
reading to her each night. Before bedtime, she read scriptures from
her mama's Bible to the family. But now with Reverend Mother and
Sister Melody fixing the evening meal, Anna had time to pick the
much-needed berries.

As Anna hummed and picked berries, a small black bear came
out into the clearing where she was bent over. She froze at the sight.
With her bucket full, she tried to run to where Juan was sleeping but
tripped over the front of her long skirt and fell facedown.

The bear became agitated when he saw Anna running. It raised
up on its hind legs and roared, lumbering toward her. Anna lifted
herself off the ground and screamed for Juan, but he only turned
over on his side. He was dead to the world. She screamed for Juan
again, but he just scratched and snored some more.

Anna raced to the nearest tree and climbed as high as she could,
still holding the berries. When the bear starting shaking the tree,
Anna dropped the bucket of strawberries. The bear sat down on his
backside and began to eat, not in any hurry to leave his feast.

~

Matt was sitting in the swing on the front porch when loud screams came from the woods. He hopped off the porch and limp-walked toward the horrific shrieks from near the stream.

Reverend Mother's voice sounded behind him. "What's wrong?"

"Screams coming from the woods," he yelled. Was it Anna? It sounded like her voice.

"Get back here. You'll break your leg," she bellowed, but he ignored her.

When Matt reached the berry patch, Juan was sleeping like a kitten. He kicked him in the behind and told him to get up. "Anna needs help!"

Anna was sitting high on a tree limb with a little bear at the foot of the tree with his paws full of berries. Tears streamed down her cheeks, and she was trembling.

The bear glanced up at the sight of him and bolted off into the woods.

He posted fists upon his hips. "Are you all right, Anna?"

She scrubbed a hand across her face and nodded.

"Juan, get over here and help Anna down."

Juan wiped the sleep from his eyes, climbed the tree, and offered his hands to lower Anna down into Matt's waiting arms.

Matt slipped his arms under Anna's knees and threw her over his shoulder. He didn't know if he could walk without falling flat on his face, but he was going to do his best. But first he needed to rest his leg. Matt plopped down on a log with Anna sitting on his lap. His leg hurt like the devil, but he didn't care. He had his wife in his arms, and she wasn't fighting him for a change.

Reverend Mother dashed into the clearing but stopped when she saw Matt. He winked at her, so she tapped Juan on the shoulder and motioned for him to follow her to the house. "Let's give the lovebirds some privacy."

"Are you hurt anywhere, sweetheart? Did you hurt yourself when you fell or climbed that rough tree?"

Anna continued to cry, her voice coming out in a babble of words. "That little bear, then I tripped, then I dropped the basket." A fresh wave of shuddering sobs came out.

"Shh, baby, you're safe with me. I would never let anything

hurt you." Matt leaned down and wiped her face with the palm of his hand, enjoying the proximity of her lovely face. He might not get a chance to be this close to her again any time soon. A close look showed her smooth complexion, and with her eyes closed, he saw her tiny black eyelashes spread delicately above her cheeks. Her lips looked like tiny rosebuds.

Suddenly, he lowered his face and kissed her wet lips. Surprised, Anna pulled him close and matched his kiss. Loving her was just like breathing. Matt was in no hurry to carry Anna back to the house, so they sat there on the log until her crying abated.

"I'm sorry. Can't believe I'm crying like a child. It's just that I've been upset all afternoon about Pedro leaving without a word to anyone. The boys are like my real brothers, and I am so worried that something bad has happened.

~

Sister Melody had set Susie and Jamie down in front of the fireplace with a story book. They were pretending to make sounds like all the animals in the pictures. This gave her a chance to slip into the kitchen to finish cutting up vegetables. Humming, she set about her task until something rustled behind her. She spun around.

A big, strange man stood by the back door mere feet from her.

"Who are you? What are you doing in this house?" Melody held a large spoon that she had been using to stir the beans like a weapon.

"You must come with me. Your uncle needs to see you," the man demanded and lunged at her.

"I don't have an uncle, and I'm not going anywhere with you." Melody jerked her arm away from the beast and tried to run from him.

The next thing she knew, something hard hit her head, and she felt herself being lifted onto the man's shoulder as he carried her out the back door. Then the world went black.

~

When Reverend Mother and Juan entered the house, they both smelled something burning. Hurrying into the empty kitchen, Juan removed the pot of beans off the burner of the stove. "Wonder where Sister Melody went off too," he said.

"Susie, do you know where Sister Melody is?" Reverend Mother asked the small girl who was reading a book by the hearth.

Susie pointed to the kitchen. "She's in there cooking. After supper she's going to read to Jamie and me."

~

Anna opened the door for Matt as he was back to using his crutches. He hated being such an invalid, but his leg was killing him. Reverend Mother was standing there with her hands on her hips. "Did you see Sister Melody outside when you were coming back from the woods? Juan and I have looked the house over and outside, too. But, it looks like a herd of large animals trampled over our garden." Reverend Mother said, looking very puzzled.

Matt hopped outside and looked the summer garden over. "Juan, come outside, please."

Juan and Matt followed the large hoof prints and saw that two horses had cut across the garden and went right through the chicken yard. The hoof prints went in the woods to the road and headed east.

Juan frowned. "It looks like one horse was carrying a heavy load while the other one wasn't."

"I believe a man came in the house and kidnapped Sister Melody, while another waited outside," Matt stated.

"Why in the world would someone want to kidnap a nun?" Juan replied.

"Whoever took Sister Melody was after Anna. This has to be her uncle's doing. He probably thinks that since Anna spent all those years in the convent that she became a nun."

"Where do you think they intend to take her?" Juan quizzed.

"If it was her uncle's men, I'm sure they are carrying her to Matamoros, Mexico—a small town across the border. It's the same place Pedro has gone to in order to spy on Moore and his gang."

The two men hurried back inside the house and told Anna and Reverend Mother what they had discovered.

"Oh, poor Sister Melody," cried Anna. "I don't ever remember seeing her on a horse. She always drove a wagon around the convent. If she went to town, she walked with all the other sisters."

Reverend Mother sat at the kitchen table. "Mr. Jenkins, how are you going to rescue Sister Melody and bring her back unharmed, I pray?"

"I am going to leave Juan here with you and Anna, round up some of my men, and we'll be on their trail as fast as we can pack our gear." Turning to Anna, Matt said, "The only place I want you to go is to the café. Juan will be with you, and I will instruct Herman to have his shotgun ready at all times. If a stranger comes into the café, you go back in the kitchen and let one of the men wait on him."

"But, are you up to riding? You still can't walk without your crutch," Anna said. Matt lumbered to his room, but Anna followed on his heels. "Matt, I need to go with you and your men. You know that I can ride and shoot as good as any man. I could be a big help with Sister Melody."

With a double take at his wife, he said flatly, "No."

"Give me one good reason why not?" She craned her neck around him to see his face.

"It's too dangerous for you to be on this rescue. These are bad men, and they will shoot to kill to prevent us for catching them. I want you to stay here where you'll be safe. Your uncle only wants the bank money, and I'm not giving it to him." Grabbing his bedroll and the crutch, he limped out of the bedroom and into the kitchen. "I'm leaving now, Reverend Mother. Please take care of Anna." With an awkward gait, Matt stormed out the front door.

Chapter 20

Sister Melody woke up on damp ground. She opened her eyes to see moving black clouds and a dim moon shining behind them. Hearing voices, she quickly closed her eyes, pretending to be asleep. Soft voices talked about her.

"You don't think you may have killed her? That bruise on the side of her face looks pretty bad."

Slowly Melody slipped her hand up to her face. Just the slightest touch rushed pain through her body. Then she remembered. The ugliest man she had ever seen demanded that she go with him. Then he knocked her to the floor and carried her out. Her jaw felt as if was broken and, moving her tongue around in her mouth, she tasted blood and felt something sharp. The fool most likely broke a jaw tooth, too. But, she silently thanked God that she was alive.

"That long-legged gal ain't dead. I did hit her hard, more so than I intended, but she was about to scream, and I had to shut her up. Tucker said the sisters would do whatever you asked, remember? Well, that skinny gal wasn't about to go with us, so I had no choice, but to clamp up her mouth."

"I know, but Moore said to bring her back unharmed. He might not like it one bit that you nearly knocked her head off,"

"I ain't afraid of that man. He talks big, but he will pay us for bringing his niece back to him or else. I ain't a woman killer, but I won't hesitate to put a bullet through him, or that weasel Tucker either," Someone spit loudly into the fire.

"Hey, Bull. I see movement coming from the woman. She's awake. I bet she's been listening to us talk." Someone crawled over to her and poked her leg through her skirt.

Sister Melody jerked her leg back and slapped his hand. "Don't touch me!"

"I see the little gal still has some spunk in her. I might need to slap her again to keep her in line," one of the men said as he stood and glared down at her with his one good eye.

"You'd better not hit me again. I think you already broke my jaw." Melody tucked both of her legs under her and sat up off the ground. "Who are you and why did you bring me out here where monster mosquitoes can eat a person alive?"

"I ain't got the first mosquito bite," replied one of them.

"Of course not," Sister Melody shouted. "Not even a bug would want to take a bite out of your stinking hide."

"Hey, you'd better watch your mouth. I haven't had time to bathe like a proper lady for several days."

"You can slip off your horse while we're crossing the Rio Grande River. I know your horse would appreciate it, too," The taller man snorted.

"You still haven't told me who you are and where are you taking me?" Sister Melody questioned.

"I don't guess it's gonna matter one way or another if you know where we are taking you. We work for your uncle, and he's paying us to bring you to him. He is across the border in a small town waiting for your arrival."

"How did you know I was his niece?"

"Golly, ma'am, he said that you was a pretty, young nun. How many nuns are living in that small town of Livingston? We've been scouting around, and you are the only one—so, here you are," Willie said.

"Uh, I need some privacy," Sister Melody said.

"Willie, go with her to the edge of those large bushes. If you try to run, we will have to tie your hands and feet. Believe me, lady, you won't like it."

After several minutes, sister Melody walked back to the fire ring that held a coffeepot. "May I have a cup of coffee and something to eat?"

"There's coffee but no food. We didn't plan our small trip very well. But we'll be leaving at daylight and be in town pretty early. Then we'll all enjoy a nice, hot meal."

"Coffee will be fine," Sister Melody said, slapping a large mosquito off her arm. "Did you bring an extra blanket in your bedroll that I may use for the night?"

"Sure, you can have mine," Willie said getting up and shaking it out for her.

"Thank you," she replied, taking the light blanket from the young man and wrapping it across her shoulders and arms. "Now, maybe I won't be eaten alive while I rest." After drinking her coffee, Sister Melody stretched out on the ground close to the fire and tucked a piece of the blanket over her sore jaw. She prayed silently for God to protect her from Anna's uncle. Surely, he would know that she wasn't his niece. But what would he do to her when he discovered the truth?

Early the next morning, the tall man named Bull and Sister Melody trailed after Willie who was scouting ahead before they reached the border.

Willie rode his horse to a full gallop back to them. "There's a big posse hiding in the woods where everyone crosses the river. We're going to have to go down river and find another place to cross. We'll have to hang onto our horse's tail and let them swim us across where the water is rough and deep. That's the only way we will reach the other side without being seen."

"How do you know this will work?" Bull asked.

"I have done this before. It's not easy, but horses are strong swimmers. You just have to keep your head up out of the water. Let them take the lead."

"Let's get going," Bull said.

The threesome took off their boots and shoes and tied them to their saddle horns. Bull insisted Sister Melody climb on his back and held tight. Willie led his horse into the water, wrapping his hand around the horse's tail. He slapped the animal on the rump, coaxing him into the water. Within a few minutes, both horses were climbing on the opposite bank of the river.

Sister Melody looked like a drowned rat, but she was alive. The men actually looked and smelled much better now that their hair and clothes were clean.

When Willie saw her shaking, he threw his wet blanket over Sister Melody's shoulder.

"We'd better get going," Bull said. "The sooner we get to town, the better we'll all be."

~

The streets of Matamoros were quiet and empty except for a few store owners sweeping bottles and other debris off the boardwalks. The men never looked up from their work as the three rode straight to the tavern where Claude was staying. He'd told Willie to take the girl around to the back of the building and wait for him to come and get them.

Bull tied his horse to the hitching rail and slowly pushed open the bat-winged doors. Sunshine was peeking through the dirty glass panes as he focused on the drunks in the room. Laughter came from the corner of the room. Bull spotted Claude Moore and Tucker eating a hearty amount of food. "Howdy, fellows," Bull said, looking down his nose at the men.

"Well, I see you made it back. Why are you alone?" Claude asked.

"I didn't think you wanted me to drag your niece in here, all soaking wet, dirty, and hungry. She's out back with Willie." Bull said, disgusted and hungry himself. He felt like grabbing the bacon and swallowing the plate.

"Let's go get her. She can have my room while she gets cleaned up." Claude said, leading the way to the back of the cantina.

~

The back door banged open, and Sister Melody jumped up from the barrel and looked at the man who was supposed to be her uncle. They locked eyes on each other. She knew that she looked pitiful with her black and white head covering flat against her hairline, her long black dress dripping water all around her, and tears filling her swollen eyes.

Claude examined her with a slow stare. "Hair's still as black as a raven and those same green eyes. You're the vision of my sister, your mama," he said. Stepping closer, Claude took her hands and kissed them. "My Anna, oh how I am missed your sweet smile."

"Please, I'm not your Anna."

"I know that you're angry with me, my pet, but I will make up all the years to you. Come now. We'll have your clothes laundered and a hot bath drawn for you, I'll send a platter of food up to your room."

"Something soft to eat, please. My jaw hurts."

Claude turned her face toward him with his pointer finger. "What happened to you?"

"Your man hit me when I refused to come with him. It is better now but still hurts."

"I'll send the town doctor to have a look at your face after you're decent enough for company."

"Thank you," mumbled Sister Melody as she followed him up the stairs to room number ten.

Chapter 21

Matt limped to the livery and called to Smithy to bring him his horse.

"Sorry, Sheriff, you let Pedro take your black sorrel. He hasn't come back yet."

"That's right, I forgot. Do you have another horse I can use for a while? You'll be paid each day I have it."

"Sure, I have a good horse out in the corral. I'll go get him. You gonna need a saddle too," Smithy yelled, as he went out the barn door.

Matt stood in the center of the barn when Jim Martin, his deputy, entered.

"I thought I saw you limping this way. What's up?" he asked

"Thank goodness you're here. Would you round up the other men and meet me in front of the dry goods store? I need a small posse to help me go after Claude Moore. A couple of his men came into town and kidnapped Sister Melody. They intended to nab Anna but took the sister by mistake."

"Absolutely. See you in a few minutes," Deputy Martin said, as he turned and raced down the street.

Smithy came in the barn with a big brown bay and tossed Matt a horse brush. "I'll grab you a blanket and saddle. You'll be on your way in just a few minutes."

Matt and several men headed out of town toward the border. The dark clouds opened up and flooded the trails, but the men continued riding for hours. The rain stopped and the men rode as quietly as they could to the border of the Rio Grande, looking for Sheriff Watkins and his posse. It wasn't long until Matt saw a young man waving a red bandana at him.

Sheriff Watkins stepped out of the trees and motioned for Matt and his men to follow him into the dark underbrush away from the main trail leading into the water.

"What brings you here, Matt?" Sheriff Watkins asked. "Are you well enough to be riding?"

"Didn't have a choice. Moore's men came into Anna's house and took Sister Melody by mistake. Anna was out in the woods picking berries, and the men came in the back door and grabbed Sister Melody thinking that they had Anna. I figured Moore thinks because Anna lived at the convent for ten years, she probably joined the sisters and became a nun."

"Yep, I can believe that. Poor woman, I bet she's scared to death."

"I don't know what he'll do to her when he finds out he's made a mistake," Matt said as he took a cup of hot coffee from a member of the posse.

"You know, Matt, we haven't heard a word from Pedro. I know he's still in Matamoros," Sheriff Watkins said, as he counted Matt's small posse.

"I can't wait for Pedro to come back across. I am going across early in the morning with my three men. We'll separate before we ride into town. I need to rescue Sister Melody before Claude harms her," Matt said, as he stood waving his hands back and forth in front of the fire. He was chilled to the bone and his leg wound hurt something awful.

"All right. My men and I will continue to stay here, watch, and wait. If he discovers he has the wrong nun, he will have to try to cross the river. With the hard rain we had last night, it won't be easy for him or your men."

"I know, but we'll just pray our horses are good swimmers."

"Pray? When did you become a praying man?"

"Since I married a godly woman." Matt smiled and turned away to talk with his men. After they made plans, Matt walked to the water's edge and soaked his bandana. Finding a secluded area, he dropped his pants and saw blood on the bandage. He lifted the gauze and tape and placed the cool, wet rag over the bloody area. It felt like heaven. Maybe this would hold until he found Sister Melody. He could only hope and pray.

~

Pedro sauntered into the tavern early the next morning and

asked for a hearty breakfast with hot coffee. The barkeep looked Pedro over like he was a prize horse. "First time here?"

"First time I've had to run and hide from the law. Now, will I get some food or do I need to go down the street?"

"Coming up," the barkeep said. "Have a seat at the tables, and the senorita will bring it out to you." Pedro took a seat and picked up an old newspaper.

While waiting for his food, he could hear two ladies speaking Spanish on the stairs above. "You'd better iron that black robe and the head piece. It has to be special for the sister. The man will pay more if we bring it to him early this morning."

Pedro pretended not to have understood what the ladies were saying. His face was buried in the newspaper while three men played cards nearby. Who was the sister the ladies were talking about? Surely, Anna's uncle hadn't already taken her and brought her here, he thought.

A lovely senorita placed a plate of tortillas with fried eggs covered with spicy tomato sauce and a small bowl of salsa in front of Pedro. She quickly returned with steaming hot coffee. "If more, just wave," she said in broken English.

Pedro smiled and mumbled thanks. She waltzed around him, patting his shoulder, and dragging her long nails across the back of his neck, sending cold chills down his spine. Pedro knew that she was trying to entice him, but he was on a mission and couldn't fool around with the gal.

He ate fast, scanned the cantina and hurried upstairs to his room. As he raised his window, voices came from the next room. "I had breakfast brought up to you along with your clean clothes. The old woman even pressed your woman's things, too." Pedro heard a man say.

"Thank you for the food and clean clothes, but what do you want with me?" The woman asked. Pedro leaned closer to the window to hear the woman's voice.

"Why, Anna darling. I have missed you so much."

"I told you, Mr. Moore, I'm not Anna. Please take me home." Sister Melody's voice.

"Now, Anna, what name has the sisterhood given you now? I learned that nuns are given other names when they take their vows. Why do you keep saying that Anna isn't your name?"

Pedro held his breath as the woman started to answer, but before she could, someone burst into the room next door.

"A sheriff posse is in town. We need to get out of here."

~

Sister Melody reached for her clothes and hurried into the water closet to dress. She could hear Mr. Moore speaking with the man who entered the room.

"How many men have crossed the border?" Claude demanded. She could hear the click of his pistol and the whir of the cylinder spinning around.

"Not sure, but we have to get out of here before they learn where we're staying."

"You're right," Claude responded, then he banged on the door of the water closet. "Get out here, Anna, before I have to take you in your undies."

Opening the door she said firmly, "I'm dressed." She straightened her head gear and pulled on her long black and white wimpie.

Claude stared at his niece. "What a lovely nun you are in that getup."

Sister Melody didn't smile or respond to his comment. "Where are we going now?"

"Don't worry your pretty head about our travel plans. You just cooperate and come along without causing any problems."

Pedro inched his bedroom door open and peeked around the room. As Claude and sister Melody came out the door, one of his men said, "Go back. Two of the sheriff's men are standing at the bottom of the stairs."

Claude turned to Sister Melody. "Don't move from this spot," and he dashed down, his pistol ready to shoot.

Pedro crept up behind the sister, placed his hand over her mouth, and pulled her into his bedroom, locking the door quickly.

She whirled around, then looked up. "Thank you, Lord. Pedro, I am so happy to see you, but you're in so much danger. Those men will kill you if they find us together."

"Go into the water closet. Leave the door cracked, and when he comes in here, pretend to be sick to your stomach. I'll do the rest."

Suddenly, there was a banging on the door. "Open up or I will shoot the lock off," Claude's voice.

"Just a minute." Quickly Pedro messed up his hair, while tossing the quilts off the bed. He unbuttoned his shirt while pulling it out of his pants. Banging continued as Pedro jerked the door open. "What?" he yelled into Moore's face.

"I'm looking for a woman." Claude pointed his pistol straight at   Pedro. "There's only one here and she sick." Vomiting noises came from the water closet.

"My papa is going to kill you!" Sister Melody screamed in Spanish.

"What did she say?" Claude demanded.

"She's like this." Pedro circled his large hands around his stomach.

"You'll marry me or Papa will kill us both!" Spanish words followed.

"Let me get the hell out of here." Claude hurried through the door and down the back stairwell.

Sister Melody came out of the water closet wiping her mouth. "Oh, Pedro, I believe we fooled him—for now. I have never been so afraid, even though Anna's uncle never hurt me. The big man called Bull hit me in the jaw and knocked me out. I think I have a cracked tooth, but I'm alive. The two men believed I was Anna. Her uncle also believes that she's a nun, since she lived at the convent for many years. I tried to tell him that I wasn't Anna, but he wouldn't listen."

"You did a great job in that closet. All that splashing water and gagging sounded like you was very sick," Pedro said as he adjusted his clothing.

"The first time was the real thing. I had just eaten, and I was so afraid. Throwing up was no problem. Afterwards, I splashed the water in the bucket."

"Well, I'm going to go out this evening and buy you some different clothes. You can't go downstairs dressed like you are. We'll head to the border once it's dark, when most of the men are in the taverns."

Sister Melody made the bed. "If you don't mind, I need to rest. I haven't slept at all since they took me on this wild journey."

"Sure, you go ahead and rest. I'll go downstairs and look around. Hopefully, Moore and his men have left town."

Chapter 22

Anna had prayed and asked God to help her make the right decision. She had to help rescue Sister Melody. Indeed, she'd begged Matt to allow her to go with him to Mexico, but he declined and instructed her to stay and work at the café. Granted, she was his wife, but he wasn't her boss. And Sister Melody needed her, and by golly, she was going to help save her.

Anna packed a few snacks and filled a canteen with water, then she grabbed a small carpetbag from the pantry and packed the nun's clothes that she had worn to Livingston. Tiptoeing into the living room, Anna picked up Juan's boots. She had already sneaked into the bedroom and 'borrowed' a clean pair of his pants and a plaid shirt. Once dressed in Juan's clothes, she took his heavy sheepskin jacket and sombrero off the hat rack and slipped out the back door.

Just as she was closing the door, Susie stood in the kitchen and asked, "Where you going?"

"Oh, honey, you should be asleep. Do you want a drink of water?" Anna hoped Susie hadn't disturbed Juan or Jamie when she got up off her pallet.

"Why are you dressed like a boy? I want to wear breeches, too." Susie drank hearty and gave Anna the cup back.

"Come on and let's get you back in the bed. Sleep tight." Anna didn't want to lie and say that she'd see her in the morning.

Susie closed her eyes and was fast asleep before Anna left the room. She rushed outside before anyone else woke up. At the empty livery, she peered at the horses in separate stalls. *Gosh, which one should I take?* All the horses belonged to someone in town. She should have come prepared to leave a note for Mr. Mac, owner of the livery. Now she hoped the owner would understand. Deciding on a pinto pony, she saddled him and tied her carpetbag and canteen to the saddle horn. Peeking out the barn door first, she led him out.

Anna had never been away from the convent except to travel on a stage to Livingston. People were always talking about riding to the border where they crossed the Rio Grande into Mexico. Surely, it couldn't be too hard to find. She nudged the pony in its sides and headed east out of town.

Once out on the trail, she passed an older couple driving a covered wagon. She flagged the couple to stop and asked them if she was riding in the right direction, and they assured her that she was. "Thank you, Jesus," she said aloud.

After traveling several hours, she spotted a cluster of trees. Anna wanted to be out of sight of the main trail. Loosening her pony's saddle, she ate some of her food and led the pony over to the stream that was running beside the trail.

Just as the sun was going down, she arrived at the border. As she sat at the river's edge, a man grabbed her, but she used her booted foot and shoved him away. The man ran off into the woods yelling. She slapped her pony in its side, and he jumped into the water and began to swim. Anna soon made it across the border but didn't dare look back until she was out of sight.

~

"Sheriff Watkins, I'm sure that person I tried to stop at the edge of the river was a young girl or small woman. I had a good hold on her waist until she kicked me away. It was a gal for sure," the young man exclaimed.

"I would bet my life that the little woman was Sheriff Jenkins' new bride. They say she's a sharpshooter and can handle herself." He snickered. "Man, I wouldn't want to be that little gal when Jenkins catches up with her."

"Why do you think she is traveling alone? We all know how dangerous it is in Matamoros. Shouldn't one of us trail her or maybe catch up with the sheriff and warn him that his wife is in danger?"

"No, if he comes back across with Moore, I'll tell him. Maybe she'll return home before he does. I hope for her sake she does, 'cause she's going to be in real danger when he learns that she disobeyed his orders." Sheriff Watkins ambled over to the fire and laughed. "I'd love to be a fly on the wall when those two get together."

~

Anna slipped into Matamoros late into the night. Stars and moonlight were the only lights showing except one or two lanterns hanging from posts near a business. She tied her pony to a hitching rail and entered a quiet tavern. The barkeep kept his eyes on her as she eased over to the bar where he was drying whiskey glasses. Without raising her sombrero, she asked if he knew a man called Moore.

"Who's asking?" the man murmured.

"Is the man here?" Anna pleaded.

"No, he left after a sheriff posse arrived a few hours ago."

"Thanks, man. One more question. Do you know if Moore had a nun with him?" Anna was pleased that the man was eager to answer her questions.

"No woman was with him, only two men. One young and one big as a bull," the barkeep said, glancing at two men who stood at the end of the bar. "My information is not free," he said, as he motioned two Mexicans to surround her.

With a sudden intake of breath, Anna pulled out a twenty-dollar gold piece and laid it on the bar. "That's all I have. Take it or kill me, but I have to find the Catholic nun that was with him."

"Kill you?" The man snorted. "Git out of here and don't come back." The barkeep picked up the gold piece, bit down on it, and then waved his men away from Anna.

Anna sauntered out of the tavern and took in a deep breath of fresh air. Looking up to Heaven, she whispered, "Thank you."

Climbing back on her pony, she walked him to the end of the street. What should she do next?

A young senorita stood in the shadow of a building. She softly called to Anna. "Young boy, come over here."

Anna glanced all around and prayed that the girl meant no harm. "You want me?" Anna quizzed, with uncontrolled shivering.

"I know where the nun is being held. The man you are looking for don't have her. He run away."

"Who and where is she? Please tell me."

"Give me a gold coin and I'll tell you," she demanded as she bounced on her tiptoes.

"Sorry, I only had one and I gave it to the barkeep just minutes ago."

The girl released a long chain of the ugliest Spanish words that Anna had ever heard and started to flounce away.

"Please." Anna chased after the young woman. "The sister is in great danger. I must help return her home. Please tell me. I would give you all I have, but I have nothing of value."

More brutal, unladylike phases spewed from the girl, then she turned and said, "Follow me."

Anna tied her horse out of sight from the street and followed the girl up the backstairs of the cantina.

"Room 8," the girl said and disappeared.

Leaning up against the wall, Anna peered up and down the hallway. She eased over to the door and rested her ear up against it. Total silence. Summoning her nerve, she knocked softly on the door. She waited, biting the side of her mouth. Finally, the door flung open so fast that Anna screamed but quickly covered her mouth. Pedro stood with his pistol pointing directly in her face. His eyes widened. "Get in here." Pedro looked up and down the hall, then shut and locked the door. Sister Melody sat there eyeing her.

Anna rushed over to the bed, removed her hat, her long black hair twisted in a rope trailing down her back. "Sister Melody?"

"My gracious, Anna. Where did you come from?" Sister Melody asked.

"Are you all right?" Anna asked, taking her into a hug.

"Now, it's my turn to ask questions." Pedro stood with strong arms crossed over his chest. Clenching his jaw, he seemed so much taller than Anna remembered. This young boy has grown into a man.

"What do you want to know?"

"Anna, please don't play dumb. You're dressed in Juan's clothes and all alone. I would guess that Matt doesn't know you're here."

"Have you seen Matt and his posse?" Anna said, swallowing the lump in her throat.

"Yes, your uncle and his men were busy running out the back way. Moore had told Sister Melody to stay put while he checked how many men were down in the tavern. While Matt and his men were busy downstairs, Moore was looking for Sister Melody. I had grabbed her and locked her away in this room. Boy, was he mad that he couldn't find her."

"You've told Matt that you found Sister Melody, didn't you?"

Anna asked, hoping that Matt would give up the chase and return home.

"No, he and his men chased the men out of town. That was late last night. I planned to go downstairs and find Sister Melody some different clothes before we tried to leave town. Dressed like a penguin, she'll stick out like a black and blue thumb."

"My word, Pedro, a penguin?" Anna laughed for the first time in days, then sat down on a chair and looked out the window. "I have an idea. Why don't Sister Melody and I change clothes? She and I are nearly the same size. Besides, I brought my own nun clothes. If something happens and we get separated or my uncle grabs us before we reach the border, he'll nab me and not Sister Melody. It's me he wants anyway."

Pedro rubbed a hand across the back of his neck. "Well, that is a good idea. Your uncle believed that she was his niece. What will you say about that if we get caught by him?"

"I'll tell him the truth. Once he sees me, he will know the difference. I have a picture of my mama, and I look just like her. He will recognize me." Anna smiled at Pedro and took Sister Melody's hand. "I'm so sorry that my uncle scared you."

"He treated me well, but his big man hit me when they carried me from the house. My jaw and teeth still hurt, but I'm alive and I'm thankful to Pedro for saving me."

"My pinto pony is hitched on the side of this building. Will you go and take him to the livery? My carpetbag is tied to the saddle horn. Please bring that to me."

"Where did you find a pinto pony?"

"I borrowed him from Mr. Mac's Livery."

"You're going to be in so much trouble. Mr. Mac doesn't have horses that he loans out to just anyone." He shook his head. "Can't believe you stole a horse!" Pedro started pacing "Do you know what they do to horse thieves in Texas? They hang them."

"Hush up. I said I borrowed the pony. I'm taking him back as soon as we return to Livingston."

"Matt, your husband—if you don't remember—is the town sheriff. He's going to set the seat of your breeches on fire when he gets his hands on you. Then he will throw you in jail."

"Oh, Pedro, you know that Sheriff Jenkins will never harm Anna. He loves her," Sister Melody said.

"What do you know that I don't know?" Anna said while throwing her hands up in the air. "Love me? That's a joke. He only wants me to give him the bank money that Uncle Claude is after. He's trying to do a good job, and I'm just playing a part in it."

"Anna, you are so young and innocent, and very, very blind. We all know that he cares deeply for you. Pedro can see it, too."

"Being in love is one thing, but being a horse thief is different. Man, he's going to be so mad." Pedro snorted and headed out the door.

An hour later, after both ladies changed into their different clothes, Sister Melody helped Anna with her hair, tucking it under her headpiece.

~

When Pedro returned, he stopped dead in his tracks. "Lord, have mercy," he said as he looked at Sister Melody dressed in Juan's plaid shirt and pants. The clothes looked so different on her body than they did on Anna. Sister Melody's shirt was as tight as it could be, and the breeches were snug-fitting on her hips. She looked like one of those 'sporting women' he had seen when going into town. Pedro grabbed Juan's sheepskin jacket and said for her to cover herself. "Stay real close together. We don't want to draw attention to ourselves, so we'll go out the back to the livery, saddle our horses, and ride quietly out of town," He looked out in the hall. "Let's go."

After traveling to the border without any problems, they crossed the Rio Grande. Pedro knew that Sheriff Watkins and his posse were hiding in the woods. He whistled and several men came out of the woods with their pistols pointed right at them.

Sheriff Watkins strode out of the woods and motioned for them to follow him into the deep cluster of trees off the main trail. He looked from Anna to Sister Melody and smiled. "Would you ladies like to stand near our fire so you can dry off some? You both still look pretty dry, since the rain stopped and the river is not too deep where you crossed."

"Thank you, Sheriff Watkins," Anna said. "Pedro rescued Sister Melody from my uncle and his men. We understand that Matt and his men are chasing them deeper into Mexico."

"Matt knows that he can't go very far because the warrant he was issued was only for Matamoros, so he's most likely on his way back to the border. We'll have to wait for your uncle to cross back into Texas before we can continue our search for him."

"So, you think Matt and his men will be here soon?" Anna said, biting her lower lip and glancing at Pedro.

"Depends on how far he chased your uncle, but he should be home soon," Sheriff Watkins said. "In fact, we were breaking camp when we saw you three crossing the river. We're going home as soon as the men saddle up."

"Please don't let us keep you," Sister Melody said. "We're ready to go on our way, aren't we, Pedro? I want to return home so I can put on my rightful clothes. I haven't been dressed like this in many years, and it feels strange."

"If you don't mind, Sheriff, will it be all right if we ride along with you and your men? I'd like the ladies to have as much protection as possible. Both are good riders, and we won't hold you up." Pedro waited for the sheriff to answer him.

"Be happy to have you."

Chapter 23

Matt and his men had Moore and his two men pinned down behind some rocks. One of Moore's men had been hit, but they didn't know how badly. Firing still came from that area of rocks.

One of his men eased over to Matt. "I'll circle behind the rocks and hopefully surprise them from the rear."

"Be careful," Matt said, as another round of bullets hit the rocks in front of them. "I wish I had my rifle," Matt said.

Another one of Matt's posse yelled, "I hit another one!"

Horses' hooves sounded behind Matt and his posse. "Hold your fire."

A Mexican soldier yelled as he jumped off his brown bay. "Who are you firing upon, Señor?"

"We have Claude Moore and his two men trapped. Moore is wanted for murder, robbery, and now kidnapping."

"Who are you?"

"I'm Sheriff Matt Jenkins from Livingston, Texas, and I have a warrant to cross the border to capture this man." Matt offered the warrant to the soldier, who looked it over.

"Sorry, sir, but you are out of limits to search for this man. He is in safe ground now, and your warrant only allows for you to search as far as Matamoros."

"Can your men continue our search and take these men to jail?" Matt asked, disgusted. "No?" The soldier replied. "That's the reason bad men hide in Mexico."

The soldier turned to walk back to the other soldiers. "You must return with us as far as Matamoros."

"Can we at least see if we shot one or two of the men we were looking for?" Matt stood straight and pointed to the cluster of rocks that the men were shooting from.

"*Si*, you can do that if you hurry."

"Quick, fellows. Search those rocks for bodies." Matt was so disappointed and disgusted that he was an arm's reach of Moore and had to let them get away.

"Matt," a man called. "We killed the big guy, but the younger one is hit and bleeding something awful."

"Wrap the dead body in a blanket, and we'll bury him when we find softer ground. I'll take a look at the other one." Matt circled a big rock for a better view. Lying on the ground was a young man who was moaning and gripping his shoulder. Blood covered the front of his clothes. "Bring me a clean cloth from my saddlebags, and we will take him to Matamoros to the doctor."

After they carefully placed the injured man on his horse, Matt and his posse followed the soldiers to Matamoros. It was dark when two of his men carried the young man up the stairs to the doctor's office. One stood guard, while the other joined Matt at the livery.

"Let's find some rooms and have a good meal. I'm ready to hit the hay," Matt said. "I'll pay some locals to bury the big guy called Bull. No telling where Moore is now and what he has done with Sister Melody. I am fearful for her life, but I know he will return to Livingston soon. He still doesn't have the bank money."

"Do you think he will kill the girl?"

"No, he thinks that Sister Melody is his niece. He won't hurt her." Matt strode out of the livery and headed to the doctor's office. After a few minutes of questioning the boy called Willie, Matt realized that he wasn't going to coax anything out of him about the whereabouts of Moore. Willie did say that he was sure Moore didn't have Sister Melody with him. They had all ridden out of town together, and the woman wasn't with them.

The doctor told Matt that the boy shouldn't be moved for at least two days. If he wanted him to stay alive, he'd best let him rest because the boy had lost a lot of blood and was very weak.

Matt headed over to the hotel and told his men that after they had eaten, rested, and taken care of their horses, they could head back to Livingston without him. He was going to stay and bring the boy back with him. "Just maybe, he will tell me something about Sister Melody."

The men nodded and said that they would pull out at sunrise. It was a dangerous place for a lawman in this area.

Early the next morning, Matt waved goodbye to his men and said that he would be home in about three days. "Thanks for all of your hard work. Keep on the lookout for Moore. He has to come back to Livingston if he wants to recover the bank money."

~

Sheriff Watkins and his men, along with Anna, Sister Melody, and Pedro, rode into Livingston as the sun was going down. The town was peaceful compared to Matamoros. Pedro led Anna and Sister Melody to the livery where Mr. Mac stood with his hands on his hips. Anna shifted as she sat on the borrowed pinto horse.

With flaring nostrils, Mr. Mac hurried over to Anna. "Well, gal, you have a lot of explaining to do. Mr. Rogers would have had a posse out on your tail, if one had been here. It's a good thing Sheriff Jenkins was out of town chasing that murderer, Moore."

"Mr. Mac, Anna needed a horse, and you wasn't here for her to ask you if she could use one. I know that's not an excuse for her taking Mr. Rogers' pinto, but I'm sure he will understand once he speaks with Anna. The pinto is not harmed in any way."

The livery owner's frown ebbed a bit. "Well, the sheriff will have to handle this mess. Rogers will have his horse back in the morning, and I'll try to explain things to him."

"Climb off, Anna, and let me put the horse in his stall." Pedro walked over to Sister Melody and helped her down. Anna and Sister Melody stood together while Pedro cared for the animals. "Come, girls, let's go home. I'm starved," he said, grinning at both of them.

~

Reverend Mother and the children were sitting on the front porch when the trio walked toward the house. They raced to the picket fence, and Jamie opened the gate for them to enter. "My prayers have been answered," Reverend Mother said, as she made the sign of the cross. "Oh, my girls, are you all right? My goodness, Sister Melody, even in this darkness, I can see the side of your face is black. What brute did this to you?"

"We'll talk about our *adventure* when the children are in bed. Right now, Pedro is starving, and I believe Anna and I could eat something too."

"Come, children, let's go in the house." As the girls walked in front of Reverend Mother, she asked, "Sister, how come you're in men's clothing?"

"That's part of the adventure, Mother. We'll tell you all about it." Sister Melody entered the house and immediately raced into the bedroom that she shared with Reverend Mother.

Pedro and Reverend Mother went into the kitchen. Pedro placed an armful sticks of wood in the stove while Reverend Mother took a platter of chicken and a loaf of fresh-baked bread and placed them on the table. Filling a pot with water and coffee grounds, she pulled the pot over the hot eye of the stove. "I made several pies while you were gone and there's plenty left. The two kids and I didn't eat much of what I cooked."

Sister Melody came out of the bedroom wrapped in her robe. "Now I feel like myself again," she said with a little laugh. "Juan will be glad to have his clothes back."

Anna was still sitting at the kitchen table, dressed in her nun's clothes. "Aren't you going to change, my dear?" Sister Melody asked.

"I guess, but I feel so natural in these clothes. I have a lot to think about now that we are safely home," Anna said, still remaining at the table.

"Where is the sheriff?" Reverend Mother asked. What did Anna mean about feeling natural dressed like a nun?

"He's chasing Moore and his men. We came across the border with Sheriff Watkins and his men. I'm sure he will be back home soon," Pedro said.

~

Later, after Anna tucked Susie and Jamie into bed, Pedro went into town looking for Juan. Anna and Sister Melody filled Reverend Mother in on what had taken place from the time Bull, Moore's man, had kidnapped Sister Melody until Anna borrowed the pinto and went out on her own to search, then finding Pedro who had rescued Sister Melody in the hotel room.

"All we know now for sure is Matt and his men chased my uncle and his gang out of town. We met Sheriff Watkins and his men at the border and came home with them. We must pray for Matt and the other men with him that they will return home safely," Anna said.

"We must be prepared for your uncle to come back here. He wants that money, and he will try again to force you to give it to him," Reverend Mother said.

"I know. I have been thinking, and I believe the best thing for us to do is to travel back to the convent. We have always been safe there, and it is the best place for me. I want to study my vows, and when ready, I want to become a nun. I feel that God is calling me to become one of you," Anna said as she wiped tears away.

"But dearest, you're married to Sheriff Jenkins," Sister Melody said before Reverend Mother could respond.

"Sister Melody is right. You are already married; therefore, you can't become a Catholic nun."

"I can. Our marriage can be annulled. We've never lived as man and wife," Anna said, with much determination in her voice. "Besides, Matt doesn't love me. He's only close to me because he thinks my uncle will come around. Matt wants to be near so he can catch him. Don't you see? After my uncle is caught, he will be glad to be rid of me."

"Anna, you don't really believe that, do you?" Reverend Mother asked. "We all know that he cares deeply for you."

"He hasn't shown me any affection. All he does is order me around. Do this, do that or else." Anna said with a jerk of her finger. "Reverend Mother—" Anna placed her hand over Reverend Mother's aged one. "Let's go home, back to the convent. Remember, you said if I was unhappy, I could return."

"Are you so unhappy that you would give up your freedom here? Being able to come and go and work at the café. Your pie and pastry business is doing very well." Reverend Mother sighed. "Are you willing to turn your back on your marriage and pretend it never took place?"

"Yes, to all of those questions. I want to leave here as soon as in the morning. We will take Susie and Jamie with us." Anna's face was resolute as she stood facing the woman she loved like her second mother.

"All right, we'll pack in the morning and let Mr. Godwin at the café, Henrietta at the store, and Preacher Stubbs know that we're catching the stage home. We can't just sneak out of town when these people have been so good to you." Reverend Mother stood and strode toward the bedroom. "We all need to turn in because we have a lot to do tomorrow to prepare for our trip home, and we have to close up this house."

~

Pedro and Juan entered the dark front room. They both walked softly into the kitchen. Juan hugged Anna and gave Sister Melody a big smile. Before they could say anything, Anna announced that they were all returning to the convent.

"You boys are grown men, and you can choose to go or stay."

Neither one said anything at first. Finally, Juan asked, "Can we give you our answer tomorrow?"

"Of course. If you want to stay here, I'll allow you both to live in this house. You are like brothers to me and what's mine is yours."

"That's a load off our shoulders, if we decide to stay," Pedro gazed at Anna, then turned to Juan. "I'm ready to go to bed."

Anna remembered that Pedro didn't stay at the house earlier. "Pedro, aren't you hungry?"

"I had some supper in the kitchen while Juan and Mr. Godwin were cleaning the café's kitchen. Thanks anyway." He lumbered into the living room.

"Anna," Juan said, "I can't believe you're going to abandon Matt. He is going to be hopping mad when he gets back to town and you're gone. He's very fond of you, and now that you're his wife, he will come after you."

"That's wishful thinking on your part." She shuffled into the bedroom, realizing she had the bed all to herself.

Chapter 24

The next day was heartbreaking for Anna. She slogged to the dry goods store and waited until Henrietta finished filling an order for one of her regular customers.

"I'll be with you in just a few minutes, honey. Be sure to look at all the pretty new ribbons that came in yesterday. Susie will surely like them." A few minutes later. "Now, young lady, tell me why you're dressed in that nun's outfit." Henrietta looked Anna up and down.

"I came to tell you that I am going back to the convent on tomorrow's stage. Reverend Mother, Sister Melody, and I feel that I will be safer there."

"Now child, you know that Matt will be home soon, and with Juan, Pedro, and Deputy Martin, you're plenty safe here. Sheriff Watkins and his men will be here for several more weeks, too. So, there no reason to leave," Henrietta said matter-of-factly.

"I have to go. Matt can continue to search for my uncle in peace, if I am not here. Besides, he can go on with his life after I get our marriage annulled."

"Annulled? Matt is not going to allow you to do that. You're his wife and he loves you."

"Please, you don't know that to be the truth. He has only spent time with me hoping that my uncle would show up and he could capture him," Anna said. "Now, I do need a few things to take on our trip home. We are going to take Susie and Jamie with us. If their parents show up, you can tell them where they are. I won't give them up easily because I love them like they are my own."

Henrietta reached for Anna's list and wiped a tear from her eye. "I'm going to miss you, gal, that's for sure. I will pray that you have a safe journey home."

"I'll return for my things in a little while. Now I have to say farewell to Mr. Godwin and Reverend Stubbs."

~

Mr. Godwin was thrilled to see Anna walk into his café, but very unhappy and almost angry with the news that she was returning to the convent. "I guess my best helper, Juan, is going with you," he said, trying hard not to show his disappointment.

"Pedro and Juan haven't said if they are leaving with us or not. We are catching the stage out tomorrow morning."

"My dearest Anna, my heart breaks. Your friendship has meant so much to me and mercy, your desserts and other dishes have brought in so much business. I will probably have to close after you depart our town."

"Please, Mr. Godwin, don't place so much guilt on me for doing something I have to do," Anna stuttered. With a quivering chin, she gave him a peck on the cheek and raced out the door. Wiping away tears, she continued down to the parsonage to say goodbye to Reverend Stubbs. After knocking, the tall, bearded man answered the door.

"Come in, my child. What brings you to see me so early in the morning? I understand that you rode to the border to help Sheriff Jenkins look for your uncle. Is that true?"

"I didn't go to the border with the sheriff, but I did go in search of Sister Melody. My uncle's men had kidnapped her, thinking that they had taken me instead." The man only looked at Anna, waiting for to continue her story. "Pedro recovered Sister Melody, and we are all home now except the sheriff. He is still searching for my uncle and his men."

"I see, I think. It is good to hear that you and the other sister is home safe and sound. So, what can I do for you this fine morning?"

"I came to tell you goodbye. We are returning to the convent in Whitmire, Texas, tomorrow. I just wanted to thank you and your wife for your friendship. I am also going to study to become a nun as soon as I can, once we return."

"A nun? But my dear, I married you and the sheriff. How can you give yourself to God when you are a married woman?"

"I am going to have our marriage annulled," Anna said. "Now, I must return to the store and get my supplies and hurry back to my house. We have a lot to do before we can leave in the morning. Thanks again. I shall always remember you and Mrs. Stubbs."

With tears streaming down her rosy cheeks, Anna was glad to be wearing the heavy nun's clothes. She had left the house without a shawl or jacket. The strong north wind was blowing her headpiece nearly off.

"Anna, Anna," Susie had run to the fence to greet her. "Is it true me and Jamie are going to go on a trip with you and the other penguins?"

"Susie, don't you dare refer to them as penguins again. They are sisters and nuns to you, understand?"

"Yes, ma'am, sorry, but is it true?"

Anna stooped down to eye level with Susie. "Would you like to go and live with me and the other sisters at the convent?"

"I don't know what a convent is, but I want to be wherever you are."

"It's settled then. Jamie is going with us, too. There will be other children there, but you two will be my responsibility."

Susie grabbed Anna's hand and they walked into the house. "I'm back and I picked up some goodies for us to take on the trip. I said goodbye to everyone, so now we only have to give the animals away. I may want to sell this house later, if the boys decide to go home with us," Anna said to Sister Melody and Reverend Mother.

"Anna, the boys are going to ride with us on the stage home, but Pedro wants to return and continue working at the livery. Mr. Mac was teaching him to shoe horses and learn to be a blacksmith. Juan hasn't said if he will return here once we get home," Sister Melody said.

"That's wonderful for Pedro. We will give him the key to the house, and he can live here rent free," Anna said. "Since he'll be living here, we don't have to do much but hire someone to care for the chickens and the cow. We need to drain the water from the icebox, and when he returns, he can purchase another block of ice."

"Let's all pack our things and cook a nice farewell dinner. We need to use all the fresh food we have in the kitchen, and I will bake some pies. Juan can take Mr. Godwin and Henrietta one each of them to enjoy."

Early the next morning, Anna purchased seven stagecoach tickets for Whitmire, Texas. Both Juan and Pedro had decided to travel with the girls and children home. Pedro said that Señor Carlos would have skinned them alive if they hadn't made the trip. He'd given them instructions to protect Anna, which now included all the others.

After traveling for five days, the sisters arrived safely in Whitmire, Texas. Juan jumped down and ran to the livery to rent a large wagon to take everyone and their baggage to the convent. Everyone was dusty and very tired.

Once Juan drove to the front of the convent, a big celebration had been planned for Reverend Mother's return. All the convent sisters and children were waving and shouting their greetings. Once Reverend Mother was down on the ground, many of the people reached out and kissed parts of her dusty black robe. Tears of joy were in the eyes of all the sisters.

Reverend Mother waved and shook many of their hands. She seemed overjoyed and surprised with the homecoming welcome. She held on to Sister Melody and Anna's hands as they entered the wide door of the convent.

~

In the crowd that had gathered outside of the convent, Claude Moore mingled with the street people. He was unrecognizable with a scraggly, thin beard, stringy hair trailing his neck, and dressed in Mexican clothes with a decorated sombrero. He watched the three nuns receiving hugs from many other sisters. Which woman dressed in a black robe and white headpiece was Anna?

~

Once all the sisters were inside the convent, Anna took the children's hands and led them to the kitchen. "Hello, ladies," Anna called to Betsy and Sadie.

"Oh, my goodness, look who's come back home!" Sadie cried as she ran to Anna's waiting arms. "Look at you. You haven't change one bit, except how you're dressed. Gracious, girl, what are you doing in that black garb?"

"Oh, it's so good to be home with you two, and I have missed baking pies for the sisters and the children at the school." Anna suddenly remembered the two children she'd brought into the kitchen with her.

"Betsy and Sadie, I want you to meet my two little ones, Susie and Jamie. They are my new charges, and they will be living here with me." Anna pulled Susie and Jamie to stand in front of her. "Say hello," Anna encouraged the children to be polite.

"Something smells good," Jamie said to Anna.

"My goodness, I bet this growing young man is hungry. Bring them both to the bar and sit them right up there. I will give them a treat before dinner."

Susie and Jamie broke loose from Anna and climbed up onto bar stools and sat waiting patiently for something to be served to them.

Betsy poured two cold glasses of milk while Sadie placed two large sugar cookies on a small plate in front of them. Both of them dived into the cookies as if they were starving.

"When was the last time these young'uns had something to eat?" Sadie asked laughing.

Jamie attempted to answer with his mouth full, but Anna stopped him. "It has been several hours since they had anything on the stagecoach. They'll be ready for dinner, a bath, and bed soon. It was a long five-day trip, but today seemed the longest."

"Here, you sit and enjoy a treat, too. I remember you could eat anytime." Betsy said as she placed another plate on the bar.

After Anna shared the evening vespers with the other sisters, she went to tuck in the children. Looking in her room, she saw there was only one bed. She had asked for two cots to be placed in her room. Walking down the hall, she stopped and looked into the girls' dormitory and saw Susie standing at attention in front of a nun.

"Give me your hand, young lady," she said to Susie who was still dressed in her day clothes. She had not had a bath, either.

Susie held her hands behind her back, "No. I am not going to let you hit me like you do that girl."

Anna looked around the room and saw another child crying under her covers.

"Give me your hand or you will get twice the licks I planned on giving you," the nun said through clenched teeth.

"What is going on in here?" Anna demanded. "Why are you wanting Susie to hold out her hand?"

The older nun slipped the heavy ruler back up her sleeve. "She will not get in bed like I instructed. Susie must learn to follow the rules." The older nun appeared like an Army sergeant.

"Oh, Anna, she's mean. She hit that girl with a big ruler on the hand over and over, and now she wants to hit me. I told her that I was supposed to sleep in your room, but she said I was a liar."

"Where is the ruler?" Anna looked at the nun, but she didn't move an inch.

Another child in the next bed jumped up. "It's in her sleeve. She hides it there."

Anna jerked the older woman's right arm and shook it. A long piece of wood dropped to the floor. She picked it up and examined it. "You have been punishing the children with this board?"

"These children must learn discipline. They are heathens and have no manners when they come to us. I have to whip them into good Christian children."

"Get out of this room and retire for the night. I will see to the girls." Anna said, as she pulled Susie into her body and held her tight. Everyone watched the old nun leave, and as soon as she was out of sight, the little girls cheered.

"Shh, girls. You don't want her to think that I cannot tuck you in bed," Anna said, smiling at all the sweet faces. Anna examined the little girl who had been punished by the older nun. "Does your hand still hurt?"

"It burns, and this little place hurts the most." The child pointed at one of her knuckles.

"Please put on your robe and come with me. Susie, why aren't you dressed in your night clothes? Did you have a bath?"

"No, I wouldn't allow them to touch me. They scared me so I waited for you to come for me. Then that old woman grabbed me and made me come to this room with all the other girls."

"Gather your things and we will go and have a chat with Reverend Mother," Anna said as she ushered the two little girls down the hall.

After expressing her concern to Reverend Mother about the treatment that the older nun was administering to the girls, Reverend Mother asked to speak to the children.

Susie came running to Reverend Mother and hugged her around the neck. "I'm not sure if I am going to stay here," she whispered in her ear.

Reverend Mother shook her head. She asked if she could ask her and the other little girl some questions.

"Ask away. You're the boss lady here," Susie said.

"Thank you, Susie. My first question is to Marie. That is your name, isn't it?

"Yes, ma'am."

"Marie, you have been with us for a while now. Has Sister Delores ever struck you or any of the other girls with a ruler?"

Marie held her head down and murmured, "Yes, ma'am."

"Does she ever read bedtime stories before lights are turned out?"

"No, ma'am."

"Does she hit the other children with her hands or a belt?"

"Both, ma'am. She slapped me in the face once, and I had to stay in bed and miss going outside."

"Why did you have to stay inside?"

"My face was bruised, and she thought I should stay away from the other sisters."

"Marie, how old are you?"

"I'm a big girl now. I'm five years old," Marie said.

"Anna, you can take these children back to their beds now. Please don't worry about them any longer. It is my responsibility to care for these children, and I will be doing a better job, I can assure you. Starting now."

"Reverend Mother, Jamie and Susie will be staying in my room until they decide that they are too old. May I get two cots and some blankets from the supply room?"

"Yes. Take whatever you need to make your wards feel safe and comfortable." Reverend Mother stood while Anna curtsied to her and left the room.

~

Turning to the cross hanging on her wall, Reverend Mother said quietly, *"Forgive me, Lord, for not protecting your children from harm. I promise from this day forward, the children will be protected and loved."*

Before the sun was up the next morning, Señor Carlos and Sister Delores were headed to the convent across the border in Matamoros, Mexico. Delores spoke fluent Spanish and was raised twenty miles from that area. She would be near her family, if she chose to be.

Chapter 25

Sheriff Matt drove the wagon to the office door of Dr. Adams. He lowered himself down on the ground, being careful not to hurt his aching leg. Glancing over into the bed of the wagon, he saw his prisoner was still asleep. Several people gathered around the wagon bed and wondered who this young man was.

"Pete, go and tell Doc Adams that I brought him a patient and please come out." Sheriff Matt asked several men if they would assist him in carrying the boy inside the office.

"Hi, Matt," Doc Adams greeted the sheriff. "Who you got there? Has he been shot?"

"This young boy was with Claude Moore's gang, and he was shot in a shootout several miles from Matamoros. He's lost a lot of blood. I will post a guard out or inside your office, whichever one you want. He's not dangerous right now, but later he will be."

Several men grabbed arms and legs and carried the prisoner into the office. Doc Adams waved them outside while he hovered over the boy's chest. "I hate to cut his nice clothes off, but I don't want to move him around too much more."

"Jim will stay with you and bring you anything you need to care for my prisoner. Be sure to order your meals and have them delivered here." Sheriff Matt walked to the door, placed his hat on his head, and said he would check back in a few hours. He drove the wagon to the livery and asked Mac to give his horse a good rubdown and extra oats. "He has worked hard the last few days." Matt patted his horse's neck. Looking around the barn, he asked, "Mac, where is Pedro?" Mac continued to work as if he didn't hear the sheriff. "Mac, where's Pedro," he asked again.

"He might be at his house resting." Mac wouldn't meet his eyes.

Matt headed to his office and was greeted by Deputy Martin.

"Welcome home, boss. I heard you brought in a member of Moore's gang. Is he still alive?"

"Doc Adams seems to think that he'll live. How are things here since I have been gone?"

"Quiet," he responded but didn't make eye contact. "I'd better go and make my rounds. See you later," he said as he dashed out the door.

Matt watched him hurry down the boardwalk into the café. Yawning, Matt decided to go by the café and say hello to Anna and Juan before he went to the house to take a nap. As he entered the café, he noticed that the place was nearly empty. Another glance around the room, and he didn't see any pastries or pies in the glass case.

Pushing the kitchen door open with his back, Mr. Godwin came out of the kitchen carrying a platter with two plates of food on it. He stopped when he saw Sheriff Jenkins standing at the door. Mr. Godwin continued over to the table and served his customers their food, then hurried to the kitchen.

Matt called to him, "Mr. Godwin, where's all your help?"

"They're not here," he said, the door closing behind him.

"Yep, I can see that," Matt mumbled to himself as he turned and walked down the boardwalk. Why was everyone acting so strange? It seemed that no one wanted to talk with him. He'd just go over to the house and get something to eat. Sister Melody and Reverend Mother always had something hot and ready.

As Matt passed the dry goods store, he waved at Henrietta through the open doorway. Suddenly, she turned her back on him, wiping her eye with a big hanky. As fast as she could, she raced into the storeroom. He stood looking in the doorway, hoping she would come out and speak with him, but she didn't. As he turned to continue down the boardwalk, he ran into Reverend Stubbs. "Hello, Preacher," Matt said.

"Welcome back, son. I heard you brought in a prisoner?"

"I did, but I am heading home to see Anna. Give my best to your wife."

"Matt, you haven't heard?"

"Heard what?" Matt asked, hoping he might get some information from the reverend. Everyone had been acting so funny.

"Your wife, the other nuns, along with Pedro and Juan, all

boarded the stage a few days ago and left for the convent in Whitmire." Reverend Stubbs wiped the inside of his hat brim with a checked handkerchief.

Matt didn't wait to hear any more from the preacher. He took off as fast as his sore leg would allow him, hopping and skipping all the way to Anna's little house. He tried the door, but it was locked. Reaching over the doorsill, he took the key down and opened the door to an empty, cold room. "Anna?" Matt called but received no answer.

He walked from room to room and found no one. The fireplace was set for a fire, the kitchen stove was cold, but the wood box was full. Both beds were made up, and the extra quilts and pillows were stacked against the wall. The longer he stood looking around, the madder he became. *That little witch thinks she can run out on me, she has another thing coming. She is my wife and she will remain my wife. I will tell her when I am ready to end our marriage.*

Tossing a match in the fireplace to warm the house, he stormed into the bedroom, kicked off his boots, and crawled into the neat bed. After tossing and turning from anger, he finally fell into an exhausted sleep.

Early the next morning, Matt decided to travel to Whitmire by horseback instead of taking the stagecoach. He could make the trip in three days, two fewer days than the stagecoach. Matt asked Mac for the loan of a horse, packed a carpetbag of clothes, and prepared a good bedroll with an extra quilt, since the nights were really cold. He stopped in the dry goods store to buy supplies for his trip— coffee, sugar, a slab of bacon, fresh bread, a link of sausages, and a big hunk of bologna.

Henrietta filled his order and tossed in some dried fruit and nuts. "Matt, I tried to talk Anna out of leaving. She was so sad and determined to make you a free man. I told her that you didn't want an annulment, but she wouldn't listen. I love that little gal. Are you going to bring her back home?"

"We're going to settle a few things between us, that's for sure. If you don't mind, please look in on my prisoner and make sure he is receiving good care. He's just a kid. I have no idea how or why he was mixed up with Moore." Sheriff Jenkins saddled his horse and looped a saddle blanket on the extra horse and placed some of his supplies on its back. He left town and hoped to be riding up in

Whitmire in three days or sooner.

~

With the grace of God and good weather, Matt Jenkins rode safely into the livery stable in Whitmire, Texas. He left his two horses and paid the owner to watch over his saddle and other belongings. "Do you know where I can buy a nice, covered wagon with four strong mules?" he asked the nice owner. "I need one in a day or so, two at the most."

"I will search around for you. Do you pay a commission if I find it for you?"

Matt smiled at the old critter. "Yes, sir. It has to be in good condition and the mules healthy and sturdy."

"Si," the man nodded. "The best for you."

Before the man left, Matt asked if the convent was close enough for him to walk.

"Si, it's just up the road. You can't miss it." The man hurried to take care of Matt's animals.

Matt stopped in The Golden Goose tavern and asked for a room and a hot bath. "Do you serve food here, too?"

A senorita whirled around his tall frame and smiled. "I can get you whatever you might want."

The girl was the prettiest young senorita he had seen in a long time. The young lady had long midnight black hair, painted red lips, and dark pink cheeks. She batted her long eyelashes and showed her pearly white teeth. Too bad he was only interested in one young lady, his wife, who was a beautiful girl with a clean face even in a long, black dress. "A room, hot bath, and food are what I would like for now."

Taking a key from the bartender, she wiggled her little finger for him to follow her upstairs. Swinging her small hips from side to side, she opened his bedroom door and entered quickly, but just as fast, Matt took her arm and pushed her out into the hallway.

"Just knock when you have my dinner." Matt smiled, went over, and pressed down on the mattress. "Nice," he said out loud. Later, feeling human again, Matt walked to the convent and was led into Reverend Mother's office.

"Oh, Sheriff Jenkins, how nice to see you again. You made good time," she said.

"You were expecting me?" he asked, giving her a puzzling

look.

"Anna's here, isn't she? She's your wife and you love her. Why wouldn't I expect you to come and take her home where she belongs?" Reverend Mother pointed to a chair in front of her desk. She skirted around it and took her chair.

"You believe that Anna should be with me, too?" Matt asked.

"Very much. Anna is confused because she is young. She believes that you used her to catch her uncle. Because of that belief, she has decided to take her vows and become a member of our order." Reverend Mother laughed. "I have allowed her to study and dress in the white clothing that the others wear while waiting for their ceremony of marriage to the church. Anna has lived here for ten years, and in all that time, she's never wanted to become a sister. She hates all of our rigid rules."

"Where's Anna now? I plan to take her back to Livingston and court her for a time before we become man and wife. I do love her, and I promise you I will take care of her as long as I live."

"Believe me, son, I know that to be true, or I would never let you take her from me. I raised her as my own daughter, and I love her very much." Reverend Mother stood, walked around the desk, and took Matt's hands. "Anna took Jamie and Susie fishing at the back of our property. She hasn't come back, so I guess they are having a good fishing day." As she walked Matt to the door, she said, "Please let me say goodbye to her before you leave with her and the children."

"Yes, ma'am," Matt said and leaned in to kiss the lovely old woman on the cheek.

Chapter 26

Anna took Jamie and Susie to the creek on the far end of the convent. Jamie had never been fishing before, but Susie enjoyed playing at the edge of the water, watching the tadpoles swim around. Jamie took a worm in his hands and held it so tight that he squeezed it into. She laughed and then instructed him on how to place the wiggly creature on his hook and swing it out over the water.

Within a few minutes, he caught a flapping brim that was larger than his hand. Using her glove hand, Anna unhooked the fish and ran it onto a fishing line.

After several hours of fishing and enjoying a picnic, Anna packed up their fishing poles and carried the string of fish back up the trail toward the convent.

As the kids ran ahead, jumping and kicking pinecones as if they were balls, they suddenly stopped. "Anna, look! There's Sheriff Jenkins." Susie ran straight to the tall, handsome man wrapping her dirty, wet hands around his tall leg. "I missed you so much, Mr. Matt."

Anna froze on the trail and watched the interaction with Matt and the children. She wanted to run to him too, relieved he had returned to town from the border unharmed.

"Did you come to take us home, Sheriff?" Jamie asked. "I like fishing, but I want to go home—away from these high walls."

"Children," Anna called to them. "Take our fish to Betsy in the kitchen."

"Are you staying with us, Sheriff?" Susie asked. It was obvious that Susie cared deeply for Matt and was very happy that he had come to the convent.

Matt patted her on the shoulder but didn't say a word. He just kept his eyes on Anna.

"Susie, do as I asked and take the fish to the kitchen. Matt will talk with you later."

Anna and Matt watched as the children raced up the trail dropping the string of fish on the ground. They scooped the fish up and ran into the back door out of their sight.

"Let's take a walk back to the creek where we can talk privately," Matt said, as he gripped Anna's arm a little too firmly to suit her.

"You're hurting my arm," she cried as she tried to make him turn her loose.

"I haven't begun to hurt you yet, my disobedient wife," Matt growled.

His long legs made giant steps, and Anna was practically hopping to keep up with his pace.

He stopped beside a fallen log and gave her a little shake. "I can't believe you dressed like a boy and rode into Mexico all alone when I forbade you to leave. If I had thought it was safe, I would have allowed you to go with me. But no, you waited and plotted until I left town. You have no idea how I felt when I learned that you were down in Mexico looking for Sister Melody. I had your uncle cornered in that same cantina you were in. If I could have gotten my hands on you, I would've tanned your backside, which I'm going to do right this minute."

"Don't you dare touch me!" Anna stepped backward and looked for a place to escape. I'll scream so loud a hundred men will come and shoot you." She lifted her chin, with her hands on her hips. Just let him try to touch me, Anna thought, and he'll be sorry.

Before Anna knew what had happened, she was lying face down on Matt's knees with her white skirt and shift over her head. He slapped his large hand down on her pantaloons three or four times before she could squeeze the first scream out of her mouth.

"Scream some more, my runaway wife. You are going to learn that I mean business." Another slap on her practically bare rump brought a shriek. "When I give you an order, you will obey me. Do you understand?" When Anna didn't answer, he slapped her bottom again, this time harder.

"Yes, yes, I understand," she replied, fighting back tears. Her bottom was on fire, and she wanted to jump into the creek to cool it off, but she wouldn't dare let him know how bad he had blistered her backside.

Matt jerked Anna around on his lap holding her tight, so she couldn't slip away. "Another thing, young lady. You're my wife. How dare you try to put me in competition with God? You can't marry him because you married me first. There will be no annulment. I am your husband, whether you like it or not." He pushed Anna off his lap and strode a few feet away. "Get up and start packing your things. You and the children are coming home with me in the morning. I will be back with a covered wagon. The stagecoach is too crowded to carry our growing family." Matt whipped around toward the trail, but he turned around. "Don't get any ideas about running away from me again. You think your bottom hurts now? There won't be any place I won't look for you, and when I do find you, well, you get the idea." Before turning to leave, he stopped and looked down at Anna. "I love you, Anna Knight Jenkins."

Anna sat on the ground in a state of shock and watched as her handsome husband stalked toward the convent. *He said he loved me.* Anna looked up toward Heaven and said, "Thank you, God, for answering my prayer. I love Sheriff Matt Jenkins, too." Pulling herself up off the ground, she rubbed her backside. She dusted leaves and damp dirt off her skirt and legs, then pulled off her white head covering and wiped the tears in her eyes. She didn't need to go back to the convent with red-rimmed eyes and looking like she had wallowed around in the grass with Matt.

Susie and Jamie ran to her as they saw her coming up the trail.

"Are we going back to your house with Sheriff Matt? I wanna go, Anna. Please, let's go," Susie whimpered.

Anna bent down on one knee so she could look Susie into her tear-filled eyes. "Yes, sweetheart, we are going back to Livingston. You too, Jamie. Both of you will continue to live with me and now with Sheriff Matt. We will make a good home for both of you." Anna hugged both of the children. "Now you both know that your folks might come back for you. If that happens, we will pray about how we will handle your future."

"I ain't going back!" Jamie said. "I'll run away first."

"My mama don't want me, so I ain't going to fret about leaving you, Anna."

Anna shook her head. "I just wanted to remind you that this

might happen, but Sheriff Matt will help us, if it does. Let's go and take a good bath and start packing our things."

~

When Matt reined up in front of the Catholic convent early the next day, he was surprised to see Pedro and Juan standing beside the hitching rail. Jumping down from the wagon, he smiled broadly. "You boys coming back to Livingston with us?"

Juan gave a stony-faced nod. "I was glad to be back home, but Pedro wants to return and continue working with Mr. Mac at the livery. I can't let my brother leave me here all alone. Guess I'll work with Mr. Godwin at the café. He was teaching me to cook." Juan glanced toward the first door. I have to protect Anna, although I was a little late in doing that yesterday. Did you beat her?" Juan narrowed his eyes at Matt.

"Juan," Pedro called. "I told you that Anna received what she deserved from her husband. Besides, I wanted to tan her hide when I opened the door where I was hiding Sister Melody in Matamoros. She had placed herself in danger when she was ordered to stay home."

"Juan, I didn't beat Anna. I would never do that, but I did paddle her backside for disobeying me. She could have been killed." Matt breathed in slow and even.

~

While the three men were discussing Anna's behavior, Claude Moore was across the road in a patch of trees keeping watch. He was sure he could tell which nun was his niece since he had been with her while in Mexico. She was taller than his sister, and he thought she favored her papa more. Claude had hoped that she would have been friendly to him while they were in Matamoros, but she was quiet and never asked him a question.

The men disappeared inside and came out carrying carpetbags, quilts, and pillows. Two other men carried rifles, fishing poles, and two large bags of oats. With all the supplies, they were going to be traveling for a while.

Once he learned their destination, he would go into town and hire a few men. He could always dispose of them after he retrieved the stolen bank money from Anna.

After the wagon was filled to the brim with the needed supplies, all the sisters and children came outside to hug Anna and wave goodbye to the boys. "Have a safe trip back to Livingston," Sister Melody called.

Livingston? Claude Moore heard a pretty, tall nun call out. She looked familiar. Yes, that's Anna, he thought. So Anna was not leaving the convent, he thought. Good, if Anna stayed here, he wouldn't have to hire any men to help him reclaim the bank money. Suddenly, another nun came out the door, arm in arm with an older woman. All the sisters curtsied, and the men took off their hats as the pair walked by them. Oh, that's Reverend Mother, Claude remembered. The older woman kissed the young woman on each cheek and said something to the sheriff as he helped the girl up on the bench.

No wonder, he thought, the sister that Bull had kidnapped kept saying her name was Sister Melody. They had the wrong girl all the time. The young nun on the wagon seat was his niece. Using his eye glass, he could tell that the younger girl was the spitting image of his sister. His sister was petite, short, and had a lovely smile. He would bet his last dollar that this girl had long black hair under that headpiece.

Chapter 27

Matt climbed up on the bench in the covered wagon. He didn't even look at Anna. "I'm not going to ask why you're dressed in that black garb again. Guess Reverend Mother felt you would stay safe from strange men and even me."

"Why would my outfit make me feel safer with you?"

"Girl, you're so innocent. Sporting a black robe and that ridiculous headpiece would turn any man off," he scoffed.

Anna reached up and felt her white wimple. "My headpiece has been worn by other sisters for decades. How dare you make fun of it?"

Matt refused to react. He leaned over to the side of the wagon to make sure Juan and Pedro were trailing close beside them. As they drove through the quaint town of Whitmire, shop owners were sweeping the boardwalk and chatting with each other. The dry goods owner was arranging displays of goods next to the wall. Each one stopped and waved as they passed.

The sun had come out from behind the dark clouds, a few chickens were darting here and there in the road, and a cool breeze was kicking up dust. Children were tramping to the schoolhouse. The little girls were giggling and whispering secrets while the boys chased each other with their wooden guns.

Susie and Jamie watched the children from the back of the wagon. "I can't wait to go home and play. I wish I was old enough to go to school," Jamie said.

"I liked working in the café with Anna. She was teaching me to make pie crust. I could twirl the dough around and around," Susie sighed and flopped back on the quilts that were piled high.

The weather was nice all day. Juan had ridden ahead and scouted out a clearing for them to camp. He reined in his pony next to the wagon and twisted around in his saddle. "There's a small stream and a cluster of trees up ahead where we can stop."

In less than thirty minutes, Pedro helped the kids out of the wagon, and they ran to the trees to relieve themselves. Matt helped Anna down and instructed the children to gather firewood. "Be careful and watch for snakes," he yelled.

"Snakes? They don't need to be wandering around in those woods if there are snakes," Anna said to Matt.

"Anna, you fish, hunt, and ride in the woods. You know that there are snakes and other critters out there. The children know the same thing. I was just cautioning them to be careful. If you are worried about them, go and help them." Matt walked to the lead mules and unhitched them. Juan unhitched the other two and they walked to the stream. They waited until the animals had their fill, then led them to the cluster of trees and hobbled them nearby. "Juan, why don't you start the fire and put up the tripod for Anna. The frying pan and Dutch oven are packed in the rear of the wagon with other utensils. I'll feed the mules some oats."

The children had gathered two big bundles of sticks for the fire and walked down to the stream. Jamie tossed rocks in the water while Susie took off her shoes and waded.

"Oh, it's so cold," she said. As she started to climb out of the water, she slipped and flopped backward in the stream. A current grabbed her and, although she screamed and flapped her arms, it carried her down the stream at a whirling pace.

Matt heard the screams and was the first one to the water. He pulled off his boots and raced down the bank until he was sure he could jump in and reach the child.

As she was still flapping her arms, Matt stepped in the water and nabbed the long white apron that she wore over her dress. "Got you!" he yelled. "Hold on to me."

"I'm so sorry, Mr. Matt. Don't lock me up in your jail," Susie cried as she rested her head on his shoulder.

"You're not my prisoner, silly little girl." He carried Susie to the creek bank which now held a crowd. Tears streamed down Anna's and Jamie's faces.

"Get her out of those wet clothes. That water is very cold. Wrap a quilt around her and let her sit close to the fire. But not too close. She might want to play in it."

"I told her not to get in the water," Jamie said.

"You didn't! You're a liar," Suzie spouted back at him.

"You two had better keep quiet. I am upset with both of you for going in the stream without an adult. Susie, I hope you learned a lesson today." Anna removed Susie's clothes during the tongue-lashing.

Pedro laughed while he and Matt sat around the fire. "This is the first of many adventures we're going to have on this trip with those kids."

"I hope this is my last dip in cold water. My feet are frozen," he said while keeping them close to the fire.

After a plate of stew and cornbread, Anna put the children to bed on the floor of the wagon. She and Matt would sleep on opposite sides while the boys slept underneath. Each man would stand guard for four hours.

~

In Whitmire, Texas, Claude Moore sat at a table at the rear of the Golden Corral saloon. From the back corner of the room, he could view all the men that came through the door. He was hunting for two desperate men who wanted to earn some fast and easy money, no matter who got hurt in the process. All the men had to do was take Anna away from those three men who were taking her to Livingston. If need be, the men might have to shoot the sheriff and the two young men. He wanted that money, and no one was going to keep him from getting it.

A young senorita was dancing around the room and giving him seductive looks. He was glad that he had visited the men's bathhouse and stopped in for a haircut and shave. It made him feel almost human again.

The girl sashayed over to his table, whirling around like a young ballerina. He grabbed the tail of her colorful skirt and pulled her onto his lap. She ran her smooth hand over his face. He seized the hand and kissed her palm.

"Later, room 6."

She slid off his lap and threw him a seductive smile as he stuffed a few dollars down her ruffle-collared blouse.

Claude waved the barkeep over and continued to watch the door. "Hey, you," he said to the heavyset man, setting the whiskey and a glass in the middle of the table. "You know any bad men who can keep their mouths shut? I might have a job for them."

"How bad?" The man looked around the smoked-filled saloon.

"As bad as they come." Claude grinned and flipped him a silver dollar.

"I'll see what I can do for you," he said, his expression impassive.

Claude placed a booted foot on an empty chair at his table and continued to size-up all the dirty ramrods and tough-looking locals who walked through the door. In less than an hour, word had spread that two of the nastiest killers to haunt the border were sleeping upstairs. Claude decided to wait and meet with them later in the evening.

~

Matt shivered when the cold breeze hit him in the face as he traveled the sixth day toward Livingston. He was pleased that the weather had been good for their travel. Being late into November, the weather had finally turned. He had told Anna to sit inside the wagon to avoid the frigid wind. The children were looking at storybooks and making animal sounds.

Pedro rode up to the covered wagon and waved for Matt to stop and climb down. "Walk with me," Pedro said as he waited for Juan to join them. "We have three men trailing close to us. Before they were in front of us, but now they've dropped back behind. They're up to no good."

"Do you think they might be Moore and a couple of men?" Matt asked.

"After they set up camp, I'll try to get close enough to hear them. Should know right away if they are just cowboys traveling to Livingston, or something else."

Chapter 28

With the temperature going down, the three men built a large fire and camped early, close to Anna's covered wagon, but hidden.

Pedro slipped on his soft moccasins, removed the coins out of his pockets and anything else that would cause a distraction, then left to go spy on the three strangers. He went on foot through the woods until he spotted three horses tied to a picket line, then circled around to the other side of the camp so the horses wouldn't sense the smell of fear close by.

The men huddled near the fire talking. Like a snake, he slithered on the ground, moving his body closer. Listening to the men, he was shocked to hear one man say that they might have to kill all three men just to grab the gal.

"What about the young'uns?" A voice asked.

Pedro froze and held his breath as the leader of the group finally said, "Leave 'em be."

Scrambling backward away from the men's campsite, Pedro crawled a good ways before he noticed that the sky slowly faded into a dark purple landscape. He felt safe enough to stand and run the remaining way to Matt's campsite. Out of breath and with a cramp in his side, he sneaked into the camp and motioned to Matt and Juan. Matt stopped at the water barrel and dipped a cup into the clean water. He carried it over to Pedro and waited for him to drink.

"We're going to have to get ready for an attack tonight. Moore has two of the nastiest men with him. They want the money, and they're planning on kidnapping her and killing us."

"How much time do we have?" Matt asked.

"They want us to be caught off guard, so they'll make sure we're bedded down and asleep." Pedro peered at Juan, praying silently his little brother wouldn't be hurt.

"I have a plan. Juan can dress in Anna's habit and sit in front of the fire with her Bible and gun, of course. Once they ride into the camp, one of them will try to grab her and carry her away, but it will not be Anna but you, Juan.

We'll fix our bedrolls with our boots at one end and sombreros covering our pretend heads. Pedro, you and I will be hidden and open fire as they shoot our dummy bedrolls."

"Where will Anna and the children be during the attack?" Juan asked Matt.

"Yes, where are you going to tuck away the children and me, Sergeant Jenkins?" Anna cringed as Matt walked near her.

"Anna!" Pedro stepped toward her. "Keep quiet, I just saw your uncle and his men. They mean business. Matt has a good plan laid out. We need to be ready for them. You and the children will lay low in the wagon bed and cover your heads. Of course, you will have a gun to protect yourself, if need be."

Anna's shoulders slumped. "Sorry, Matt. I was so worried about all of us. I'll do what's needed—undress and give Juan my nun's outfit. I'm sure he will be irresistible."

"I'm never going to live this scheme down, if we survive."

~

After the campsite was made ready, Juan headed over to Pedro. "What do you think our chances are in fighting off these men?" Before Pedro could answer, Juan's voice broke. "I'm scared, Pedro. I fear for our lives."

"I know, little brother. Me too. But let's pray right now that God will protect us. We're not killers, but those men out there are. Remember, they are coming after us to take Anna and murder us. What we do when those men arrive will be what we have to do to protect Anna."

When Anna and the children were safely in the wagon, and Matt and Pedro were stationed on both sides of the area. Juan took a seat on a tree stump in front of the fire with his head bent low, as if he was praying. He ran his fingers under the neck piece several times, hoping to stretch it so he could breathe easier. His face and hands were cold, but the rest of his body was hot under the long black robe. How the sisters could bear wearing these heavy outfits, he'd never understand.

Juan said amen a few times and made the sign of the cross, pretending to be a real nun, as he sat like a sitting duck. *Just let one of them grab me and, boy, what a surprise that fellow will have if he happens to carry me away!*

Horses' hooves galloped close. Juan cocked his pistol and glanced over his shoulder. Suddenly, two men appeared from out of the bush and blasted their guns at the dummy bedrolls. A strong man grabbed Juan up off the ground and attempted to place him in front of his saddle.

Juan reared backward and bucked the man nearly off his horse. Firing only one time, Juan shot the man, and he loosened his hold. Falling to the ground, Juan rolled away from the stranger's horse's hooves. The man lay low on his horse's neck and disappeared away from the campsite.

The other two men were lying near the fire, both dead. Matt raced over to the dead bodies and using his foot, he flipped both men over to get a good look at them. Neither man was Anna's uncle, Claude Moore.

~

Anna came out of the covered wagon and grabbed Juan and Pedro both. "Thank the Lord you three are all safe." She had prayed so much her throat was nearly raw.

Matt tromped over to Anna. "Your uncle got away again, but Juan did shoot him. He's left a bloody trail."

Anna knew that Matt was a dedicated lawman and would want to follow the bloody trail. She only wanted to go home. "Please, Matt, let him go. Take us home tomorrow and you can send the bank money to wherever it belongs. We can spread the word that the money has been returned."

"And you think that your uncle will just ride away and forget you, period?"

"Why not? He left me for ten years, and he only used me so he could get the stolen money. I don't mean anything to him."

"Matt, I agree with Anna. Let's head home and try to forget about Moore," Pedro said. "We are exhausted but alive. Chances are if we keep up the chase, somebody is going to get hurt. Let's just lie low for a while. If he's shot, Moore might not be alive very long anyway."

Matt peered down at the two bodies. "Well, boys, we'll pack

these two on my horse and take them into Livingston. There's a handsome reward on both of these criminals. I will see that each of you receive the money."

"But, Matt, you helped with this attack. You deserve part of the reward," Juan said, as he wiggled out of Anna's clothes.

"It's my job to hunt and kill, if necessary, bad men. I get paid by the townspeople. Besides, I wouldn't have survived this brutal attack without your help. Just think, you will be able to get a fresh start with a nice nest egg."

Matt took Anna by the hand and said, "I'm tired. Let's go to bed."

Anna lay on her side and looked across the children at her husband. *Her husband*, in name only. She wanted him to have his freedom, but he would have to decide to leave this time. They would be home tomorrow and hopefully, he would move back to his place, return to work, and let her get on with her life. She raised up on her elbow to start a conversation about their relationship when she heard a soft snore coming from him. Well, another time soon, she thought.

Chapter 29

On the remaining trip home, Matt took charge of the reins and drove the covered wagon all the way to Livingston. He deliberately moved his right leg to touch her skirt every chance he got. She would jerk her body over and act like he never touched her.

Susie climbed through the canvas curtains and sat between them for miles as Jamie slept in the back. She chatted until she couldn't hold open her eyes. For miles, Anna held her in her lap until Matt stopped the mules and placed Susie on Anna's bed.

Anna stretched her back and murmured thanks. "That little girl is growing," she said.

Matt only nodded and continued looking forward. A few miles down the road, Matt motioned for Juan to ride ahead and asked Pedro to find a place to stop for a while. "The children need to get out, and the mules need a rest."

Anna jumped down and pulled some supplies out to make a quick soup. The weather was very chilly, and hot soup would taste good. Juan built a fire while the children ran around and chased each other. Matt walked back to speak with Pedro and make sure the dead bodies were still wrapped tight and secured on his horse.

After everyone had stretched their legs and filled their bellies with hot food, it was time to make the last miles to Livingston. Once the children settled down for a long nap, Matt and Anna sat on the wagon's bench.

"You know, Matt, I really don't know anything about your life or your family. Don't you think I should know something about you?" Anna leaned forward, tucking her legs under her long black robe.

"If we're going to stay married, sure, but if not, you don't need to know anything about me." Matt held a hand up as to say *No way.*

"Our marriage is something to settle in the future. I was just pondering about you, but if you don't want to talk, fine." Anna stared at the road ahead.

"I'm from Portland, Texas. My family has a big ranch there, but my dad and I didn't see eye to eye on things. I wanted to raise horses, and he wanted to grow corn. So one day, I had enough of his back-breaking orders and I left."

"Do you have brothers and sisters?" Anna quizzed, happy to see that Matt was willing to talk.

"I have two sisters. Both are married now."

"So, you keep in touch with your family?"

"After being gone for a couple of months, I broke down and wrote my mom and let her know where I landed. I had no intentions of ever talking to them again, but I was in church, and the minister's words hit a nerve and made me feel guilty about not contacting my folks. So, Mama and me write."

"That's good." Anna sighed. "Before being dropped off at the convent, I really missed my parents. Uncle Claude was good to me, so I stayed busy working the garden, washing, and cooking. But, after he was gone, I had time to think about my mama. I miss her so much, but to be fair, Reverend Mother filled the hole in my heart. She has always been so good to me."

"I miss my mama and, to be truthful, I miss Pa, too. He was good to me, but he just wouldn't listen to new ideas."

"Have you ever thought about returning to Portland?"

"Sure, I've given it a lot of thought, and I will one day. They're getting older, and I would like to visit with them before it's too late."

"Don't wait too long. Each day is a blessing from God. As we both know, he has really blessed us on this wild trip."

~

Right before dark, Matt drove the covered wagon in front of Anna's small house. He signaled for Pedro to ride up beside him. "Take those men by the sheriff's office and let Martin see them. Afterward, take them on down to the undertaker's office. He will give you a receipt, and I'll pay him later. Juan and I will unload the wagon and take it and the mules down to the livery." Matt sat still for a minute, then he took both of Anna's hands in his. He leaned his face toward hers. She slid back a few inches. "Welcome home, darling, to the simple life." Whispering, he said, "You know what I want most from you is a taste of your…juicy pies."

Blushing bright pink, she shoved him, nearly knocking him on the bench. "Oh you, help me down this instant before I hurt you."

Matt howled with laughter. He was happy to be back to Anna's—his home now—with everyone safe and sound. What a trip, he thought.

~

Late in the evening, Anna had fried the last of the bacon that they had on the trip and made fresh bacon and egg sandwiches. Thinking about her chickens, she glanced outside to the empty chicken pen. First thing tomorrow, she would go and purchase several dozen sitting hens and two roosters. She would ask Juan to ride out in the country and choose a nice milk cow. Milk, eggs, and butter were the main ingredients for making pies and growing strong, healthy children.

Matt came back in from walking the short distance from town and sat at the table with Susie and Jamie.

"Mr. Matt, are you going to be my new pa?" Jamie asked.

Susie jumped out of her chair and screamed at the top of her lungs. "No, he's going to be my pa first. Anna is my new mama and now Sheriff Matt will be my pa, not yours."

Anna hurried out of the kitchen with a dry dishrag in her hands. "What in the devil is going on?" Narrowing her eyes, she looked at Susie.

Susie edged closer to Matt as he wrapped his arms around her small shoulders. "We are having a discussion about fatherhood."

"Fatherhood? What in the world." Anne eased down into the vacant chair.

"It looks like these two both want me to be their new pa. Since you have claimed them as yours, and they already call you Mama, they want to call me Pa." Matt grinned at Anna's open mouth. "I'm willing to be their guardian, unless the court says different."

"The court?" Anna asked as she felt a tightness in her chest.

"We can't just continue to keep the children unless we are granted guardianship and later, are able to adopt them. The court will want to be sure that their parents won't come back for them."

"We need to talk about the children in private not in front of them." Anna stood and stormed back into the kitchen with Matt directly on her heels. She whirled around and looked over his shoulder at Susie and Jamie still sitting at the table. "Why are you talking about being their pa? You and I are not really married, and you aren't going to be in their lives for long."

"Let me tell you something, Missy. We are legally married and we're going to remain hitched. We have been through hell the last couple of days, and I wouldn't have put Sister Melody, Pedro, or you through any of the misery that we have endured chasing after your thieving uncle if I didn't care about what happens to you. You, my little pretend nun, are my wife until death do us part."

"I want you out of my house now. Go, get your things and leave. I may be married to you but in name only, and it's going to stay that way until I can convince a judge to have it annulled."

"Now, you listen to me, Sweetheart." Matt strode toward Anna as she shifted away from him. He advanced in one large step and stood nose to nose with her. "This is still your uncle's house, but it will never be yours. It will be mine, and everything you own is mine, too. As your legal husband, you even belong to me. You can't buy anything without my signature, and another very important thing—those children in the other room will never belong to you without me in your life. Got that?"

"Are you having your first fight?" Susie asked, as she and Jamie stood in the entranceway of the kitchen with wide eyes.

"Of course not. We are having a disagreement," Matt said.

"Are you going to hit her, Mr. Matt?" Matt turned to Jamie, his face hot from embarrassment. He got down on one knee and pulled Jamie close. "Jamie, men don't hit ladies and boys don't hurt girls," Matt said.

"When my pa yelled, he would hit my mama a lot. She would cry. Please don't beat Miss Anna," he said as he raced to Anna and shielded her body.

~

Matt couldn't believe that he had lost his temper in front of these babies. Both of them had lived with bad-tempered people who abused them and others when they were angry. Now, he and Anna were raising their voices at each other. He felt so ashamed, and he could tell that Anna was embarrassed.

"Come, children. Let's sit down in front of the fireplace and let Anna and me hold you both until you fall asleep," Matt said as he lifted Susie into his arms. Anna held Jamie's hand and led him to the big rocker.

After an hour, both children's feet were dangling almost to the floor. They were sound asleep. Matt looked at Anna as she placed Jamie on a pallet. He carried Susie over to a pallet that was laid out beside the little fellow.

"Let's go to bed, too. The boys will be home soon, and I know that they are tired. We've all had a long day." He glanced at Anna and held up his hand. "No more talking tonight."

Anna went into the bedroom and Matt followed. He lifted a bag that held his personal items and walked to the dry sink in the kitchen. Matt dipped water into a round pan and soaped a white washcloth, then unbuttoned his shirt and pulled the top of his union suit overhead. Tossing them both on the floor, he splashed water on his face and began scrubbing his armpits, neck, and chest.

~

Anna had hurried and changed into her nightgown and jumped into bed, covering herself from head to toe with the quilt. She knew better than to demand that Matt sleep on the floor, and he would never allow her to sleep on a pallet, like she did while he was recovering from his leg wound.

As Matt stood in the kitchen, she could see his every move. Her eyes were glued to him as he prepared to clean up. She had never seen his bare back before. His back muscles were visible and his shoulders very broad. As he washed his arms, they were so chiseled she wouldn't be able to place her hands around the top part. When she had moved him from the ground into the wagon, she knew he was a tall, well-built man, but he was fully clothed then. My word, she thought, if he ever hit her like Jamie's pa hit his mama, she wouldn't live to tell about it.

The kitchen went dark, and Matt came into the bedroom and set his bag down on the dresser. Then he sat down on the bed and slipped off his boots and trousers. The mattress sagged as he stretched his long frame out and pulled up the quilt. Sighing he turned over on his side facing Anna's back. He cradled her body and nuzzled the back of her neck.

Anna lay perfectly still but was aware of everything. A soft snore came out of Matt's mouth, and he was sound asleep.

"Thank you, Lord," Anna said.

Chapter 30

Matt watched as Anna cooked breakfast, dressed the children, and hurried out the door. She'd wanted to visit with Henrietta at the dry goods store and check on her job at the café. He had a full day and was out the door as soon as breakfast was over. He spoke low to Juan as he left, giving him instructions to keep an eye on Anna. He was still worried about Claude Moore trying to kidnap her.

~

"Lordy mercy, child, let me look at you. You look wonderful," declared Henrietta as she entered the store. Both of the children rushed to the candy jars and placed their noses on the glass case. "I was afraid Matt wouldn't be able to convince you to return with him," she said, as she stood holding Anna's hands.

"Matt has never taken no for an answer, so here I am." She laughed and avoided mentioning the paddling he gave her and that she wasn't given a choice whether she wanted to return with him or not.

"You know that young man really loves you. He was in a near panic when he found out that you had gone back to Whitmire."

"I'm not sure he loves me. We might kill each other before love develops between us." Anna gave a shy grin. "I do have a list of supplies if you don't mind filling it for me while I go and see Mr. Godwin. Hope he will allow me to have the same arrangement that we had before I left. One day I want to have my own bakery."

"You run along, and I will collect your supplies. Maybe John will be here when you return. I know he was upset to hear that you had gone back to the convent to live."

"Oh, he is a nice young man." Anna was happy that John worked hard to keep the dry goods store running for his mother after his pa had died.

Looking over her shoulder, Henrietta whispered, "John would kill me if he knew I told you, but when he found out you weren't a real nun, he took a shine to you. You know he's only a year older than you, but he could provide a good life for you and me with this business," Henrietta said.

Anna blushed and smiled. "John will make a good husband for the right young lady. The way Matt and I were forced to marry doesn't happen every day, thank goodness. He will get to choose his wife."

Henrietta gave a hearty laugh. "I'm sure you are right. I know that you and Matt are going to have a great marriage one day, you just mark my words."

"God will have to lend a hand," Anna said, as she gathered the children and walked out the front door heading to the café.

Mr. Godwin nearly dropped the two platters of food he was carrying when he spotted Anna standing next to the dessert case. "Anna, my dear, you're back, I hope for good this time."

"I believe so, Mr. Godwin. We only returned home last evening, and I came to see if I could have my old job back. I really miss making pies and other sweets."

"Yes, please come work for me, like before. Everyone has been asking for your pies, and now they will be happy again. I was beginning to think I might have to close my door and retire. Business dropped off so bad after you and Juan left."

"I can start in the morning, if that is all right with you. Can't speak for Juan, but I believe he will come and work, too. Tonight, I'll make pies to have ready to sell in the morning," she said. "I'd better go home now. See you tomorrow."

Once all the supplies were put away, Anna placed a roast in the oven for the evening meal. Green beans, mashed potatoes, and hot rolls would round out the meal. Anna placed a tub of laundry to soak on the back porch. She really missed Sister Melody and Reverend Mother visiting with them. There was so much housework and cooking that went into taking care of two children and three grown men.

The chickens had arrived, and Juan had put a new milk cow in the small stall beside the chicken yard. Tonight, she would ask the boys to gather the eggs, feed the chickens, and milk and feed the cow each day. That would be a big help.

Once the clothing had been hung on the line to dry, Anna put Susie and Jamie down for an afternoon nap. Jamie protested that he was too old to sleep during the day like babies did. Anna told him that she would think about letting him stay up, if he didn't become too grumpy during the day.

When the dishes were cleaned and put away, Anna announced that she would be making pies tonight, and tomorrow she would begin working at the café. "I'll take the children with me."

Matt opened his mouth to make a comment, but before he could, Anna interrupted. "I know you said I didn't need to work, and I should stay home—you being the head of the house and providing for all of us." Anna backed up to lean against the table, eyeing him as he walked toward her.

Grinning, Matt had obviously been thinking about Anna's safety while he was at work. Actually, she would be a lot safer at the café surrounded by people coming and going.

"Let me ease your mind, my dear wife. I agree that it will be a good idea that you work during the day at the café," he said, as he poured water into the wash bowl.

~

Sunday morning Sheriff Jenkin's new family were in church. The tension between Matt and Anna eased a little, no doubt, because of the children sitting between them.

As they sat in the pews, Anna felt every eye in the church on her. Probably because she wasn't dressed in the Catholic habit as they expected her to be. Many of them still believed she was a sister of the order, no matter that they'd been told different. She should stand up and cry, "Boo." That would get their goat. Preacher Stubbs would most likely faint if she stood up and made a scene. It was all she could do to sit still and contain the laughter building up in her throat.

Matt glared at her, as if she was a misbehaving child. "What?" He mouthed to her. Grinning, she only shook her head and closed her eyes as if praying.

After the service, Henrietta grabbed her arm before they exited. "Anna, wait," she called. "Will you and your family have Sunday lunch with John and me today? I have cooked a ton of food and it's ready except for the yeast rolls."

Anna looked to Matt as Henrietta repeated the invitation. "Please Matt, bring everyone to my house."

"Sounds good to me, if you have enough for the Juan and Pedro too."

"Mom has cooked plenty, so please come so I won't have to eat leftovers all week," John said.

Henrietta served a feast for Sunday lunch. Ham and sliced roast, little red potatoes, fresh baked yams, green snap beans, lima beans, and hot fluffy rolls were on the stove waiting to be eaten. Strawberry pie and a special treat, bread pudding with a rum sauce, were the desserts.

~

John sat next to Anna and treated her like a princess. Every time she moved, he was at her beck and call. Matt noticed all the kind gestures. A jealous streak flew through him. *Surely John knows that Anna is my wife.*

Afterward, as the men and children sat in the parlor, Pedro told them that he might buy into the livery stable. "Mr. Mac mentioned that he is thinking about retiring and selling his business. I want to talk this over with Anna before I decide."

"Why do you need a woman's opinion?" John asked. "Women don't have any business sense."

"Anna is a very important person in my life. I have never done anything without discussing it over with her." Pedro looked at Matt and saw him smile and nod in agreement.

"That's silly. You're a man. Do what you want and don't let a silly gal tell you what and how to do anything," John said, as he settled back in his chair with exaggerated casualness.

"John, I think you've said enough. Pedro has a right to talk to whomever he wants about anything, whether it's man or woman." Matt stared at the young man until he looked down at the floor. "I think we'd better get our silly gal and head home. These children are asleep on their feet."

Anna entered the parlor. "It's time to go home. Thank you, John, for being such a gracious host and to you, Henrietta, for the wonderful meal."

Matt reached for Susie while Pedro picked up Jamie and placed him on his shoulder. Everyone said thanks again as they loaded up in Matt's wagon.

On the way home, Anna gushed over John. "He was so sweet."

"Yep, I thought for a minute he was going to spoon-feed you," Matt snarled.

"What do you mean? He was so gracious." She glared at him.

"Bull," Pedro said from the back of the wagon. "You didn't hear how he talked about women. If you had, you would have wanted to black his eyes."

Anna whipped around on the bench and looked down at Pedro. "Tell me what he said."

Matt cut a glance at Pedro. "No. Pedro, forget what he said. You keep talking to Anna like you always have. Now, let's just remember what a nice lunch we had and forget all the others."

Chapter 31

Claude Moore could watch the whole town from his view upon the mountain. He had returned to the cave and was well hidden in his spot that overlooked Livingston. People came and went from the shops and homes. Carpenters were entering his little white house that Anna was living in, and the sheriff was returning home from his job. He was sure that the young woman that ushered two young children to town was Anna. She was not dressed in the Catholic's nun black dress and headpiece. Why, he pondered, was she was parading around in regular clothing?

From all the activity taking place at his house, Anna appeared to be having additional rooms added to the small frame. He had no idea why those children were living with his niece. They weren't her children, he was sure of that because they were too old, and nuns didn't give birth. He really needed a partner to investigate the situation.

Sitting on the ledge, he squeezed his right hand with a small bag of sand. The hand wasn't broken, but he could hardly open and close it. The doctor told him to exercise his hand, and slowly it would get well. The gunshot wound to his shoulder was healing to the point that he wasn't having to wear a sling. He was lucky to be alive after that blundered plan he and his two men attempted. Someone had tipped off the sheriff and his men that they were going to ride into their camp. Fortunately, he was attacked by the youngest boy, so he managed to get away. He was disappointed that his two partners were killed, because he could use one of them now.

Everyone left the house while the carpenters remained. If everyone was living in his house, they'd need more bedrooms for sure. He wondered if Anna was using his money to pay for the remodeling. She had better not be spending the bank money.

When the time was right, he'd ease down to the house and catch Anna and the children alone. With a gun pointed at one of the children's head, Anna would do whatever he wanted.

~

Matt sat in his office, flipping through new wanted posters and catching up on other reading that piled up while he was chasing Anna's uncle.

Deputy Martin came through the door with a fresh bag of coffee beans. He walked over to the black potbelly stove and filled the pot. "Oh, Sheriff, I almost forgot. Leonard gave me this telegram for you."

"Thanks." Matt tore open the piece of folded paper and read and re-read the message.

"Bad news?" Martin asked.

"Yes, I believe it is. My sister writes that my father is very sick, and I am needed at home."

"Where's home? You haven't ever mentioned where your folks live."

"Portland, Texas. A small town outside of Corpus Christi."

"Are you going? What about your job and your new family? Man, you have a lot to think about." Martin checked the coffee and poured a cup for each of them.

"I need to send my sister a note to find out how bad my pa is or if they need money. I'll be back soon. Don't mention this telegram to anyone, please." After a few hours, Matt received an answer to his telegram. His pa was on his deathbed, a few of the hands had quit, and there wasn't anyone to run the farm. His sister begged him to come home.

Man stood in the telegraph office, staring at his hands. How could he uproot Anna and the children? Sheriff Watkins entered the office and was surprised to see Matt.

"Matt, I was on my way over to your office. We need to talk seriously."

"I just received bad news, and I was wondering what I was going to do. Maybe, this will take my mind off it and I can think about it later."

The two men walked side by side into the sheriff's office. Deputy Martin leaped up out of Matt's chair and said howdy to

Sheriff Watkins.

Matt said, "Martin, the sheriff and I have some business to talk over. Would you please go and make the rounds?"

"No, Matt, the deputy needs to hear this news, too." Sheriff Watkins said.

"Go ahead," Matt said, uncertain that more bad news was coming.

"Well, I don't like to boast, but I have been promoted to Marshal. I have a new assignment."

"Congratulations, man. You deserve the position. Where is your new assignment?" Martin asked, eager to hear more about the new job.

"Here," he said, unsmiling. "In Livingston."

"Why would you be assigned here when this town already has a sheriff?" Matt asked, a queasy feeling growing in the pit of his stomach.

"This is the part I don't like. You, Matt have been reassigned to be the sheriff in Brownsville. The town needs a good man who can help catch all the bad men who are headed to the border."

"Brownsville?" Matt shook his head. "Every lawman who tries to clean up that town is murdered. I'm not a killer, but to stay alive down there I would have to shoot someone all the time. I have heard that from many men who have ridden through here. Sorry, but there's no way I'm going to take on that job."

"I'm sorry, Matt. Here are your orders." Sheriff Watkins placed a large envelope in Matt's hands. "You write headquarters and give them your answer."

Matt held the telegram from his sister in one hand and his new sheriff's job in the other. His future rested in his hands. Then he knew. "Well, Marshal," Matt grinned at Sheriff Watkins. "Thanks, but no thanks. I'm needed at my folks' home in Portland. What about Deputy Martin?"

The deputy glanced from Matt to the new marshal. "If he wants, he can keep his job, but he will be working for me."

"I have a few things to gather out of the back room, then this place will be yours. I need to go home and tell Anna about me losing my job before she start hearing rumors."

"Oh, Matt, one more thing. Here's the draft for the reward money for Anna."

"Anna?" Matt frowned and gave the marshal a questioning look.

"Slim Smith was a wanted man, and he had a reward on his head. Five hundred dollars. Since Anna shot him, she is entitled. Also, I have the reward drafts for Pedro and Juan for killing Bull and that youngster called Willie. They had five thousand dollars on Bull and five hundred on the young man. Tell them to take the drafts to the bank and they will receive their money."

"This is good news, at least." Matt held the envelopes in his hand. "Believe me, I need some good news to tell them today."

After gathering his few items from the small room that he lived in before Anna came to Livingston, he placed his Stetson on his head and walked out onto the boardwalk. He stopped and glanced at the saloon across the street. If he was a drinking man, he could drown his troubles. *God, I feel that my world has turned upside down. I need your help today for sure. Please help me find the right words to convince Anna to go with me to Portland. I don't want to force her to go, but I can't leave her, especially with her uncle still running loose, Amen.*

Chapter 32

Matt carried his few personal belongings into Anna's house, but no one was home. Anna, Juan, and the children were still at the café, and Pedro was working at the livery. Placing his items in the bedroom, he went into the living room and built up the fire in the fireplace. The house was chilled, but it would be warm when the others arrived home.

Home, a sweet word, but this house wasn't going to be their home for much longer, he thought. His folks' farm in Portland was a very nice place. The house was large with plenty of rooms and a huge kitchen. The farm was a busy place. His pa had over twelve men working the fields, feeding the cattle, and milking the cows. At harvest time, his pa hired about ten more men to help gather the corn and replant the fields with oats or hay.

Matt remembered how he pleaded with his pa to buy horses and let him train them for cattlemen to pull wagons and carriages, or use as recreational horses. His pa wouldn't even listen to the idea. If he was going to move home, things would have to change. He didn't object to running the farm, but he wanted to enjoy some of the work, and horses would make him happy.

As he sat in the rocker in front of the fire, he heard the children running up the path to the front door. Anna and Juan were directly behind them.

"Hi, Mr. Matt," Susie said as she jumped into his arms while Jamie stood next to the rocker, waiting to be noticed.

"Hi, yourself. Were you a good girl today?"

"Yep," she said.

"I was good, too." Jamie spoke up. "Anna made Susie sit in the corner for saying a bad word."

"Jamie," Anna's stern voice came from the doorway. "What

have I said about tattling?"

"I'm hungry." He scooted behind the rocker that Matt sat in. "When are we going to eat?"

"Hello, Sheriff Jenkins," Anna said. "How was your day?'

"Probably didn't go as well as yours. After dinner, I need to have a private conversation with you." He knew he had left her confused about what was coming.

Once the children were bathed, fed, and tucked into bed, Matt and Anna walked into their bedroom. Anna sat in a straight chair while Matt made himself comfortable on the edge of the mattress.

"All right, Matt, out with it please. Did the law catch my uncle today?"

It never crossed Matt's mind that Anna would think about her uncle when he asked to have a conversation with her. He felt bad he had worried her all evening. But he was so concerned about his folks it hadn't crossed his mind. "Anna, I'm sorry that you were thinking about your uncle all evening. But to answer your question, no, your uncle hasn't been captured. My news is about my folks. My pa is very ill. I received a telegram today from one of my sisters. She said I was needed at home."

"Did she say what was wrong with your father?" Anna asked, her expression matching his.

"No, she said he was on his deathbed." Matt paused for a minute. "Some of the men have quit, and there is no one to run the farm."

"I see. So, what are you going to do? What about your job as sheriff here?"

"Sheriff Watkins came to see me this morning. He has been promoted to Marshal, and he will be working from Livingston. I was reassigned to another town as sheriff." "Where?" Anna demanded.

"A border town, Brownsville," he said softly.

"No," Anna screamed. "Surely, you don't want a job in a town like that?"

"Anna, please sit down. You're right. I already told the sheriff, I mean, Marshal Watkins, that I will not take the job down there." Matt stood and walked over to the window and looked out at the full, golden moon. "I am needed in Portland, at my folks' home. Pa is dying, and I must go and help Ma. And I want you and the children to go with me." Matt paused and looked at Anna as she watched him move back to the bed and sit down.

"Anna, you're my wife and I care deeply for the children. In time, I want us to be a real family. Just maybe, you and I will learn to care for each other." Matt reached and took Anna's hand and held it tight. "Please say that you will come with me."

Anna sat silently in the chair without even blinking an eye.

"I want the boys to come with us. There's plenty of work on the farm, and they will get paid. They are part of your little family, and I care for them."

Anna's shoulders relaxed a little when she learned that the boys were welcome to go with them. "When do you need an answer?"

"I need to know that you will go within a few days. We will travel on a private stagecoach. I know it will be harder on the children, but since I will be driving it, we can stop as often as needed."

"I never heard of a private stagecoach."

"Money can buy anything, Anna. If the boys agreed to come with us, then the trip will be easier on all of us. We can take turns driving." Matt sat on the corner of the bed watching for Anna's reaction to all he had thrown at her. He wanted her to say she would go. He didn't want to force her, but he didn't have a choice. One thing he knew—he couldn't and wouldn't leave her in Livingston with her outlaw uncle trying to kidnap her at every turn.

"Matt, you know we should have an annulment. Our marriage isn't real. You were practically unconscious, and the men made me agree." Anna waited for a rebuttal, but when none came, she said, "All right, I'll go with you if you promise that I can leave with the children if I'm not happy. You will grant me an annulment, and we both can go our separate ways. No one needs to know of our arrangement except Juan and Pedro. I tell them everything."

"I promise you, Anna Knight Jenkins, if I can't make you happy living on my folks' farm, I will arrange for you and the children to go wherever you want." Matt stood and took Anna's hands in his. "But be warned, my little nun, I am going to do everything in my power to make you happy. Now, let's go and talk this over with the boys. I do have something for you and the boys that will make all of you happy." Matt opened the bedroom door, and Anna walked into the living room where the boys were lying comfortably in front of the fire.

"Juan and Pedro, please join us in the kitchen for some coffee and doughnuts," Matt said.

After a long discussion about Matt losing his job, his pa being very sick, and how he needed to help run his family's farm, the boys asked several important question. Juan wanted to know if he still could learn to be a smithy, and Juan was concerned if he could still learn how to run a café.

Matt assured Pedro that if he was able to buy horses, he was going to need someone to run their livery. He said he would hire a man to come and teach Pedro all he needed to know about caring for animals and making other things out of iron. As for Juan, he said that he was sure his mother would love to have Anna and him help her to feed all the farmhands. With their good food, men in town would be fighting for a job on their farm. Matt also told Anna that she could still make pies and other desserts and sell them in town. The old café would be happy to sell her pies, and maybe one day, she could open her own bakery.

After everyone quieted, he reached into his vest and pulled out the surprise. "Anna, I have a bank draft for you. Remember that man who shot me? Well, he was wanted and had a reward on him. Here it is. All yours. It's five hundred dollars."

Matt handed Pedro an envelope and he just held it. "Boys, those two men, Bull and Willie, were both wanted men with rewards on their heads. That man called Bull was a really bad one, but the younger man had only killed one man."

Pedro opened the envelope and showed it to Juan. "Five thousand, five hundred dollars." Pedro grabbed Juan, and they hugged each other.

Juan whispered, "Now we can help Señor Carlos."

"Yes." Pedro grinned. "But we need to take care of this money, so we can be set for life."

Matt chuckled. "You boys are something else. First thing you want to do is give some of it away and then save the rest. I knew you both had common sense."

"Señor Carlos has been like a father to us over the years. He has done without to care for us. Now, we can repay him with money. Of course, he will not want to take it, but Reverend Mother will see that he does."

"I want to thank you three for agreeing to go home with me. I promise you that you won't be sorry. My folks are good people, but I am worried that my pa may die soon. With that said, we need to leave in about three days. I know it is going to be hard to tell Mr. Godwin

goodbye again, and Mac at the livery, but they will understand."

Anna stood and placed the cups in the sink and told the boys goodnight. After she was out of hearing, Matt spoke to the boys. "You both know that we are going to have to be very careful on this trip. Anna's uncle is still running free, and he will stop at nothing to get to her. Of course, you know that. But I am going to purchase a stagecoach and six strong horses for our travel. We'll take turns driving and go so much faster than the covered wagon. And we'll stop at stage outposts to spend nights. In fact, we should reach the farm in three days if the weather holds."

~

The long three days took four days and nights, but on the morning of the fifth day, Matt drove under the arched wrought-iron sign that read, "Jenkins Farm." Several men rushed out of the barn and held onto the lead horses' heads to keep them calm while Anna and the children were helped out of the stagecoach.

The men greeted Matt with big hugs and pats on the back. He rushed to Anna and tucked her arm in his when he saw his mother standing on the large front porch. She was a petite woman with rosy cheeks, gray hair, and twinkling blue eyes. Wearing a wide smile, she held open her arms to greet her long-lost son. Tears streamed down her cheeks as she looked from Matt to Anna.

"Mama, this is my wife, Anna."

Anna was wrapped in this stranger's arms just like she had always belonged there. The warm greeting thrilled her all the way to her toes. She immediately felt like she belonged at Matt's home place. "I hope your husband is doing better. We have prayed all the way here for him," Anna said, as she looked for Juan and Pedro.

"Thank you, my dear. He is some better, but only time will tell. The doctor doesn't give him much of a chance for recovery."

Susie and Jamie raced to Anna, wrapping their little arms in her long skirt. "My goodness, Matt, who are these little ones?" his mother asked.

"This is Susie and Jamie. The big boys are Juan and Pedro. We are one big family, and we have come to help you and Pa."

"God has answered my prayers. Your sisters are in town purchasing supplies, but they have to return to their families soon. I have imposed on them enough."

"Mama, I am sure they don't feel that way," Matt said.

"Oh, but they do. My girls hate this farm and country living. They have homes in the middle of Houston. Both girls were thrilled to learn you were coming home. They are already packed."

"Well, we are here now, and we can help with everything. Is Pa awake? I would like to see him."

"He was a little while ago. You go on in while I show everyone their rooms. This is a large house with plenty of bedrooms upstairs. Your father is in the one at the bottom of the stairs."

"Something sure smell goods," Juan said.

"I am cooking a roast, but I will have to prepare more food." Mrs. Jenkins looked embarrassed. "We haven't been cooking big meals since Mr. Jenkins took ill. The men have been cooking for themselves. That's the reason some of the men have quit."

Anna stepped forward. "Mrs. Jenkins, Juan and I will clean up from the trip and get busy helping prepare dinner. We do not intend to be a burden to you. Matt told us that you need help with Mr. Jenkins and the farm. We will do whatever we can to ease the workload off your shoulders." Anna smiled at Juan.

"God bless you, child. I don't know where my son found you, but I am so pleased. Now everyone, follow me and I will show you the bedrooms upstairs. You can pick your own rooms. There is a bathroom at the end of the hall. Mr. Jenkins had a man put a pulley outside the window so water can be hauled upstairs. I'm sure Matt remembers how it works."

~

Anna chose the first room for Juan and Pedro. It had two large windows, a stone fireplace, and two oversized single beds with a dresser to match. A smaller room was next door—perfect for Susie and Jamie. It also had two nice-sized beds with a matching dresser and many bookshelves against one wall. Down the hall was a large room with a king-size, four-poster bed with a lovely quilt and a stack of pillows. A stone fireplace with two rocking chairs sat in front of it. Anna wondered if this room belonged to Matt's folks before his pa took ill.

~

Matt entered the kitchen and heard someone drive up to the back door of the house. His two sisters, Jennifer and Martha, and a big burly man sat outside in a large flat-board wagon. The back of the wagon was filled with sacks and barrels of food. Matt hurried outside and greeted his two sisters.

"It's about time you came home, brother. Now that you are here, we are leaving. Our own families need us. At least, we will be appreciated."

"Jennifer, I had hoped that you and Martha would stay for a while. I would love for you to get to know my wife, the two children that we are going to adopt, and the two young men who grew up with Anna."

"That's impossible, but we'll say hello and goodbye. We will be leaving in the morning. You will see why we're in such a rush to get away if Pa gets better. He hasn't changed one bit, Matt, and you'll be ready to leave soon, too."

"But Jenn, Pa is on his deathbed. He's as weak as a kitten," Matt said.

"And meaner than a snake. We aren't going to be sorry one little bit when the good Lord calls him home. This place and Mama will be better off without him." Martha posted a fist on her waist.

"I can't believe you girls feel that way. Pa has given you so much over the years, and now you're not showing any respect to him." Matt frowned at his two sisters. "With a lot of care and many prayers, it is possible that God will give him another chance at life. I want to do my part in helping him recover."

"Pray all you want, brother dear, but before he took to his bed, he made Jenn and me cook tons of food for the old man who brought his threshing machine here along with his whole crew of men. Three big hot meals a day. We slaved over that stove to feed those dirty men.

Pa was proud of the bags of oats, barley, and wheat he had stored in the loft of the barn. The farmhands worked beside the men from daylight to dark, plus doing all their other chores. I know they were as happy as we were to see that big ugly, loud machine crisscross over to someone else's fields. Pa never thanked us for a thing we did, just gave orders to Mama to make us cook and clean."

Martha took another breath and said, "Now, you write us a letter and let us know how things are after you have been here for several weeks." She flounced inside the house and raced up to her bedroom.

After a hearty dinner with all the family around, Jennifer told Anna that she wished that they had come sooner. "You are a wonderful cook, and I love your pies. I know Mama will appreciate your help."

As the girls helped clear the table, Matt and his mother went to Pa's room to check on him. Matt and his father had a long talk about the farm. His father was exhausted and fell asleep as Matt talked. He was also struggling to breathe, and this worried Matt.

~

"Yes, Anna, Mama is one of the sweetest people in the world, but our father is a tyrant. He has nearly killed Mama with the workload he piled on her. I hate leaving her, but she won't leave Pa and the farm and come and live with me. My husband and four children need me. I am so happy that Matt came home and brought you." Martha wiped her eyes, then rushed back up the stairs to finish her packing.

Later that night as Anna tucked Susie and Jamie in bed, they couldn't stop talking about seeing all the farm animals. "I'm going to collect eggs every morning and wash them in a big bowl," Susie said, yawning.

"I'm going to learn to milk cows. Do you know you have to wash their teats before they give milk?" Jamie commented, as he pulled the cover over his shoulders. "Can't wait."

"Goodnight, my little farmhands. Sweet dreams." Anna said a prayer over the children and kissed both of them.

Standing outside the children's bedroom door, she whispered, "Lord, I hope that I will be as happy here as the children seem to be right now. Amen."

Chapter 33

Early the next morning, Anna gave Juan a list of food supplies she needed after he helped the two sisters with their luggage. He'd volunteered to take the girls into town to catch the stagecoach. "And will you look over the café and restaurants? I'll visit with the owners if the places are nice later in the week. And I'll need to take Susie and Jamie into town and have them fitted for some work boots, heavier pants, and western hats. No reason why Susie can't wear long pants while playing outside in the cold. I might even get myself a few pairs."

~

With the crowd gathered at the stage depot, a tall stranger stood leaning up against the building. When he spotted Juan, the young boy who was always with his niece, he knew he had found her. Lowering his head as Juan and the girls passed, he didn't let the boy out of sight.

~

Juan visited several small cafés and one large eatery. He didn't order anything but just looked the places over. His evaluation was based on how large the dining room was, the number of people eating, and the cleanliest of the building. Afterwards he stopped in the dry goods store and had Anna's list filled. Placing the supplies in the back of the wagon, he drove the ten miles back to the farm.

~

The stranger followed close behind Juan without being seen. He wanted to check out the place where Anna was staying and how many people were around her. Once the boy pulled around to the back of the farmhouse, the stranger tied his horse to a tree limb and lay down in the tall grass where he had a good view of the back.

Several men hurried outside to unload the wagon while two children danced around Juan. He stooped down and slipped both of them a candy stick. They laughed and ran over to the barn. Two men came out of the barn doors, and one man picked up the little girl, laughing. The stranger immediately recognized the sheriff of Livingston. So, he thought, the rumors must be true that Anna married him. He should have known. She would have never traveled this far with a man without being his wife. But how could she be a nun?

The stranger counted the men he saw on the farm. Five or six, not counting the men working the fields. He was going to need a man to help him kidnap Anna. They would catch her alone, and with this farm being so big, she wouldn't be missed right away. Yes, he needed to hire a good man who would keep his mouth shut.

~

Matt didn't want any more of the men quitting because of poor meals after working all days in the fields. That was something else he planned to change. With the scorching sun in the sky, he asked the men if they would like to rest after lunch until three o'clock every day and then work until six each evening. After dinner, the rest of the evening would be their free time. He always hated never having any time for himself when he worked for his pa. A rested man could accomplish more than one who was beaten down from the hot sun or freezing weather.

The men readily agreed and asked if they could ride into town and take care of business or buy supplies. Matt assured them the free time was theirs, but be ready to work each afternoon.

Later in the evening after Matt had watched his mother and Anna wait hand and foot on his pa, wash and clean clothes, and prepare a meal for nearly twenty people, he called Anna into his pa's office. "Anna, when I asked you to come to my folks' farm, I never intended for you to be a workhorse. I never realized how much work has to be done to keep this place in good working order. We need to interview some women to come here and help with the cleaning, washing and ironing, and the dishes after the meals. You and Mama are killing yourselves taking care of Pa, the children, and cooking. The other ladies can do the rest."

"I must admit your pa does take a lot of care. Sometimes, even when he's sleeping, he needs someone to sit with him. I am worried about his deep breathing. The doctor needs to come and check on him more often."

"I'll have Juan put up a notice at the post office and the dry goods store for help, and he can stop by the doctor's office and ask him to come out to check on Pa. Maybe you can prepare a special pie for him to take back with him?" Matt stood and walked around the big oak desk and took Anna's hands in his. "Are you and the children happy here so far?"

"I miss Reverend Mother so much, but I do like it here. I would like to go horseback riding sometimes and see the rest of the farm. We have been so busy that I've hardly walked out of the house."

"How about a date with me right after breakfast in the morning?" Matt walked with her into the hallway. "I have some bills to pay, and then I'll be up to bed. Morning comes early here on the farm."

"I haven't had any trouble convincing the children to go to bed at night. They run all day from collecting eggs, milking the cows, and playing with the pigs. Jamie wants to learn to ride, too. They are exhausted after their baths each night."

~

Anna took her time with her toiletries and dressed in a new white nightdress with rows of cotton lace on the bodice. She had washed and dried her hair in front of the fireplace. Before she thought about it, she dabbed vanilla behind her ears.

She and Matt had been sharing the bed in their room with rows of pillows placed down the center of the mattress. Matt had stood at the bottom of the bed and warned her, "I can't promise to behave myself more than six nights. After that, my little pretend nun, beware that I might blow my trumpet and overtake your protective Jericho wall."

Matt had kept his promise to stay on his side. He turned and faced the wall, even without saying goodnight. But tonight, she felt it was time to remove Jericho's wall and see what happened. What would Reverend Mother say about Matt knowing about the Jericho wall in Joshua chapter six?

After an hour of sitting in front of the fire brushing her long black hair, she peered into the dark. What was keeping Matt? She put on a matching robe and went downstairs.

"Oh, Anna." Mama came out of her husband's room wiping streaming tears from her eyes. She rushed into Anna's arms. "He's gone."

"Oh, I'm so sorry," Anna said. "Is Matt in the room with him?"

"Yes," she said, sniffing and wiping at her nose.

Pedro and Juan came into the hallway, waiting for Anna to finish her conversation. Finally she joined them. "Oh, Pedro, Juan, would you ride into town and get the doctor? Tell him that Mr. Jenkins has passed."

Anna walked the boys to the door and leaned close. "If the post office is still open ask if any ladies have answered our notice about working here. We could use the help right away."

"Should we tell them to come out here—in the morning?"

"Yes, that would be fine. Tell them to come to the back door and ask for me."

Matt walked out of his father's bedroom and closed the door. He stood next to his mother who was sitting in her favorite chair weeping, her shoulders shaking. "I guess we should tell the preacher," she suggested.

Matt patted her on the shoulder. "The doctor will tell him when he returns to town. We'll need to prepare the grave and get things ready for the service. Will you want to have everything here?"

She nodded. "The small cemetery needs to be cleaned. Weeds and tall bush are taking it over. Your pa wanted to be buried on his farm."

Matt stooped down next to her chair. "Mama, I will prepare whatever you and Pa want. I don't want you to worry about anything. Anna will help me arrange everything." Matt stood and took her arm. "Why don't you get some rest before the doctor arrives?"

"Yes, I am tired, son. Please let me know when the doctor arrives." Anna took Mrs. Jenkins' elbow and led her upstairs to the guestroom. After making her comfortable, she hurried into her bedroom and removed her new gown and robe, donning instead a day dress and slippers.

Back downstairs, Matt hugged her, then they walked into the kitchen. She put on a fresh pot of coffee. Matt had a smug look on his face when she sat down next to him. "I liked your pretty nightclothes. Did you wear them for me?"

"Please, this is no time to discuss *us*. We have plans to make for your father's burial," she said, her shoulders heavy.

"I know, but seeing you in that made my heart feel alive again."

He reached across the table and squeezed her hand.

A warmness grew within Anna. She wanted to fall in his arms and cry her heart out for him. To lose someone you love was so heartbreaking, and it took a lifetime to get over it. She was young when her parents were murdered, and she still missed them. With God's help, and Reverend Mother' teaching, she finally grew to accept that they were in heaven.

She knew that Matt felt guilty that he had become angry at his pa and left in anger, only to return to find him on his deathbed. At least his father was conscious and knew Matt had come home to care for him, his mother, and the farm. His pa had told him that he was sorry that he made him run away from his home. Matt had prayed for his pa's recovery, but the good Lord had other plans.

Chapter 34

Fortunately for Anna, two middle-aged ladies came to the farm early the next morning. Anna learned that Myrtle and Heloise Jackson, the ladies, were cousins and lived in town. They had packed a carpetbag, just in case the farm had a place for them to live in. She asked if they would share a room until better arrangements were made for them, and they readily agreed.

Anna gave them long white aprons to wear over their best dresses they'd worn for their interview. With Mr. Jenkins' funeral service in two days, she gave them a list of things to ready the house for all the guests that would attend the service. She was sure many people would come out of curiosity more than to mourn the man.

The farmworkers set about preparing the small cemetery, and two of the men were building a coffin. Mrs. Jenkins said that she had plenty of leftover white satin in the storage closet. She had made Jennifer's wedding dress and had ordered too much material. Heloise said that she worked as a seamstress, and she knew how to line the inside of the coffin.

Anna was thrilled that all the necessary tasks were being handled. The new maids were a blessing. When they weren't waxing the furniture or staircase, they were shining the silverware or taking out the best china to put out for the day of the funeral. Anna was busy making desserts and pies to serve while looking over her shoulder at the children. They both seemed to know that this was a sad time for Matt and his mother, and they were well-behaved.

Juan came into the kitchen and helped prepare the meals. The maids seemed to be happy to have the sweet, young man working alongside them as they peeled bags of potatoes, carrots, onions, and snap beans for the twenty people who lived on the farm. They fried four chickens and dozens of pork chops for dinner. The men didn't complain when sandwiches were served for lunch with cake and pies for dessert. For now, the farmhands took their meals in the bunkhouse, but Matt had mentioned he wanted to add a spacious dining room for special occasions onto the back of the main house.

The day finally arrived for the service for Matt's pa. Anna was exhausted from all the preparations, but she was pleased with how the house looked. The preacher and his wife arrived early to spend time with Mrs. Jenkins. After she dressed the children in their new clothes, with instructions not to go to the barn, Anna needed some fresh air.

Anna walked out the back door and took in a clean breath of fresh air. She glanced over at the corral. In one hand Matt held an apple for his favorite pony, while patting it with the other. He seemed to be relaxed, and she knew he would be happy to see this day end. He was wearing a new shirt and vest, with shiny new boots. *Golly, he's sure one handsome man.*

Looking down at herself, she was the only one without new clothes. She didn't have time to shop, so she put on her long black nun's dress with a soft white scarf tucked in around the neckline.

A crowd of men gathered beside the barn. The farmhands had led the wagon and carriages to an open field and opened a corral for the saddlehorses. Almost all the men with their families were strangers to Anna, but Matt seemed to know most of them; however, she heard him ask, "Who's that man? Has he lived in our area very long?"

~

The man was quick to say he didn't know, but before Matt could confront the stranger, he had disappeared. Matt had an uncomfortable feeling in the pit of his stomach. When he saw Anna on the porch, he rushed over, taking her arm to lead her inside. He didn't want Anna being left alone with so many strangers attending his pa's funeral. "How are you doing, my pretentious nun?" He smiled while looking over her attire.

"Sorry, I didn't have time to shop for a new dress. I hope I won't embarrass you in this garb, as you once called it."

"Anna, you could never embarrass me. You're the most beautiful young lady here—with or without clothes." He choked back a laugh.

"Oh, you. Behave yourself," Anna said, blushing bright pink.

"I will have to tell all our guests that you're married to me."

"Oh, there you both are." the doctor came into the kitchen. "Right before I left town, I was given this telegram to pass on to you. I do hope it's not bad news."

"It's most likely from one of my sisters. I was afraid that since they only left a few days ago, they hadn't made it home in time to receive the message about Pa." He started to tear open the small brown paper when he noticed it had Anna's name on the front. "Sweetheart," Matt said softly, "this is for you."

"For me? It can't be for me. I don't know anyone who would be sending me a telegram." Anna touched her throat and swallowed deep.

Matt handed her the telegram. "Let's go in the pantry while you read it."

Anna ripped open the folded paper and read, "Anna—stop—Reverend Mother retired—stop—Wants to come and visit you—stop—Coming with her—Señor Carlos—stop—Arriving Tuesday."

"My goodness, this can't be. Reverend Mother has retired. Retired? This is unimaginable." Anna said, passing the telegram back to Matt with bewildered eyes.

Someone was clapping their hands in the kitchen. "It's time we start the service. Everyone, please come outside and take their seats." He turned to her. "Come, Anna. We have to attend to our guests. We'll discuss this later. Be happy Reverend Mother is not sick. And she is coming for a visit." Matt smiled, placed his arms around Anna's waist, and led her to the front row of chairs that were set up on the front lawn. He sat next to his mother and positioned Anna on his other side, holding her hand tight.

Parson Mason spoke sweet words over Matt's father and read many scriptures from the Good Book. The choir from First Baptist Church of Portland sang two songs that lifted everyone's spirits. After a lengthy prayer to close the service, the family members stood and tossed flowers on the coffin as they filed out of the cemetery. Parson Mason announced that dinner would be served at the house. Many of the ladies of the community lifted the hem of their skirts and rushed into the kitchen to help serve the many casseroles, turnip greens, collards, small red potatoes, corn, peas, mashed potatoes, fresh sliced bread, and cornbread. Another two tables sat covered with cakes, cookies, and pies.

The ladies carried platter after platter of food to tables set up outside. This was easier for the guests to serve themselves. The women had also set up a table with hot coffee, tea, lemonade, fresh water, and apple cider. A special table was set up for Mrs. Jenkins, Matt, Anna and the children, along with the preacher's wife and children. Anna insisted that the farmhands and housemaids sit and eat along with the guests.

After almost everyone had said their condolences and left for home, Matt walked with the parson to his carriage and gave him an envelope that contained fifty dollars. "Mama said that she can't thank you enough for the many hours you spent with Pa. Because of you, he had my sister write and ask me to come home. I will always be grateful to you. We patched up our differences before he passed."

"I'm so happy to hear that," Parson Mason replied. "Please don't feel you have to pay for my services."

"Your job is not an easy one. Believe me, working as a sheriff is close to your line of work. You save people's souls, and I try to keep them from killing each other." Matt smiled. "Please use this money as you see fit for yourself, your family, or the church. I wish it could be ten times more. Thanks again, and I hope to see you in church Sunday."

~

Later into the evening, after everyone had left the farm, Anna and the two housemaids worked diligently to put all remaining food away and clean the kitchen. The two children went to bed without a fuss. They had run and played with many of the neighbors' children until they were tuckered out.

Before Matt went back into the house, he walked to the barn and spoke with Luther, one of the farmhands. He thanked him for helping his mother care for his pa. "Believe me, Luther, I know you had your hands full, but Mama couldn't have managed without you." Luther looked down to hide a shy smile.

After checking on the horses in the corral, he went into the bunkhouse and thanked the men for everything they did while his father was sick. He praised them for all the extra work they did to help prepare the farm for the funeral. "Later, I will show you my appreciation."

For an hour, he sat in mama's room, allowing her to talk until she fell asleep. She told Matt she was glad to have him home with

Anna and the children. His two sisters had not been happy being there, and they fussed about everything. They would not enter Pa's bedroom.

"I thanked God for Luther every day." She confessed she was happy to see his sisters go home to their own families.

Matt pulled a quilt over his mother's frail body, turned down the lanterns, and went into the kitchen. Anna might still be in there, but one of the maids said she had just retired. He thanked her for all of her hard work and went up the backstairs to the second floor.

A light shone from under the bedroom door, but when he stepped inside, Anna was fast asleep. She was wearing an old night dress, snuggling a piece of the Jericho wall against her breast.

He smiled to himself and undressed. After a visit to the water closet, he eased under the covers, trying not to wake Anna. She had worked like a champ caring for all of the townspeople who had come to the funeral. He wanted to tell her how much he loved her, but now wasn't the time.

Chapter 35

The following day, Matt and his mother had an
appointment to meet with his father's close friend and lawyer. Anna
and Juan wanted to go check out the town's café and bakery. She
wanted to make pies and hopefully sell some at one of the
establishments. Matt wanted Anna to come with him and his mother,
but she felt that the lawyer's business was private, and he could tell
her what she needed to know once the meeting was over. She and
Juan would go and visit the bakery.

"Good day, Matt, Mrs. Jenkins," Mr. Talbert said. "This awful
business of reading a will won't take long., Mrs. Jenkins, your
husband, was very straightforward as to what he wanted to do with
his money and farm."

Matt reached for Mama's hand as Mr. Talbert cleared his throat
and wiped his hanky across his mouth. "Matt, do you want to look
this over to make sure it is your father's signature before I begin?"

"No, please continue. My pa trusted you, and I have no reason
not to."

"Mrs. Jenkins, your husband has left everything he has to Matt,
except some money to his two daughters. This includes the farmland
and most of his savings, but there is one condition." He lifted his
eyes over his wire-rimmed glasses and peered at Matt's surprised
face. "The one condition is that Mrs. Jenkins has a home at the farm
as long as she desires. You, Matt, will be her guardian and make
sure she has everything her heart desires, within reason of course."
He sat and waited for their response.

"Mr. Talbert, my mother should have inherited everything, not
me. What was Pa's reasoning for this?" Matt shook his head.

"Your father only wanted what was best for his dear wife."
Turning to his mother, he said, "Mrs. Jenkins, your husband knew

that you didn't need to worry about the farm. He knew that Matt loved you as much as he did, and you would be taken care of for the rest of your days. He was only thinking of what was best for you.

Now, Matt, your father left your sisters the sum of one thousand dollars each. I will make a draft and mail it to them. If they have any questions about the will, they can contact me. I will try to explain everything to them. Your father knew that they had a great dislike for him and even greater hatred for the farm. So, he gave them money, nothing more."

Matt shifted in his chair. "They will have a lot to say, but I will tell them to contact you. I love my sisters, but I witnessed how unhappy they were when we arrived. I tried to talk to them, but they only wanted to return to their families," he said.

"Here's a copy of the will. You can go to the bank and have his funds transferred into your name. I will have the farm's title transferred into your name as well. Do you want to have your wife's name placed on the deed, too?"

"Can I do that?" Matt asked, because he was told a woman couldn't own any kind of property.

"Yes, the law is more lenient than before," Mr. Talbert said.

"Yes, I want her name on the deed. It's Anna Knight Jenkins," Matt stated, as his mother smiled sweetly.

"Mama, are you sure this is fine with you? I know you worked right beside Pa, helping to build up our farm. Everything he has should be yours," Matt said holding her two hands in his.

"From the day you left home and threatened never to return, your pa never smiled again. He told me that a man is nothing unless he has a son to leave the result of his hard work, and his land. On his deathbed, he smiled again because you came home. And Matt, my dear boy, I couldn't be more pleased that you will live on the farm with your family and me."

"Thank you, Mama. You will never need for anything. Anna and I will see to that." Matt stood and said, "Let's go the bakery and enjoy a treat and some coffee."

~

Anna and Juan met Mr. Erwin Jackson, the owner of the bakery. He was eager to taste one of Anna's pie or the special breads she baked. "I have to close every day right after lunch because I run out of goodies," he said.

"I will try to deliver some to you tomorrow. If you like my pies and goodies, please give my man your order, and I will deliver them myself as soon as possible. Maybe one day a week, I can come into your kitchen and cook pies. May Juan and I see your kitchen?"

"Anna, I need to go to the barber for a haircut. I won't be long. Now stay with Mr. Jackson until I return. Promise?" Juan said.

"Of course. Matt and Mrs. Jenkins will be coming soon anyway." She followed Mr. Jackson into the large kitchen. After looking around, she was excited about the large counter and the two ovens placed side by side.

"Now, Mrs. Jenkins, all I need is a good baker to help me out, and I shall retire one day a rich man."

"Yes, you have a fine work space. I hope my husband will agree to me working here with you. We have a lot of farmhands to feed, but I like working in town and selling my goodies." While Anna was looking over Mr. Jackson's cookware, she heard him speak harshly, "Who are you? What are you doing coming in my back door? Get out this instant!" Anna spun around and saw Mr. Jackson pointing toward the back door with his eyes on a stranger that had entered his bakery.

"Shut your trap, old man, before I shut it for you. This lady is going with me." The stranger seized Anna's arms and shoved her toward the door.

Anna glanced back at the tall stranger with the same crystal blue eyes her mother had. "Uncle Claude? I can't believe it's you. How...how could you have done all the things people are saying you did? Robbing and killing people. I didn't want to believe those things about you, but—"

"Keep believing I'm the good guy, sweetheart. But now I need for you to come with me."

"No, you aren't the man I knew, and I would never go off with someone like you. Take your hands off me before I scream this place down!" Anna tried to jerk her arm loose from his grip.

"Take your hands off Mrs. Jenkins. She said she isn't going with you. Now, leave this kitchen before I have to toss you out."

In a flash, Mr. Jackson was lying on the kitchen floor with a gash on his head.

"You beast! How could you hit him with that rolling pin? What did he do to you? You might have killed him," Anna said, dropping to her knees over the baker.

Claude jerked Anna to her feet, turned her toward the back door, and shoved her out onto the porch. He whistled, and a rider came from the trees with two horses.

"I'm not getting on that horse. You'd better get out of here before it's too late." Anna kicked at his legs and hit him with her reticule.

~

"Mouthy witch, isn't she?" Claude's partner cackled.

Claude drew back his fist and hit Anna in the jaw, then grabbed her before she fell off the porch unconscious. "Shut up and hold her while I get on my horse."

~

Matt and his mother entered the café to find one man hurrying past them. A man yelled for someone to get the sheriff, and a woman demanded a pan of water and some clean rags.

Matt sat his mother down at one of the tables and rushed into the kitchen. Anna and Juan weren't inside, but Mr. Jackson lay on the floor. He looked dead, but the woman attending to him said he wasn't.

"What happened here?" Matt asked.

"We won't know until we bring Mr. Jackson around. He was hit really hard with a rolling pin."

"How do you know the weapon was a rolling pin?" Matt asked like the former lawman he was.

"Because it was lying near him with blood all over it. Surely, he wasn't preparing pastries with it," replied the woman who was placing a cold cloth on Mr. Jackson's face.

~

Juan approached the café feeling like a new man with his fresh haircut but stopped at the frenzy around the café. He hurried over to the table where Mrs. Jenkins sat waiting for Matt and Anna. "What's happening? People are scurrying everywhere out on the boardwalk," he said.

"I am not sure. Matt went into the kitchen looking for Anna."

Juan rushed into the kitchen in search of Matt and Anna. "Where's Anna? I left her with Mr. Jackson while I went to the barber," Juan said as he looked around the room. He noticed the worried expression on Matt's face.

"I'm not sure who hit Mr. Jackson on the head, but Anna is gone. Her uncle or some stranger has taken her—where, I am not sure. I don't believe he will hurt her. He just wants the bank money. Still…there's the blood." He listened to Matt as Mr. Jackson's opened his eyes.

"What happened? Who hit you, Erwin?" The sheriff asked.

"Mrs. Jenkins' uncle. She didn't want to go with him. I told him to leave the café and tried to stop him from forcing her out the back door, but all of sudden, everything went black."

"You were hit with your own rolling pin. You're lucky to be alive," the sheriff responded.

"Mr. Jackson, my name is Matt Jenkins. Anna is my wife. Are you sure the man that took Anna was her uncle?"

"Yes, she called him uncle and appeared upset to see him. She mentioned something about him being a wanted man and he wasn't the man she remembered."

Matt and Juan stepped onto the back porch of the bakery and looked around. On the ground, Matt discovered Anna's reticule. Juan had jumped off the porch and saw horse prints near the steps. One set of prints had a loose horseshoe. With every step the horse took, he left a trail that was easy to follow.

~

Matt entered the kitchen and told the sheriff that he was going to gather some men and go after Claude Moore and his wife.

"Now, Mr. Jenkins, I'm the law here, and I won't tolerate a lynching party." The sheriff stood straight and lifted his pants with both sides of his hands.

"Claude Moore is wanted dead or alive, but I only want my wife back safe and sound. If he has hurt her in anyway, there won't be any lynching. I will kill him with my bare hands." Matt returned to the table where his mother waited. Outside on the street, he placed his mother in their carriage and instructed Juan to ride ahead and tell Pedro and several of the men to pack bedrolls for a few days out on the trail. "I need them to help me find Anna."

On the way home, Matt told his mother all about Claude Moore and Anna's relationship. He told her a little about Anna's life at the convent and how she loved Juan and Pedro like brothers.

She told Matt not to worry about the farm. Luther would keep things running smoothly while he was gone to bring back Anna.

He also told her to have a man go into town early Tuesday morning and escort Reverend Mother and Señor Carlos to the farm. He tried to explain Anna's relationship with both of them. "They'll be staying with us for a while. Reverend Mother will be a big help. Please put her up in the guest bedroom, and Señor Carlos won't mind bunking with the men. He's a father figure to Juan and Pedro. I am sure the two new maids will not mind sharing the smaller room off the pantry. After I settle this business with Anna's uncle, I will try to have a guesthouse built, but for now everyone will have to pull together with the living arrangements."

"Son, you only have one job to take care of, and that's finding Anna. I am not helpless and I can manage everyone. You just take care of your wife." Mrs. Jenkins patted her son on the leg and gave him an encouraging smile.

~

Juan had ridden the ten miles back to the farm as fast as his bay horse would carry him. He rushed to the barn and waved to several men in the corral. "Come quick, Miss Anna has been kidnapped and Matt will be here soon. He needs men to pack bedrolls, grub, and canteens of water to last for a few days. Don't forget your rifles. We're going to rescue her from those men."

~

Jamie was sitting on the corral fence watching the men work the horses. He watched the men drop everything they were doing and rush around saddling up their horses and packing bedrolls. "Miss Anna is hurt," he said aloud. Rushing over to the back porch, he whispered to Susie, "Miss Anna is hurt, and some bad men have taken her away. We have to help the men find her."

"Ain't nobody gonna let us go with them."

"You're right. After Matt and the men leave, we will follow them. I'll saddle my pony—"

"You ain't got no pony," Susie said, rolling her eyes.

"It's almost mine. Pedro won't care if we take him and ride double. Now are you going with me or not? Because I'm going after those bad men. Miss Anna is good to us, and we can't let somebody hurt her."

"All right. I'll pack some food while you get the pony ready. It's nearly suppertime, and I'm hungry."

Chapter 36

After two long days of following the trail, Matt and his men were tired and cold. The weather had turned colder than usual for late September, and the men had not thought to wear their jackets. No one complained, because they were all worried about his wife.

"They have to be hiding out somewhere near here. A shack or cave is my best bet, but where? Let's all spread out and walk if necessary. The horse prints are too clear for us not to find them," Pedro said. A few of the men stood guard while others lay on their bedrolls for a few hours.

Matt headed deep into the forest and found a big fallen log. He checked for critters, sat down, and folded his hands over his face. He didn't know when he had been so afraid. Anna had come into his life nearly six months ago, and now tears stacked up in his throat. Taking out his handkerchief, he swallowed hard and wiped his mouth. Never had he dreamed a girl dressed in a nun's outfit would steal his heart.

Anna's heart was filled with love for Reverend Mother, Pedro, and Juan, but he was desperate, almost sorrowful, for her to love him and accept their marriage as real. She had shown nothing but kindness to his pa while he was alive, something his own sisters had not done. His mama already love Anna because of the way she had taken charge of the house and prepared meals for everyone, including the farmhands. "Lord, please help me find my wife before something bad happens to her," he prayed, remembering God's care, and said, "Amen."

His chest tightened, and thoughts of Anna's uncle, Claude Moore, raced through his mind. Anna wouldn't be safe as long as he was alive. Claude wanted the stolen money, and he didn't care who he had to hurt to get it. Unfortunately, there wasn't any money because it had been turned over to the bank of Portland.

~

After leaving the farm, Jamie and Susie followed the men closely, but it wasn't long before they were miles behind the men. Jamie's pony couldn't keep up with the men, so they took shortcuts through the thick forest.

The first night they huddled close together to keep warm, because they didn't have matches or flint to build a fire. All night, Jamie stayed awake and fought mosquitos. He wrapped his small arms around Susie because every time an owl hooted she cried out. By the next day they had traveled miles from the farm. Stopping at a creek bed, Jamie loosened his hold on his pony reins as he drank the cool water. Suddenly, the pony jerked his head and raced away. Jamie chased after the pony but to no avail. He fell to the ground and pounded his fists. His horse was hungry, he guessed, and wanted to go back to a warm barn and plenty of feed.

When Jamie returned to the creek bed, Susie began to whine. "Jamie, I can't go no more. Your pony has done went back to the barn, and I bet we're going to get a good paddling when we get back home for being gone. I wish I had packed more than two apples and a couple of peppermints sticks."

"Hush up. I'm tired and hungry too, but we have to find Miss Anna," Jamie said. "I saw a shack while I was running after the pony, and I want to go look inside. Maybe we can spend the night there out of the cold. You stay right here under these bushes until I return."

"Okay, but hurry. I don't like being left alone out here." Susie laid her head down on the soft grass.

Jamie walked through the thicket of trees and underbrush until he came upon the shack, but it didn't look empty. There were two horses tied around the back. Who was inside? Sliding on his belly like a snake toward the shack, he listened under the window. Two men were talking. He eased up on his tiptoes and saw Miss Anna tied to a chair. Suddenly a door opened and a man stood on the small front step, relieving himself. Jamie quickly crept through the stone foundation and climbed under the shack. He fought back spider webs, heard rats scurrying everywhere, and prayed he didn't step on a snake.

Footsteps sounded overhead, and men's mumbled. He didn't

care what they were saying. All he knew was he had discovered where the bad men were keeping Miss Anna. *I need to find Mr. Matt.* As quiet as a field mouse, he hurried back to Susie. "I found her, Susie. Let's go get Mr. Matt." But first he flopped down on the ground and tried to catch his breath.

"I can't hurry nowhere. I am too sleepy. Let's go tomorrow," she groaned. Susie lay back down and refused to move a muscle.

"All right, you stay hidden, and I'll be back soon." Jamie jumped up and retraced his steps. Hours later, night had fallen and Jamie was all turned around. Tears trickled down his face. He fell to the ground and prayed, "Please Jesus, help me."

~

The guard was moving around the campsite to keep awake. Something sounded like a hurt animal. Taking his pistol out of his holster, he tread softly until he discovered Jamie lying on the ground nearly asleep, crying.

"Hey, fellows, look who I found." The man scooped Jamie up in his arms and headed toward the campsite. Jamie started struggling to be put down until the man said, "It's all right, fellow. I'm Hank, and I work for Mr. Jenkins."

Jamie relaxed and wiped the tears and snot away from his face with his sleeve. "Really, I found Mr. Matt?"

"Sure thing. What in the world are you doing this far from home? Does anyone know that you've left the farm?" the man asked as he continued carrying Jamie.

"I have to see Mr. Matt because I found Miss Anna. Please take me to him," Jamie pleaded as he wiggled to get down from the guy's arms.

Matt was sitting close to the fire ring drinking a cup of coffee alone as the men slept all around the fire.

"Hey, Matt, look who I found lying in the underbrush. It's Jamie."

Matt leaped to his feet and rushed over to see the child. "Lord have mercy, son. What are you doing way out here all alone?" Matt took him out of Hank's arms.

"We're looking for Miss Anna," Jamie said, out of breath.

"Take it easy now and start slowly," Matt said. "Who is with you?"

"Mr. Matt, please listen. I found Miss Anna. She's in a shack with two bad men. I heard them talking, and when I peeked in the window, I saw Miss Anna tied to a chair. They didn't see me, but I have to go get Susie."

~

"Susie? Little Susie is with you?" Matt felt like he might scream, but he didn't want to scare the child.

"Where's Susie now," demanded Juan.

"I left her under some bushes. She's hiding. Susie was too tired and hungry to keep moving. See, I borrowed the pony that I ride on the farm, but he got loose and ran away, most likely back to the farm."

"Was Anna all right? Did she look hurt?" Matt was so excited to hear this wonderful news even if it did come from a five-year-old.

"Yep, she had rope around her shoulders. She didn't see me, but she was looking around," Jamie said, as he pulled on Matt's hand. "Let's go now, before the bad men take her somewhere else."

"Did you tell Myrtle or Heloise where you and Susie were going?" Juan asked, furrows forming on his forehead.

"No sir," Jamie replied, hanging his head down to his chest. "We had to find Miss Anna and we did too. Let's go and get her!"

"Yes, we will do that right now," Matt said and patted Juan on the back. "Take it easy. We'll find them all very soon." He turned to Hank. "Gather all the men. Tell them to saddle up and to be quiet."

After all the men stood together, Matt explained that Jamie has discovered the shack where the men are holding Anna. "It's not very far from here, but it's nearly morning now. Once we're close, we'll surround the shack."

~

Susie was lying in the bushes where Jamie had left her. A big boot nearly stepped on her, and she gasped. Suddenly, an ugly man stooped down and stared at her. She eased back further into the brush, but a long arm jerked her up. He held her over his head, while she held her arms bent at the elbows, hands formed into fists. "Put me down, you big turd, before I pee on you," Susie said.

The man dropped her onto the ground and growled, "Girl, do your business and be quick about it. But you'd better watch who you're calling names."

In less than two minutes, the man grabbed Susie around the waist and carried her like a sack of potatoes inside the shack. "Look what I found outside in the bushes. Can't decide if I want to toss her over the big ridge outback or cook and eat her."

~

Claude looked up at his partner and noticed Anna had turned as white as a sheet. "Shut up, and let the young'un alone." Turning to the tot, he asked, "Who are you, little girl?" He was sure the little girl was the one who was with Anna in Livingston.

"I'm hungry. Do you have something to eat?" the girl said, lifting up her chin.

"Sorry, kiddo," Claude said. 'We ate all our grub. We need to go to town and get some more. Would you like to go to town with us?"

"No, I'd better run back home now." Susie headed to the door, but Claude beat her there and blocked her. "Anna, I am sure this little stage actress is the girl who was living with you in Livingston. We can use her as a hostage."

"I don't want to be a *holeage*," Susie bellowed, her fist on her waist. "And I can't go to town with you. I have to go home."

"Tie this mouthy brat next to Anna. I am sure Anna will cooperate now that we have her precious little girl. Right, Anna?" Claude walked over to Anna and slid down the bandana that covered her mouth. "So Anna, love, now will you tell me where you have hidden my money?"

"Susie, come close to me. Please be good so they won't have any cause to harm you," Anna said, without answering.

"No harm will come to either of you if you just tell me where the money is located. I know you have been spending it."

"You're wrong. Before I discovered you were a thief, I only spent what you sent me for passage and living expenses. Afterward, I earned the rest of the money from the sale of my pastries."

"Where is the big package of money I sent to the convent?" he remarked, lifting a single eyebrow.

"I'm going to tell you one time and one time only. I don't have your money. Sheriff Jenkins turned the money over to the Portland Bank the day after we arrived at his farm."

He slapped her across the face. With a choked voice, she said, "Did that make you feel better?" But before he could comment, Susie flew at him and bit down on his upper thigh as hard as she could through his pants. Claude kicked her to the other side of the room. "What have you taught this child?" He rubbed his leg as he advanced on Susie, but Anna's pleading stopped him.

~

"Please don't hurt her again. If it is money you want, I have some in the bank."

"Really, little girl? How could you have money, living in a convent for the past ten years?"

"I am not lying. In the bank of Livingston, I have five thousand dollars. I will give it all to you," Anna said, as she watched Susie crawl across the floor to sit at her feet.

"Did you sell your folks' farm to get that much money? I tried to sell it, but the judge in Whistler wouldn't let me because my name wasn't on the deed. The only thing I received was the money in my brother-in-law's bank account because I was your guardian. Poor fools. They only saved four hundred dollars. It really wasn't worth the trouble I had hiring those drunken men to come in and kill them."

Anna couldn't believe what he had done. She sucked in her breath. "You . . . you had my mama—your sister—killed? I can't believe you were that desperate for money." Looking down at Susie, then back at her uncle. "My mother loved you so much. She didn't want you to be alone. It would have broken her heart to see the rotten, scum-of-the-earth, human being you are today. I can't stand to look at you." She slumped forward so she wouldn't have to look at him.

"Anna," Susie said softly, "I've got to go to the privy, now. Tell them."

Anna cleared her throat. "I have been tied for hours, and we need to go outside to the outhouse. Untie me now."

"Anna, my dear, where are your manners? How about saying please?"

"You don't deserve any kind words from me, and none will be coming. So untie me now so I can take care of this child."

Claude laughed. "You are still the feisty child I took care of for several years. Many times I wanted to beat you, but I was afraid I would have to cook my own meals."

"If I had known you were responsible for the death of my parents, I would have poisoned you," Anna said without humor in her voice.

Claude looked out the front window of the shack, then walked over to Anna and untied the rope, pulling her to her feet. Susie grabbed her around the waist, but Claude held onto Anna's elbow. He pushed her out toward the outhouse. "I am watching your every move. Don't try anything cute, my dear niece. I would hate to have to shoot that little tyke hanging onto you."

Anna and Susie went into the outhouse, and both held their noses as they did their private business. Peeking through the cracks, Anna saw movement in the trees. Matt and his men? "Susie, when we go outside, I am going to pretend to faint. When I bend over and make a funny noise, I want you to run as fast as you can into the woods. Don't look back at me."

"Hurry up in there, before I come inside and get you," Claude barked as he knocked on the outhouse door.

"But, I'm afraid of the woods. I don't want to leave you," Susie pouted.

"Please, be brave and do this for me."

The door jerked opened and Claude stood there staring at the two girls. "About time. Get going back to the shack," he said as he turned his anger on his partner. "Put out that stinking smoke."

Anna took several steps in front of her uncle. Suddenly she grabbed her stomach, moaned loudly, and slowly buckled her knees and fell to the ground. Both men stood staring down at her, not paying any attention to Susie's flight.

"Anna, what's wrong?" Claude's voice held concern.

Out of the blue, seven men with guns came out of the woods, surrounding the area where the two men stood staring down at Anna. "Don't move a muscle. You both are under arrest," Matt shouted.

As fast as a striking snake, Claude jerked Anna off the ground and placed his pistol next to her head. "Now, Sheriff Jenkins, if you want this girl to stay alive, your men had better back away. Turn my partner loose."

Matt swallowed hard and glanced at his men. "Do as he says."

"Jumbo, get our horses and bring them around here. Now!" Claude waved his pistol at the men. First one of you to try to follow us will cause this little prize's death."

"Listen to me, Moore. You're a dead man. If you harm a hair on Anna's head, you will never have a good night's sleep. I will follow you to the end of the earth, day and night, until I kill you with my bare hands," Matt seethed, as he flexed his fists.

"You talk big. I could kill you right now, but I am going to let you live. Believe it or not, I don't want to be responsible for tearing Anna's heart out."

Jumbo brought their horses around from the back of the shack. Claude sat Anna up in the saddle. He leaped up behind her, holding his pistol next to her neck. He walked his horse out of the yard to the tree line and stopped, turning to face the men. "Remember what I said. You'd best not let me hear . . . Ouch!" Claude yelled, as he batted at arms and legs that enveloped his head. Falling to the ground, he rolled away from the horse, the small boy who'd encircled his head hurled into the air.

Anna jumped off and slapped the horse's flank to move it away from the child. The men rushed to Claude and stood over him with their guns pointed. Claude sat up, shaking his head and batting at the air.

Matt rushed over to Jamie who lay sprawled out in deep leaves. He was as still as death. "Jamie," Matt whispered, "Jamie, do you hear me?"

The young boy began to moan and reached for Matt's arms.

"Thank you, God, for this small miracle."

Two of the men appeared from the woods with Jumbo, his arms tied behind his back.

"Jamie, how do you feel, son?" Matt wiped dirt and leaves away from his hair and forehead. "Are you hurting anywhere?"

"Am I your son, Mr. Matt?" Jamie looked up with expectant eyes.

Matt pulled the boy to his chest and hugged him tight. "If you want to be, you can."

Anna knelt beside Matt and brushed a kiss on Jamie's head. "Oh my goodness, baby. You could have been killed, but you saved me."

"That's what I wanted to do. Susie and I left the farm to save you from those bad men. Looks like we did it." Jamie's broad smile spread across his face.

Matt carried Jamie to the yard of the shack and gave him to Pedro. "Watch him for a head injury, please. I have business to take care of." Then he rushed over to Anna. He hugged her, then held her at arm's length. "Did they hurt you?"

Anna shook her head. "My uncle is not the man I remember."

"I have never been so afraid as when I discovered you had been taken by him. God answers prayers for sure." Matt sat down on the small step of the shack and pulled Anna onto his lap.

"Oh, Matt, Claude killed my pa and mama. He told me. I couldn't believe the words coming out of his mouth. He hired men to raid our farm and kill them. My mama loved him so much. I don't think I will ever be able to forgive him. Although I will because God requires it, but it won't be easy."

Matt ran his thumb under her eyes and wiped away her tears. He rested his chin on top of her head and spoke softly. "In time, sweetheart. Time helps to heal a lot of things. Don't think about how you should feel. God will help you."

"Ever since I arrived in Livingston, I have been nothing but trouble for you. If I stay at your farm, I promise to make things better." She sniffed. "Let's go. I'm starved, and I know Susie and Jamie are too."

Matt laughed. "Is that the only reason you want to go home?"

"Oh, you. There're many reasons." Anna gave him a sweet smile.

Chapter 37

Excitement was in the air as Matt, Anna, and the children rode into the front yard of the farm. The men followed, waving their hats and giving a yell at the other farmhands, letting them know that all was well as they rode straight to the corral and barn.

Reverend Mother and Señor Carlos stood next to Mrs. Jenkins on the large surrounding porch, smiling and crying at the same time. Matt leaped off his horse and helped Anna to the ground as Pedro and Juan carried the children to the porch.

Heloise and Myrtle held out their hands for Susie and Jamie to come to them. "You little scamps, you scared us to death when we couldn't find you. I should skin you both, but I'm so happy to see that you're all right." Myrtle said, as she hugged them.

"I'm a hero, Miss Myrtle. I saved Anna!" Jamie boasted. "I leaped out of a tree on top of the bad man and knocked him off his horse."

"Mercy," Heloise said.

Pedro eased behind Jamie and pulled him into his arms. "Listen to me. A real man doesn't pat himself on the back. He does not brag and tell others how great he is. Do you understand?"

"No, because I am great and brave. How come I can't tell others what I did?"

"Others will soon learn without you telling them. People will talk about it." Pedro hugged the boy. "You did great out there, but you don't brag about it."

"Yes, sir," Jamie said, as he pushed out his bottom lip.

Anna and Reverend Mother met each other at the bottom of the porch steps. The old woman said, "My child, I was so worried about you. I prayed every minute that Matt would find you, and God answered my prayers." Reverend Mother turned from Anna and reached for Señor Carlos. "Look who came with me? I want him to stay. Maybe you can talk him into it."

Pedro rushed over to Señor Carlos. "Te extraño mi amigo."

"I missed you too, my son," Carlos replied, smiling. "Remember to speak English."

"I will and I do, most of the time, but I am so happy to see you." Pedro grabbed the old man and hugged him tightly. "Are you going to remain here on the farm with us?"

"We'll discuss my living arrangements later," He took his arm, looking around.

Matt walked over to the porch and hugged his mother.

"Oh, son, I'm so happy you are home with your wife and children. Everything here is fine. Luther and the other men took care of everything."

"Do you mind if Reverend Mother and Señor Carlos are here for a while?"

"I love having them. It's like I have known Sister Margaret forever."

"Sister Margaret?" Matt asked, his brow furrowed.

"Now that she is not the Reverend Mother at the convent in Whitmire, she wants to be called Sister Margaret or Maggie."

"That will be hard to get used to." He laughed as he watched Anna, Señor Carlos, and Reverend Mother—Sister Margaret now—reunited.

The first thing Anna wanted was a hot bath. The children wanted food but fretted as they suffered through a bath and a hair wash. Sister Margaret and the two maids cooked a big dinner with Anna's favorite—chicken and dumplings.

~

Matt had to travel into Portland to file a report with the sheriff about Claude Moore and his partner who seemed to be nameless because no one ever asked him his last name.

The sheriff pulled out several wanted posters, showing Anna's uncle was wanted in several states. The U. S. Army's reward was the largest because he had murdered a conductor of the train and stolen their payroll. "Matt, since you aren't a lawman any longer, and you captured these men, you will be granted the reward. His partner is also a wanted man for robberies at several farms."

Matt listened to the sheriff, but all he heard was Anna saying *if she stayed* on his farm. This comment burned into his heart. He wouldn't let her leave him. "Thanks, Sheriff. I had a lot of help catching Anna's uncle. I'll accept the money and divide it with my farmhands. They risked their lives for my wife."

"The money will be yours, and you can do whatever you want with it." The sheriff smiled. "The country will be a safer place now that we have those two behind bars. I will telegraph the Army to come for them. It is possible your wife will never have to testify against her uncle, because he will receive the death sentence from the army court alone."

"I hope that will be the case. She is upset with him. He told her that he had killed her parents to steal their farm when she was only about eight years old. So, if she never sees him again, that would be wonderful."

"I will send a message to you when I receive the award money. Thanks for everything you and your men did."

Matt shook the sheriff's hand and walked out into the sunshine. The wind was crisp and cold, but the sun felt good on his face. Glancing down the street, he saw Jackson's café. He wanted to know how Mr. Jackson was doing, so he hurried down the street.

As he hurried down the boardwalk, a young saloon gal came out of the dry goods store. She was looking down when she bumped into Matt, nearly knocking him into the dirt street.

"Oh, my goodness," she cooed, "this must be my lucky day to run into such a handsome cowboy." She dropped her packages at Matt's feet, rubbed her body against his side, and wrapped her arm around his neck.

Matt pushed the gal away. She reeked of cheap perfume. "Thanks for the compliment, pretty lady, but I'm married and have no interest in what you might be offering me."

The girl stepped back and slapped Matt's face so hard she scraped her long fingernail across his chin. "That's all I'm offering you, big boy." She reached down and snatched up her two packages and flounced away.

Matt's face was on fire from the slap and also from the embarrassment he felt as other shoppers on the boardwalk stopped to gawk at the scene. Quickly, he continued onto the café to check on Mr. Jackson. As he entered the café, he used his handkerchief to wipe the blood off his chin. "Hello," he said to the young lady behind the checkout counter. "Is Mr. Jackson working today? My name is Matt Jenkins, and I would like to speak with him."

"Come back here, Mr. Jenkins," Mr. Jackson called to him.

"It is so good to see you working, Jackson. I know Anna has been worried about you. She remembers how you tried to protect her from her uncle."

"Well, I did try, but that man nearly killed me with my own rolling pin," he said laughing.

"Anna wants to work with you and make pies and other pastries to sell. Do you still want her to help you out?" Before he could answer, Matt commented, "I'd really like her to stay on the farm, but she loves making pies and cooking to earn her own money. So I am not going to stand in her way."

"Yes, I would love for her to work here, and that fellow Juan too. He's a great help, and all the young ladies come in just to see him. He never even notices any of them." Mr. Jackson laughed so hard his belly jumped up and down.

"I'll report your message back to both of them. Anna and Juan will come into town in a few days. They'll be happy to hear that you are in good health."

Chapter 38

Anna was in the kitchen helping Heloise, Myrtle, and Sister Margaret prepare the large supper for over twenty-four people each night. Matt motioned for Anna to come out on the back porch where he could speak with her in private. "It's a little chilly out here, Matt. What's so important that you need to speak to me out here?"

"I can't seem to get you alone anytime during the day. You are so busy. Don't you know that you're the lady of this house, not one of the servants? You don't have to work harder than our paid staff. If you need more help, I can hire more people so we can be spend time together. I miss you so much." He moved closer to Anna to steal a kiss.

Anna put her hands on Matt's shoulders and took a sniff of him "Well, it smells like you have already had a lady friend pretty close to you. Who are you spending time with? It's not me wearing that cheap perfume. Is she someone I have met?"

~

Matt's mouth gaped open as he watched his sweet wife enter the kitchen and slam the door in his face. He stormed in from the porch, stopped, and looked around for Anna.

All the ladies stopped working and watched as Anna stormed up the stairs and slammed her bedroom door.

He quickly took the stairs two steps at a time and tried the door. It was locked. Matt banged on his bedroom door. "Open this door, Anna."

Screams of her reply came, "Go away, you two-timing . . . gigolo!"

~

The ladies' mouths all flew opened. "What in the world has happened to cause her to call him names?" Heloise asked.

"I think the green-eye monster of jealousy has appeared. Let's all go into the parlor and take up our knitting until the two of them have settled down. They'll be embarrassed if they know we heard them," Sister Margaret said, trying hard not to laugh.

Mrs. Jenkins entered the parlor and heard Sister Margaret talking about Matt and Anna. "Sister Margaret, the whole farm can hear those two upstairs. What has happened?"

The ladies shook their heads and sat down in front of the fireplace when they heard a banging on a door overhead. "How dare you break down my door?" Anna screamed as she threw a vase of flowers at her husband's head. A loud shatter, then more shattering was heard until there was silence coming from upstairs.

~

Matt had entered the bedroom door and dodged several vases of flowers until he could get to Anna. "You listen to me, you little hellcat. I haven't looked or been with a woman since I met you. I fell head over heels in love with you the first day I saw you take off that thing you call 'wimpy,' and I saw your beautiful long black hair. I was thrilled when you told me you weren't a nun."

"You're lying! You stuck to me like glue so you could catch my uncle. I was just someone you used. Too bad it took you months to catch him."

"Anna, sweetheart, that isn't true. I was afraid for you. My men protected you and watched your home because I knew how bad your uncle was. I was afraid that he would hurt you. Now you have to know I was right."

"Where were all those men when that crazy fellow showed up and shot you in the leg? If your men had been close by, we would never have been forced into marriage. A marriage that I am going to have annulled as soon as I can."

"Over my dead body, little miss. We are married and we will be until death. I love you so much that I had your name placed on this farm, along with mine."

"What? You did what? But why? This farm is your mama's," Anna said softly, stunned at his words.

"No, it's mine. My pa left me everything except a little money for my sisters." Matt stepped closer to Anna as she shook her head.

"Why did you have my name put on the deed? You know I am going to leave here and go home—leaving you a free man."

"You are my wife, and I want you to share everything I have. Besides, Anna Knight Jenkins, I will never let you leave me." He closed in on her and placed his two palms on her cheeks. Leaning down, he kissed her pink lips, then carried her over to the bed. Turning around, Matt saw the busted door standing open. He quickly set the door against the hinges and placed a straight chair under the doorknob to keep it in place. Then he rushed back over to the bed.

"Matt, how can you really love me? I have been nothing but trouble since I arrived in Livingston."

"You were no trouble to me, sweetheart. When you stood on that pile of dirt, giving a blessing to Big John, my heart swelled with pride. I knew then that I had to have you in my life forever. After I tasted one of your pies, it sealed the deal—I would never let you go."

"Oh, you, that's not very romantic." Anna smiled and rubbed the scratch on his chin. "How did this happen?"

"Just like that cheap perfume got on me. A saloon gal ran into me on the boardwalk and forced her body against mine. I told her I was married, so she slapped me. Her long fingernail scratched me. I promise you that is the truth." He crawled onto the bed next to Anna. Their hands touched and their fingers entwined as he unhitched his belt. Impatiently, he began working on her buttons down the shirtwaist she wore.

Anna's eyes watched her husband with the stillness of a wild animal. Matt gazed into Anna's crystal blue eyes. "Anna, I love you with all my being. My heart is pounding. You can feel it," he said, placing her hand over his heart. "Are you ready to become my true wife?"

"Yes, Matt Jenkins, I am ready. I am afraid . . . a little, but I have all the faith in the world that you won't hurt me—intentionally."

"Never, intentionally, my love."

Epilogue

"Anna, this house is busting at the seams. We have ten people living under this roof, and we are feeding two dozen every meal. I have received the reward money from the sheriff in Portland, and after dividing it with the farmhands, we still have a sizeable amount left. The first thing we need to do is make the bunkhouse larger. It needs its own kitchen with a long dining table. I want to hire a good cook for them. There will be many times that we will share a meal, but on a daily basis, I want them to eat together in the bunkhouse."

"That's a great idea. It will give the maids more time to do other things in the house besides cook," Anna said.

"I want to build several guest houses in the back of this house—a place for Sister Margaret and Señor Carlos. Their cottage could have a kitchen and two large bedrooms, so each can have privacy. I know Señor Carlos is staying with the men in the bunkhouse, but I want him to have a room of his own."

"Oh Matt, they will love a nice little house. They will feel like they really belong here." Anna kissed him on the cheek.

"The maids need to have a place of their own, too. I want to build a cottage large enough so that when we hire another person, all three would have their space. The children and Juan and Pedro can live upstairs and have their own rooms. Juan and Pedro have never lived apart, so I know that they will share a room. Mama can sleep in the room downstairs. She hates the stairs. The big room that was Pa's can be her sitting room. What do you think?"

"I think you have planned a room for everyone. Do we have enough money to build the cottages? I have money in Livingston."

"Yes, but that is your money. When you get ready to open a bakery, you will have the money to buy a building in town or have one built. I know that a bakery has always been a dream of yours."

"Will you hire a lawyer and have him check on my parents' farm? Uncle Claude said that he tried to sell it, but his name wasn't on the deed. I am sure that I must be the only heir. The house is probably falling down, but the land must have some value. We can use whatever money I receive to help with expenses on the farm and new horses." Anna smiled at her handsome husband. "I know you have always wanted a horse ranch."

"My love, I have dreamed of a horse ranch since I was a young man, but if that dream never came true, I couldn't be happier. I have you, my little pretend nun." Matt pulled her into his arms and gave her a long, loving kiss.

The End

Linda Sealy Knowles is originally from north Mobile, Alabama (Saraland/Satsuma area). She presently resides in Niceville, Florida, near her two children and three beautiful granddaughters.

Linda's writing is a God-gifted talent that brings joy to her heart. When she receives a compliment from one of fans, it warms her soul, and she feels like a New York Bestseller.

<u>Other Books by Linda Sealy Knowles</u>

The Maxwell Saga (Five books)
Journey to Heaven Knows Where
Hannah's Way
The Secret
Bud's Journey Home
Always Jess

~

Kathleen of Sweetwater, Texas
Abbey's New Life
Sunflower Brides
Joy's Cowboy
Trapped by Love
The Gamble
A Stranger's Love

www.ingramcontent.com/pod-product-compliance
Lightning Source LLC
Chambersburg PA
CBHW061036120726
47910CB00006B/2282